PRAISE FOR *A PASTOR'S PIT*

"Our churches have been protected as part of our religious heritage. But in his intriguing novel *A Pastor's Pit*, my friend Judge Roy Sparkman paints a realistic scenario in which that freedom to preach God's Word could be quickly lost. This book is a must-read for those who cherish religious liberties—and also enjoy a fascinating story!"

—Dr. Robert Jeffress
Pastor, First Baptist Church, Dallas

"At a time when religious liberty battles are raging across America, I am grateful Judge Sparkman is not only producing a story of fiction to capture your imagination, but one focused around the crucial battle of our day."

—Kelly Shackleford
President/CEO, First Liberty Institute

"While my friend Judge Roy Sparkman's new book is a work of fiction it has been beaten out on the anvil of personal experience from his years on the judicial bench. His words are prophetic and a clear warning for all of us who hold our religious liberties near and dear. Read it...and reap!"

—O.S. Hawkins PhD
Author of the best-selling Code Series of devotionals
including *The Joshua Code* and *The Jesus Code*

"As a legislator, I loved reading *A Pastor's Pit* as it showed vividly the interplay between words in legislation, judgments in a courtroom and their combined impact on the lives of real people. It was an engaging read that captures the very real problems faced by anyone who stands on religious principles in a world that is increasingly hostile to Christianity. I highly recommend this great read for anyone who needs to be reminded of the importance of religious liberty and free speech to Christians."

—James B. Frank
State Representative, HD69 Texas

"I have been following religious liberty issues for a number of years and *A Pastor's Pit* clearly presents the next realistic attack on those freedoms. Those who love our religious freedoms must read Judge Sparkman's book to prepare for that attack! A great read!"

—Bobby Albert
Author of three books including *The Freedom Paradox*;
President of Values-Driven Leadership, LLC

"Judge Sparkman through faith and intellect and wisdom in the faith has spun a story that is real life captured in the court room drama and the pastors pulpit and the Supreme Court. Captivating from the beginning by the story telling it reveals what may be true sooner than we think."

—Bob Osburn
A Texas Trial Lawyer

"I strongly recommend *A Pastor's Pit* for anyone who values our constitutional right of religious liberty!"

—Dr. William S. Spears, Founder and
CEO, Cenergistic LLC

A Pastor's Pit

by Judge Roy Sparkman

ISBN 978-1-64663-301-2

Published by

◄ köehlerbooks ™

3705 Shore Drive
Virginia Beach, VA 23455
800-435-4811
www.koehlerbooks.com

JUDGE ROY SPARKMAN
A Pastor's Pit

A NOVEL

VIRGINIA BEACH
CAPE CHARLES

DEDICATION

Dedicated to my two preacher boys, Curt and Brent, and to all who follow them in the pastor role. During your ministry I believe you will encounter criminal threats for preaching the Bible. Stay strong. Continue to preach the truth of God's Word in love, to all people including those who attack you.

Ephesians 6:10 – *"Finally, be strong in the Lord and in his mighty power." (NIV)*

"The constitutional freedom of religion is the most inalienable and sacred of all human rights."

~Thomas Jefferson

CHAPTER 1

PEOPLE NEED THE ASSURANCE OF *what will happen to them when they die,* he thought. Pastor Preston Curtis hunched over his desk preparing his sermon which would focus on 1 John 5:13 where John says, "so that you may know that you have eternal life." With his thumb and forefinger, he pressed at the tension gathering in his forehead. Having that theological issue resolved was the ultimate question about life. What happens when we die and how does life impact their afterlife?

He looked around his office as he tried to relax. It was nothing fancy, but it was very functional. The green carpet was old, the curtains were stained and were probably as old as he, but it had a big window that let him look over the church parking lot and into the hills and wooded area beyond. His desk was small but adequate, and there were four chairs to accommodate visitors. He had become comfortable sitting at this desk where he could relax and work on sermons, confer with parishioners or comfort the hurting. He took a deep breath, began to relax and looked back at his sermon notes.

Preston knew he needed to help his congregation understand that there are many things we trust in other than our relationship with God—our jobs, our education, our families, our investments, even our religions. In his sermon, he wanted to remind them that none of those things have any value when we die.

A sadness mixed with determination settled over him as he remembered when he was twelve and a good friend was killed in a car wreck. He didn't know if his friend had been a believer in Jesus and whether he went to Heaven or Hell. As he entered ministry, Preston knew he had to passionately teach that Jesus was the only way to Heaven. He couldn't stop preaching that. He never wanted to have another person he knew die without becoming a believer. That drove him.

I love my role as a pastor, Preston thought as he pondered his sermon. *I am so fortunate. I get to guide people through both the best and worst of times in their lives.* He felt very settled in his life as a pastor.

The voice of the receptionist interrupted his thoughts when she buzzed in. "Pastor Curtis, there's an anonymous caller on the phone who says she must talk to you and that it's very important, but she won't tell me what it's about. I asked her to leave a number, but she refused and made some comment about trying to warn you about something."

Preston narrowed his eyes. "Okay, I'll take the call, thanks."

A fairly young sounding woman said, "Reverend Curtis, you don't know me. I can't tell you my name because I could be fired if my boss finds out I called you. I wanted to warn you that you are about to be indicted in a criminal action to be filed by Multnomah County District Attorney Tim Ryan under Oregon's hate speech statute for religious hate speech."

"Is this some kind of crank call? What are you talking about?" Preston said. "I don't hate anybody."

"You remember those sermons where you said Muslims are going to Hell?" she asked.

"Yes," Preston replied, "but that's not hate. I merely tried to tell them that the Bible teaches that anyone who doesn't trust Jesus is going to Hell and our religions can't save us." There was silence on the other end of the call. With his head bowed, he raked his fingers through his hair.

"How do you know I'm going to be indicted?"

"I can't say, but you need to hire a good lawyer because in the next week or two you are going to be arrested. I don't know if someone can talk the DA out of this, but unless someone does, I guarantee it will happen."

"How do I know you are not some crazy prankster? I have had some crazy people call me before making all kinds of threats."

She sighed. "You are the pastor of Grace Bible Church. You have four students who have created a big stir about not being able to have Christian meetings. You have an imam and his followers upset at you. Want me to keep going? Trust me, the DA's office has a lot on you."

"This is unreal," Preston said. "Are you with the DA's office? How do you know what they are going to do? Can you stop it?"

"No, I can't stop it," the caller said. "I tried. But Tim Ryan is determined, and the local Muslim imam is encouraging him. You can't let anyone know I called, but you need to believe me when I say, you have to take this seriously." With that, she hung up.

His world had turned upside down in a span of five minutes. He couldn't think; he couldn't focus. He sat there, stunned, his vision glued to the ticking hand of the clock on the wall. He hadn't murdered anyone, stolen money, or used drugs. But she said he was about to be indicted. What could he do? *I don't know any lawyers in Oregon,* he thought. Maybe he could call RT Glassman, his best friend from high school who was now a Texas lawyer. He hadn't talked to him in ten years. Surely he would take his call, but he didn't know if RT would be able to help him. What was he even thinking? He couldn't afford a lawyer, and he didn't know anything about criminal law.

In America, a preacher can preach from the Bible—is that not right?

His mind raced, his heart nearly pounding outside his chest. How could he tell his wife, Janie, and their kids, or the church that he was about to be arrested? He needed to go home and tell Janie about the call.

He walked past the receptionist. "Carol, I'm not feeling good this afternoon. If a church member has an emergency, tell them to call me on my cell phone. Otherwise, I'll be back in the office on Monday."

"Are you okay?" asked Carol.

"I will be," he mumbled and kept walking.

CHAPTER 2

QUIET HOVERED OVER THE LIVING area, with nothing but the muted glow of Fox News on the television. Preston entered the den and set his briefcase onto the floor, his pulse beating in his ears.

Janie was sitting peacefully on the couch, her beautiful blond hair bundling together at the base of her neck. Beyond the window before her, the landscape trailed down to the evergreen tree line. Past that, the crest of currents toppled the saltwater of their ocean view, a flock of western gulls rising and resembling something of a white moving cloud, casting their wavering shadows over the blue. She was working on the family calendar for the next six months, unaware of how Preston's world had been rocked. Preston just stood in the doorway looking at his wife. *She looks so beautiful and peaceful. How do I break the news that her peaceful world is about to be turned upside down?*

As Preston entered the room she stood, and Preston wrapped his arms around her and gave her a peck on the cheek. Instantly, he could tell the way her blue eyes locked onto his and how she cocked her head back that she knew something was wrong. He'd never been able to hide anything from her. Janie leaned into him and pressed another kiss on his lips.

"You're home early, hon." Wavy rows of concern lined her forehead that he only wished he could soothe. "What's wrong, Preston?"

"You better sit down," he said.

Janie sat back down on the couch with the worry wrinkles deep on her forehead. Preston loved everything about Janie. She was a petite, small package, but her smile could melt him, and she was kind to everyone. Preston couldn't remember her ever saying anything unkind about another person. She was understanding when he had to be out all hours of the night with church members' concerns. She would be up early, meditating and preparing for the weekly Bible study she taught, and up late meeting kids' needs. In spite of her busy schedule, she always listened.

"C'mon. Talk to me," she said and patted the couch beside her.

After sitting, Preston turned to her. "You remember those sermons where I was preaching that the Bible said the only way to get to Heaven was by trusting Jesus as Savior and I said, 'Muslims are going to Hell,' because they don't trust Jesus?"

"Yes, of course I remember them. How could I forget? There's been trouble at the church and at school over those sermons. What happened?"

"I just got a call from an anonymous caller who seemed to know all about me and what has been happening at the church. She said in the next week or two I am going to be indicted and arrested for some crime called 'religious hate speech' for preaching that Muslims are going to Hell."

Janie stared at him, speechless. Finally, she said, "What? I hear and understand the words *indicted and arrested*, but what does *religious hate speech* mean? Is this for real?" She gasped. "You're going to prison?" Tears welled and her voice choked.

"I don't know what all of this means," Preston said. "I have counselled parents whose kids got into drugs and they were arrested, but I have no idea about what happens in a situation like this. I've never heard of such a crime. If I hadn't talked to this person myself, I would think this is somebody's idea of a bad joke. She told me to call a lawyer. I don't know any lawyers here, and we can't afford one anyway."

Janie released the death grip she had on his hand. "What are you going to do?"

"I have no idea. You know my best friend from high school, RT Glassman, is a Texas lawyer, and I think I might just call him."

They sat there, stunned, just staring at each other for what seemed like several minutes. Finally, Janie said, "You have mentioned RT over the years, and I think I met him once. Tell me about him and why you think he is the person to call."

Preston leaned his head back against the couch and with a small smile began to reminisce.

"He was my best friend in high school. I grew up on a farm and I always considered him the city boy. I knew if I ever got into trouble, RT would be there. We were alike in many ways—both good students, liked baseball and went to the same church activities. We just hung out together a lot. RT would help me haul hay for my dad. He would always say 'sure' any time I asked for help. By the time we got out of high school, I was six feet tall, but RT was six feet three, stocky—not fat—but his stature could be intimidating. I always felt safe if I thought there was going to be any trouble. We would go to the Red River that divides Texas from Oklahoma, and take a round piece of wood with a shiny finish and skim it across the water and try to jump on it and ride it. I could always ride it further than him and it drove him crazy.

"We used to skip church on many Sundays by slipping out of the sanctuary and we would go to the belfry tower to visit and talk. That's how I know how to keep an eye on what the kids are up to now. Even the good kids! It's the voice of experience. We got busted one time because I accidentally kicked the bell during the middle of the church service. RT told me his mom asked him, "Why did you ring the bell?"

RT responded, "What bell?" His mom just shook her head and rolled her eyes. We had a little problem with the truth in those days. My dad had talked to the head usher who saw us run out of the bell tower, so he knew the truth. He skipped any discussion and went straight to, 'You are grounded for two days, and if you do that again, you will be grounded for the rest of your life! Understand?' I just knew never to mess with my dad. But RT and I were always together and if one of us got into something, we both did. We thought a lot alike about school, church, Dallas Cowboys, and neither one of us wanted to grow up to haul hay for a living after we got out of high school. I could always trust him. *Always.* He had my back. After high school we went in different directions, but when we would get together it was like we could pick up where we had left off the last time we saw each other. Over the years, as we both got busier, we have talked less and less. I just believe he could give me some direction. I feel like I am overwhelmed because I have absolutely no idea what to do. He is a lawyer and I hear he has been successful, but his practice is in Texas and not in Oregon."

"You are right, Preston. You should call him. And I mean call him tonight!" Janie insisted.

Preston got up, kissed Janie on the forehead and said, "I think it's too late to call him tonight. I'll do it tomorrow. Let's not tell the kids or anyone else about this until we can process it a little more. We can't solve this now. Let's pray about it, get some sleep and see if we can think more clearly in the morning."

Janie nodded, and as he turned to walk to his study she said, "Come back here." She reached up, hugged him, gave him a passionate kiss. "Don't ever forget that I love you, your kids love you and God loves you, no matter what." With a lump in his throat, Preston was speechless and returned the hug. Preston turned to go to his study and Janie sat on the couch and, after looking at the six-month calendar she had been preparing, just turned it over and realized it was now worthless. Finally, she got up and headed to the bedroom, knowing there would be no sleep for her on this night.

CHAPTER 3

AFTER TALKING TO JANIE, PRESTON sat in his home study, still unable to focus and uncertain about what to do or who to call. He knew Janie was right and he should call RT, but he didn't want to take advantage of the friend he hadn't talked to in several years. He wondered how RT would respond when he asked for a favor. In this case, a big favor. He began to reflect on his life and the path he traveled to become a pastor.

How have I gone—in just a few minutes—from having a fulfilling and happy life to having my entire world turned upside down? How did I suddenly move from supposedly being a loving husband, father and pastor to being a criminal who supposedly spewed hate against Muslims? I was just trying to help point everyone to the Jesus of the Bible and that nothing else—including any religion—can secure their place in Heaven.

It seemed his life was flashing before his eyes and his thoughts turned to *how and why did I become a pastor anyway?* He visualized being back in a church camp as a senior in high school. He was standing around the campfire singing songs and praising the God he loved with the other kids, when his youth pastor, Jerry McDonald, came and stood beside him and said, "You have the gift, you know."

Preston looked at him. "What gift?"

"Have you ever thought about becoming a minister?"

Preston just stared at him. It was like he was reading his mind because that was exactly what he had been thinking.

"Actually, yes I have. I was just thinking about that. How did you know?"

"I have thought for some time God had his hand on you and that He had a special calling in ministry for you. What's holding you back?" the youth minister asked.

"Man, I don't know," Preston said. "This sounds silly, but as soon as I take that step, people will look at me differently and call me 'preacher man' or a 'man of the cloth' or some other name. Everybody will be watching to see how I act. I don't really want to be looked at differently. I have also been told that life in ministry can be hard. Everybody in church is your boss. You don't get paid much, and your kids always have the label of 'preacher's kid.' I have just been trying to process it all. I think my parents had expectations of medical school for me. I am afraid to disappoint them."

"Preston, first of all, I heard a whole lot of 'I's in what you just said, rather than what God wants. Secondly, since you are about to graduate from high school, it is a perfect time to make this commitment. If God is calling you, don't put if off. I understand your struggles. I had those same questions and doubts, but I know I made the right decision. God will guide you and provide direction if you trust him. I also know your parents. They'll be excited that you decided to follow the path God has for you. You stay here at the campfire while the group keeps singing and you do business with God. I will be standing to the side. When you and God get through dealing with each other, come and tell me what you think." With that comment, Jerry walked away.

Ten minutes later, Preston walked over to Jerry, smiled, and said, "I just surrendered to become a pastor and tell people about trusting Jesus."

Jerry hugged him. "I am proud of you. We'll walk through this together." Jerry prayed for Preston and his journey to become a pastor had begun.

After the camp, the youth pastor met with Preston weekly to mentor him and to begin to prepare him for a life of ministry. *Over the years, through college, seminary and the early days of being a pastor, God had confirmed the call upon my life and things had gone smoothly—until now,* he thought.

About that time, Janie walked into his study.

"Can't sleep?" Preston asked.

"Nope, I'm really worried about everything. This all seems so unfair."

"Honey," Preston said, "I agree this looks totally unfair through our lens, but there's no comparison to any unfairness I might suffer and the unfairness that Jesus suffered. Jesus was crucified for people like you and me so we could have an eternal home. Plus, he warned us about these types of abuses. Remember how Jesus warned us, 'You will be hated by everyone because of my name'?"

Janie smiled and said, "They didn't warn you in seminary about preaching the Bible being religious hate speech, did they?"

For the first time since the anonymous phone call, Preston was able to smile. "No, they didn't."

"When I can stop thinking about all the negatives of this situation, you know what else I think about?"

"No," he replied.

"Some of the people you have ministered to and some of the things you enjoy about being a pastor. Name me one thing you enjoy about being a pastor. I think you need to focus on something positive right now."

Preston wondered how he had been so lucky to be married to

this woman. "Well, I really love everything about being able to help people, through both the good and the bad. I remember one of our deacons, Jim Springfield, bringing his eight-year-old daughter to my office and she prayed to trust Jesus. I love being able to talk to the kids about Jesus. But then I remember being with Phillip and Crystal Dodd when they were heartbroken as they watched their little Judy's life slip away. That was tough. I hugged them, cried with them, prayed with them, and just sat with them. That was so hard because their daughter was the same age as our son Caleb, and I could visualize it being you and me sitting there instead of them. I had no answer to all of the 'why's they asked. Even without the answers, they seemed to appreciate me being there. I just want to make a difference and for people to see Jesus through me. This indictment thing is so confusing."

"Oh, honey," Janie said, "Crystal has told me over and over that they would not have made it without your being there. You made such a difference to them in their time of pain. You gave them strength, encouragement, and hope. They needed those things in that moment. Particularly the hope of Judy being in Heaven with Jesus. Preston, you can't get dragged down by all of this hate speech stuff. You have made a huge difference in the lives of people. Remember last Sunday when three young couples brought their babies to the front of the church to affirm they would raise their children in a Christian home?

"You prayed over those babies and the parents that God would give them wisdom and encourage them in raising their children in a way to love God. You encourage people! Preston, do you remember how encouraged the homeless are each Thanksgiving when you lead our congregation to provide lunch at the homeless shelter? Last year there were tears of joy everywhere as our people passed out hugs, plates of warm food and bags of necessities to grateful people. No matter what happens, I want you to remember: you have made a difference in the lives of people. Don't you forget that Preston Curtis!"

The lump in Preston's throat wouldn't let him speak, so he just pulled Janie close and hugged her. Tomorrow he would try to come up with a game plan. He decided he would call his friend RT.

CHAPTER 4

RT'S JOURNEY AS A LAWYER preparing for the challenge of dealing with religious liberty issues had begun unintentionally in law school. As a third-year student at Baylor University School of Law, RT was sitting in his constitutional law class, but was unprepared to be called upon that day. He had been studying for the bar exam, preparing for a mock trial, and had spent a total of thirty minutes that week with his wife of six months. Plus, he wanted to practice corporate law.

There were forty-nine students in his constitutional law class, which should have meant that each student should get called on only once every forty-nine days. RT had been called on in the previous class, so he felt safe about being unprepared. But for some reason, Professor Derrell Simpson thought he should ask RT to recite on back-to-back days. *He's looking at me again,* RT thought. The dread sank in, and he kept his head down hoping to avoid the embarrassment.

"Mr. Glassman, what was the US Supreme Court holding in the case of Reynolds vs. United States?" He started looking for his summary outline of the cases which was given to him by a friend who had taken the class the previous year.

"Mr. Glassman, we are waiting!" said Professor Simpson. Finally, RT was able to find his notes and choke out an answer. "Based on the holding, it appears they concluded polygamy as practiced by the Mormons was bad."

Professor Simpson scoffed. "Can someone help Mr. Glassman out? That may be the results of the holding, but it appears the reasoning of the Supreme Court has escaped him." Finally, a friend of RT's spoke up. "The holding of the case is that there were constitutional protections of free speech and religious liberties, but there are limitations in the area of religious liberties. Therefore, in a criminal prosecution for violation of the laws banning polygamy, religious beliefs by Mormons was not a defense to prosecution. Anti-bigamy criminal statutes were held to be constitutional, and the defendant could be charged with the crime of polygamy even though his personal religious convictions, as supported by the Mormon church, said polygamy was acceptable. Criminal prosecution for polygamy represented an acceptable limitation on religious liberty."

"Very good," said Professor Simpson. "I'm glad someone has read and understood this very significant case."

He spent the next twenty minutes trying to explain the logic and reasoning of how the constitutional protection for religious liberty could be found by the Supreme Court to be limited. RT never understood why it had to take those nine Supreme Court justices one hundred pages to say the religious practice of polygamy by the Mormons was not protected by the Constitution, in spite of the language that it was illegal for the government to make any law prohibiting the free exercise of religion. Of course, he was not thinking of the case's impact on religious liberties, nor was he thinking that the constitutional issue of religious liberty would ever become an issue in his law practice. He was just trying to survive the Con Law class, graduate, pass the bar exam and begin practicing law.

Professor Simpson was not finished with his questioning about the boundaries or limits of religious liberties.

"The Mormons argued the Old Testament in the Bible permitted polygamy and they cited Solomon as an example, with his seven hundred wives and three hundred concubines. The Mormon position seemed to be that the Bible permitted it. Mormons allowed it, because in their view they were trying to prevent affairs, prostitution, and bastard children. Other people feared allowing polygamy in the name of religious liberty could open the door to other heinous things such as incest, infanticide or even murder in the name of religion. Where is the boundary between religious liberty and society's acceptable norms? One person's religious anathema can be another person's salvation. The constitutional issue for the justices was, where, in America, and in our Constitution, is that line of constitutionally protected religious liberty?"

The practical impact of limitations imposed by the Supreme Court on religious liberties went right over RT's head. He went to church regularly and had become more active in his Christian faith over the years, but he never thought his religious liberties would be limited by Reynolds v. United States, and its progeny. It never occurred to him that a pastor would one day be charged with a crime for preaching the Bible.

CHAPTER 5

AS PRESTON PREPARED TO CALL RT, he reflected on how he got to Oregon as a pastor.

He went to Southwestern Baptist Theological Seminary in Fort Worth, Texas and earned a Master of Divinity degree in preaching. Unlike undergraduate school where he felt a lot of time was spent on unnecessary classes, Preston enjoyed his seminary classes and the study of the Bible. His preaching class taught him that a sermon was composed of three points and a poem. But more importantly, he began to get a direction for his life in ministry. God confirmed to him that he was to teach people the Bible and about God's love, and also address a society that was drifting away from the view of God's design for how we should live our lives.

As his skills grew, he was called to be pastor of the Grace Bible Church outside Portland, Oregon, in a city called Pitfall. Before accepting, he and Janie talked about it at great length.

"Preston, Oregon is a long way from Texas and from all of

our parents and siblings. Do you think we could wait for a church somewhere closer to Texas? Our kids won't be able to grow up around any of their grandparents, and from what we have heard, ministry is harder outside the Bible Belt."

Preston and Janie had gone to visit the church, the committee conducting the search and the community.

"Janie, remember how lovely Oregon was with the mountains and waterfalls? I have never seen as many waterfalls as there are in Oregon. It's beautiful! We could drive a short distance in one direction and be on the beach, and a short distance in the opposite direction and be in the mountains. I think we would all love it. Plus, the people on the committee that interviewed us seemed very nice, friendly and gave us the impression the congregation loved the Lord and would love us and our family. The school system is good and should provide a good education for our kids. I feel good about it."

"The people seemed nice enough," Janie said, "but the whole process kind of gave me the creeps. We sat in this big room with five men and three women asking you questions for four hours, and I basically just sat there and smiled and nodded occasionally. Everybody was at least twice our age. One of the guys even winked at me! They said all of the right words, but I am not sure about it."

After they prayed and talked about it for two more days, they both agreed they were moving to Oregon. Their parents all expressed the same sentiment, that Preston needed to follow his calling.

Preston knew little about Oregon except that it was a long way from the Bible Belt, and it was a beautiful part of the country with a lot of people who liked outdoor activities. Somewhere in his interview to be pastor, the committee failed to tell him about the dark underbelly of some area residents and their view of religion. He naively thought if he was nice, shared God's love, and preached a good sermon once in a while, that the people would love him back.

CHAPTER 6

PRESTON AND JANIE WERE FILLED with enthusiasm for the adventure God had placed before them. Their friends had gathered to pray for them, encourage them and to wish them well. On the way to a friend's house, Preston and Janie pined about how much they were going to miss their friends. One of Preston's best friends in ministry, Philip, wanted to make a brief statement and then pray over them.

"Preston and Janie," he started, "we are going to miss you terribly. I'm really going to miss laughing at Preston's bad jokes. We all know he cannot tell a joke. But seriously, couldn't God call you to a church a little closer to Texas than Oregon?" They all had a good laugh and there were a couple of slaps on Preston's back. "But you have told us that this is what God wants you to do, and we all know you are a gifted preacher committed to preaching the truth of the Bible. Grace Bible Church is very fortunate to have you guys take up ministry there. Before you go, we thought it only appropriate to share some of your most shining moments of ministry."

From the back of the room one of the guys yelled out, "Yeah, like the time we were having communion and you dropped your cup with the purple grape juice, and it stained the brand-new carpet." Preston turned a little red, but they all laughed. "Yeah," another friend said, "or how about the wedding you were performing when your iPad went blank and you didn't have your notes to complete the wedding. I had never seen you speechless before." Again, the room erupted in laughter.

"All right, all right!" Preston laughed, "I didn't know this was going to be a roast! Nobody sent me that memo! You're about to persuade me I am going to miss some of you guys about like I would miss a bad toothache!"

"Seriously, Preston," said Philip, "we really are going to miss you guys. Your whole family is an inspiration by the way you reach out to people and you witness, pray and spend time with those who are hurting and in need of someone to minister to them. Plus, your uncompromising desire and ability to preach the truth of the Bible is second to none. We have been blessed to have you help lead us in ministry, but even more importantly, we are fortunate to be able to call you and Janie our friends. Let's pray. 'God, we pray for Preston and Janie and their family as they move to Oregon to minister in a place you have prepared for them. Thank you for the time we have been able to spend together, and for the impact they have had on so many of our lives. As they go, we pray you will protect them physically, spiritually, and emotionally and that you will use them mightily in their new ministry in Oregon. In Jesus' name, Amen.'"

Philip asked Preston to share what they could pray about for them. As Preston and Janie focused on friends gathered around them, they expressed some specific requests:

That God would go before them to prepare the people's hearts for their ministry.

That they would be able to share God's love with the people in Oregon to help them be drawn to God.

That they could see many people trust Christ as Savior as the truth of the Bible was taught and preached.

That the transition for their children would be easy and uneventful.

Preston and Janie spent three hours visiting and sharing good memories with friends. At one point, one of Janie's friends pretended she was going to push Preston into the swimming pool. Preston was able to grab her arm as they both crashed into the pool, street clothes and all. As Preston came up sputtering water, he yelled, "You don't have to drown me just because we are moving!"

Preston and Janie were both exhausted as they left the roast but also were encouraged and they felt better prepared for the journey ahead. But they both knew the hardest part was ahead of them—saying goodbye to their parents.

Janie was close to her mom and saw her nearly every day, as they only lived a couple of blocks away. The relationship had moved from parent-child, to being friends: Janie's mom was the one person with whom she could talk openly. Her mom had provided support when Janie and Preston had a miscarriage; she walked Janie through the birth and uncertainties of each child, and helped her learn how to be a nurturing mother. On those days when Janie was tired and did not want to hear the word "Mommy!" one more time, her mom would always jump in and help. Janie and her mom gave each other one last hug.

"I'm going to miss you," her mom said. "I hope you can come back often; you know your dad has had some health issues over the last couple of years, and he can't travel like he once could."

"I know, Mom," Janie said. "I don't know how I am going to do this without you. You are always there."

"Janie, you will be just fine. You will make new friends and develop new and exciting relationships. I think you will also be surprised at how you and Preston will grow as a couple being that far away from family. But you are going to do great, and we look forward to hearing how God blesses your ministry there."

"Thanks, Mom. You are my best friend, and I will miss you, but we will come back as often as we can. I love you." The reality of the separation from family was beginning to settle in.

CHAPTER 7

WHEN THEY HAD ARRIVED IN Oregon, the people in the church were very friendly and glad to have their new pastor. One day Preston was sitting at his desk in his office when three elderly ladies walked in, each holding a gift for him. One had a pie; one had two dozen cookies; a third had a chocolate cake.

"Wow," Preston said, "are you trying to fatten me up? I think I have already gained ten pounds in just two weeks!" They all laughed, and Preston gave them a hug, and after the ladies left, he wondered which of the three desserts would never make it home.

Preston and Janie quickly realized that Pitfall was an appropriate name for the suburban city. "Pitfall" as defined by Webster is a "surprising difficulty or something unforeseen or unexpected."

While the church was small with only about two hundred members, it was in the rapidly growing suburb of Portland. Despite the growing population, the inability of the church members to change such things as the style of music, their giving attitudes and ministry perspective had made growth of the church difficult. Another challenge was the people themselves. Many worshipped nature and outdoors rather than the God that created nature, which was not something Preston expected. Nor was the resistance from the elders expected.

Preston loved to call and visit members, as well as prospective members, for the church to encourage them to attend. He was committed to reaching out and trying to grow the church. He also was working with the elders to develop an advertising budget to talk about planned activities. However, when Preston would talk to non-members, it was common to hear, "We will come sometime. We usually go to the mountains or the beach on the weekends."

The concept of *tithing*—giving a percentage of income to the church—was a foreign and unwelcome concept. For many of the people, the concept of *evangelism* meant the preacher would talk to people about Christ, but their own religion should be private and demonstrated by example rather than by a verbal witness. Preston tried to use a courtroom analogy to emphasize the weakness of saying a witness should simply be seen and not heard.

"I have a lawyer friend in Texas who said every witness in the courtroom takes the witness stand and starts talking about what they know, had heard, or had seen. No judge or jury would accept the testimony of a witness who simply took the stand and claimed the judge or jury could understand his or her testimony simply by looking and observing him or her. Therefore, in the same way, we live our lives in a way that demonstrates a Christian lifestyle, but we must also be proactive in sharing Christ with our friends, neighbors and family."

Finally, making changes inside the church was slow and difficult. Most of the decisions were made by the elders. Preston had previously been in churches that had been led by either deacons or staff, but this church was his first led by elders. There were six elders besides himself. All the elders were older than he, and during his visits before he was hired, he had met them all and felt comfortable with the group. And at Preston's first meeting as pastor, Bob Martin, elder

chairman, had welcomed him as the new pastor and elder. Elder
Joshua Bernard led in prayer. Chairman Martin laid out the agenda
which included finances, personnel matters, insurance claims,
church repairs, worship services, music, sermon topics.

Preston thought as he looked at the agenda, *Interesting. I see no
topic concerning any ministry opportunities, and this list looks like they
want to either dictate or approve my sermon topics. Not a big fan of that.*

Preston typically determined his sermon topics a year in advance.
But he had never had to get his sermon topics approved by any other
leader in the church.

All of the matters seemed routine until they got to the worship
services agenda item. Preston spoke up.

"Men, I would like to see us begin to *blend* our music with some
more contemporary music—nothing too drastic or hardcore, but as
an example, Chris Tomlin's music, which could include 'Here I Am
To Worship,' or 'How Great Is Our God.' We can blend them with
some of the hymns or play some updated versions of old hymns like
Tomlin's 'Amazing Grace.' I can coordinate with our worship pastor
so the music fits the sermon for the week. Is that okay?"

Immediately, Chairman Martin said, "Pastor Curtis, our people
are pretty traditional in their worship style, and we like to sing hymns
from the hymnal. Maybe at our next elder meeting we can talk about
having one of those 'seven-eleven' songs at a service." He chuckled at
the reference, meaning a song that has seven words sung eleven times.

Preston started thinking, *This could be harder than I thought.
Growth of the church is going to be hard if we can't make any changes.*

"Now," continued Chairman Martin, "let's talk about what
sermons we want you to preach."

"I am a little confused," said Preston, "I normally choose the
topics for sermons and typically teach a book of the Bible all the
way through, except on special Sundays, like Easter, Thanksgiving
or Christmas. I explained that to the Pastor Search Committee I met
with, and no one expressed any concerns."

Preston had no issue with informing the other elders of sermon topics but bristled at the notion that these men—even as spiritual leaders in the church—would try to control the sermon topics rather than letting him do that as he was led by God. Being able to preach the truth of the Bible was not an area where he was willing to compromise.

"Well, pastor," Chairman Martin said, "we hear you and we want you to have a certain amount of freedom, but as elders of the church we are spiritual leaders, too, and we have a responsibility to also lead the church. Why don't we start by you telling us what your ideas for sermons are, and we will go from there."

"John is one of my favorite books in the Bible and that is where I intend to start. It is a book that addresses some very significant principles for life. Those themes include a lot about who Jesus is, that he is the giver of eternal life, and the importance of trusting Jesus to have that eternal life."

"Sounds perfect," Paul Reed, the senior elder, said.

Preston had noticed during the meeting that while Bob Martin was chairman and spoke frequently, Elder Reed always had the final word.

"Okay," said Chairman Martin, "that's the end of the agenda. Anybody have anything else?"

"Yes, I do," Preston spoke up. "I didn't see an item on the agenda for ministry opportunities. Can we discuss those areas?"

"Sure," said Chairman Martin. "We have Sunday school and a ministry led by one staff member to follow up with new visitors each week, and we have a great youth pastor who leads the youth program. We also have a volunteer seniors' pastor to lead the senior adults, to take them on trips and sing at nursing homes twice a year. The ministries seem to be going well."

"I know about those," Preston said, "but I would like us to expand our ministry from just ministering to our members. I would like to see us start a reading program ministry at the elementary school located two blocks from the church. I would like us to support a homeless ministry, and a pregnancy ministry for those with problem pregnancies to provide support to prevent more abortions. I would also like for us to feed the homeless on Thanksgiving Day and establish a young moms' ministry where young mothers—member or nonmember of our church—can come have childcare and a time of spiritual and social interaction with women at a similar life stage. I can keep going with a ministry opportunity list, but I would like to start with those items. Who can help lead us?" There was silence for a minute as a couple of the elders wondered whether they had made a mistake in hiring this new pastor.

Finally, Chairman Martin said, "That is a pretty aggressive agenda, and all of those sound like interesting areas of ministry. Why don't you pick the top one area of new ministry on your list and we will talk about that one at our next elder meeting."

Preston agreed, but some of the realities of trying to grow the church and expand the ministries, in light of the resistance from at least some of the elders, made the task seem almost insurmountable. *But with God, all things are possible,* he thought. Preston decided he needed to build a personal relationship with each of these men that he hoped would lay the groundwork for building bridges.

———◇———

Over the next three weeks, before the next elder meeting, Preston was determined to spend time with every elder each week to have one-on-one meetings. If they could see his heart and build a relationship, he was optimistic about their future together.

Paul Reed quickly became one of Preston's favorite elders. He was the oldest of the elders, in his eighties, and had a colorful history. He had been a pilot in World War II and had flown more than thirty missions. As with many WWII veterans, Elder Reed was hesitant to discuss his time at war. Preston had heard that Reed had been shot down. One day he finally opened up.

"War is terrible, and I don't like to talk about it. We just did what we had to do. I enjoyed flying but there was one day I thought my life was over. That experience was awful and one I will never forget. My bomber had five crewmembers, and one day, in a run over Normandy, my plane got hit with flack. I thought we might be able to make it back to our airport, but one engine had been destroyed and the rudder was damaged, so I had no control. When I finally decided we needed to bail out, I found out my gunner had been killed. The rest of us bailed out over water. When the plane crashed, the gunner's body disappeared and was never found. We all floated in the ocean for two days before we were picked up, and I really thought I was going to die. That was when my faith became real to me because when you stare death in the face, everything else that you thought was important disappears.

"One of the hardest things I ever had to do was explain to my buddy's family why he wasn't coming home. I got a Purple Heart for that mission, but I didn't think I deserved it because my friend died, and I was responsible for him, as the pilot. For a long time, I felt guilty because I survived and he didn't, but with God's grace over time I was able to move on. It took me quite a while before I could fly a plane again."

"I'm so sorry, Paul," Preston said. "I want you to know how glad I am that you are here as a leader in our church. You are a remarkable man that God has used, and I believe he will continue to use you for years to come."

A deep bond of friendship began that day between the two men.

CHAPTER 8

PRESTON COULD PREACH THE RAFTERS down, and Janie could sing like an angel. Their theme verse for ministry was based on 1 Peter 5:2: "Be shepherds of God's flock that is under your care, watching over them, not because you must, but because you are willing, as God wants you to be; not pursuing dishonest gain, but eager to serve." Care and serve was their mantra and it endeared them to the congregation.

As a young minister, Preston had learned lessons not taught in seminary about being a pastor. One Sunday, early in his tenure as pastor at Grace Bible Church, Preston baptized sixty-five-year-old Frank Norman. Unknown to Preston, Frank wore a hairpiece. Because Pastor Curtis went to a Baptist seminary, baptism had to be by complete immersion. Preston leaned Frank back into the water and was filled with horror! *Oh no!* he thought, *his hairpiece is floating off his head.* He began to try to hold Frank's head still under the water while at the same time get the floating hairpiece properly positioned back on Frank's head. He wanted to neither drown nor embarrass Frank, but the hairpiece was not cooperating. The congregation knew Frank was staying underwater a long time but had no real clue as to what was happening. Finally, Preston got the hairpiece as close as he could and brought Frank up, sputtering. *Oops!* Preston was trying to keep a straight face. The hairpiece was still not straight on Frank's head, so Preston shifted it quickly, and said "Amen."

When Preston got home, Janie said, "What was up with Frank's baptism? It looked like you were trying to drown him instead of baptize him." After Preston explained what had happened, neither of them could stop laughing. His ability to laugh at himself was one of the characteristics the congregation loved about their new pastor.

Another quality the congregation loved about Pastor Curtis was how much he loved and cared for his congregation, and how he would immediately respond when they were in need.

One of many examples was when Preston had received a call from a young church member. "Pastor, this is Brad Hart. I know you are new to our church, but Nancy is four months pregnant and having contractions and we are at the hospital waiting for the doctor to arrive. We are worried she is about to lose the baby. We have been trying for two years to get pregnant. She is very upset, scared and worried. Both of our parents live out of the state and can't get here today. Would it be possible for you to come pray for her and our baby?"

"Absolutely," Preston said. "I was just walking out the door headed to the church and I will come straight to the hospital."

"Thank you," Brad said.

When Preston got to the hospital, he found Brad and Nancy in her room. The machines connected to Nancy were beeping and the room seemed cold and sterile. Brad was standing beside the bed holding Nancy's hand and rubbing his hands through her hair. Nancy looked pale, her eyes puffy, as she lay in the bed. They looked up with fear, seeking solace, as Preston walked into the room.

"Thank you for coming," they both said. They explained that the technician had just completed the sonogram and they were waiting for the doctor to come talk to them. Preston grabbed both of their hands and began praying.

"Father, we know Jesus is the Great Physician and that Brad and Nancy love you. Father, we pray now for this sweet baby, for protection, for health and the ability to grow and live a healthy, full and productive life. Please let Brad and Nancy know you love them, you love their baby and that you will provide peace, comfort, protection, and wisdom as they deal with this pregnancy. We trust you God. Amen." No sooner had Preston said, "Amen," than the doctor walked in. Preston could tell by the look on her face that the news would not be good.

"I'm sorry," she said. "There is no heartbeat and no life. You had started a miscarriage and we will have to do a D and C to complete the process and to clear everything out. I know this is a shock to you. I am very sorry. After you get settled down, we will take you to surgery. After that, if you would like, you can make an appointment and I will talk to you about all of your questions."

"Doctor, I have to ask one question," said Nancy. "Did I do something wrong to cause me to lose the baby?" She began crying.

"Absolutely not" the doctor replied. "Sometimes this is the body's way of protecting babies that either don't or can't form properly. But you did nothing wrong. And just because you had a miscarriage does not mean you can't get pregnant again."

Preston was experiencing their pain as if his own wife had lost a baby. He hugged them both and let them cry. As they rolled Nancy away for her procedure, Preston said, "Just know we love you, your church family loves you and God loves you. We will be praying for you and I will check on you later."

As he left, he called his secretary and gave her the names of three young couples to call to ask them to reach out to Brad and Nancy. Since he and Janie had suffered a miscarriage, he could totally empathize with the couple. His presence and his prayers provided a valuable salve to encourage a hurting young couple.

On another occasion, the husband of an elderly couple died. When Preston arrived at the home, the new widow gave him a hug.

"Ms. Winston," said Preston, "I am so sorry for your loss. Jake was such a sweet man. He had become such an encourager to me. We are all going to miss him. I wanted you to know that I and our church family love you and are here for you." With that, he gave her another hug. She just leaned into Preston and said, "I'm going to miss him. We were married for fifty-four good years. He had a strong faith, so I know he is in Heaven with Jesus now. That gives me great comfort. Will you do the funeral for me?"

"Absolutely," Preston replied. He was honored to preside over funerals for committed Christians like Jake who had lived long lives serving the Lord. As he drove away, Preston observed that frequently his mere presence meant more than any words he could offer. No pious religious words would help Ms. Winston, but he knew he had brought comfort by his presence. While the long hours could be exhausting and draining, Pastor Curtis' love for Jesus and the people drove him to give more.

———◇———

Preston's physical and time limitations, combined with a shortage of other staff members, began to cause some cracks in his support. One Sunday as he was greeting the worshippers after a service, one of the elders pulled him aside.

"Pastor, sister Sanders is upset with you. Her mom lives with her and has been sick for the past couple of weeks and she says you haven't called on her. She's talking about it. My wife is trying to calm and quiet her, but as you know she has led several of our women's ministry events and is very influential with the other women."

"Yeah, I know," Preston responded. "I keep meaning to reach out to her but between hospital calls, sermon preparation, funerals, church meetings and spending a few minutes with my family, I haven't been able to get to see her. But I will call her. Thanks for the reminder."

Another crack in his support came when one of the elders

apparently told some church members that Preston wanted to have the church do some contemporary songs. One of the men caught him at the church office one day and said, "Preacher, I hear you want us to start singing those modern ditties instead of hymns. I don't like those. Those seven-eleven songs have no meaning compared to the hymns. You shouldn't push that."

"Thanks for the feedback," Preston said. "Hymns are wonderful, but there are some contemporary songs that communicate great messages about God's love. I would never try to replace the hymns, but would like to blend the music style of hymns with some contemporary songs. Hymns are for our members who worship best through the music of hymns, and an occasional contemporary song would be for those who worship best through that kind of music. You know, for forty years you have been sending your kids to youth camps where they sing contemporary songs with guitars, and the Wednesday night worship time with our high school students and youth pastor uses contemporary music. You do want us to bring young people and young couples into the church, right?"

As the man walked away, he said, "Hymns have been here forever and if it was good enough for my grandparents, my parents and for me, it ought to be good for them."

Oh boy, thought Preston, *this really could be tough.*

CHAPTER 9

PRESTON BELIEVED THE BIBLE WAS God's inspired, infallible instruction manual to teach people how to live. Because of that conviction about the Bible, he never backed down, compromised, or apologized for preaching on any topic, no matter how controversial, from the Bible. His perspective was that he had to "teach that we are to love all people no matter how unlovable, how different or unfair or unkind they may be. Christ died for them all." However, there were clear, practical, but controversial teachings that needed to be presented from the Bible. Some of the controversial topics he would preach about included:

- "God loves everyone including the unborn and opposes abortion," he would also say and assert that abortion was "infant murder."
- "Baptism is evidence of an intentional decision to follow Jesus and once you are saved, you must be baptized by immersion.

Jesus was baptized by John and was immersed. It demonstrates that God has saved you. Since babies can't give that testimony, infant baptism isn't Biblical."

- "The only way to Heaven is by a relationship with Jesus; not by a relationship with Buddha, Mohammed, the Pope or anyone or anything else."
- "Marriage is a covenant relationship between a man and a woman. Same-sex marriage is an abomination to God. Just look at how he treated Sodom and Gomorrah!"
- "You are to bring your tithes, ten percent of your income, into God's storehouse, the church!"
- "Husbands, you should love your wife like Christ loved the church and wives, you should submit to the leadership of your husband."

Being in the liberal culture of Oregon, Preston was frequently branded by outsiders, the media, and even other pastors as right wing, rigid, harsh and by some as a kook.

Preaching that the Bible was literally true and a necessary guide for the correct way to live a life had occasionally caused clashes for Preston, but he had no clue about the storm clouds that were brewing because of his sermons.

The controversy with the Muslim community began when four high school students who were members of Grace Bible Church came to visit Pastor Curtis about a problem they had at school. These four students were juniors at the local high school. They loved Jesus and tried to share their faith with students and encourage events such as Prayer at the Flagpole and FCA, Fellowship of Christian Athletes. There was constant scrutiny about their Christian activities by the school faculty and principal. The students had asked for use of a classroom for a Bible study and were told no. They were also told they could not share a devotional with the students each morning.

They asked to be able to pass out Bibles and were again rebuffed. They wanted to pass out Christian tracts to students as they came out of school and were told no. They wanted to sing Christian songs in the student talent show—no, again.

The final blow for them came when they learned about the different way in which Muslim students were treated. There was a large Muslim population in their community and a group of Muslim students was being allowed the use of a classroom each Tuesday afternoon to meet as Muslims United. During these meetings, the students frequently included guest imams, and studied and recited the Quran. Prayer rugs were brought and used as part of the educational exercise.

The four students went to visit the high school principal to find out why the Christian students were being discriminated against and the Muslim students were given such freedom. Principal Turner was generally perceived as friendly and helpful.

"What's the occasion for you coming to my office today?"

Clay, as the spokesman for the group spoke. "Mr. Turner, why can't our Christian student group meet like the Muslim group gets to meet?"

"They are not a 'religious' group," the principal said. "They are just another ethnic group meeting from another country."

"How can you say that?" the student pressed. "They carry prayer rugs into their meetings. According to my dad, the law says that if one religious group gets to meet, any other   religious group of students can also meet on campus."

"They are a small minority group, and they feel picked on and bullied by Christian students. They need encouragement. And while it is true that the federal Equal Access Act requires that if you let one religious group meet on school property you have to let other religious groups also meet, Muslims United is not really a religious group. It is just a group of students with a certain political and ethnic background that want to meet and encourage each other. They are predominantly from Turkey and it would be like if you went to Turkey as a group of students and wanted to meet as Americans United. Or think of them as a Republican or Democratic group meeting. We let those types of organizations meet without opening the door to religious groups under the Equal Access Act."

"But Mr. Turner, Muslim is the name given to followers of the Islamic religion, and they are teaching and practicing their Muslim religion in those meetings. They have the imams come in and teach them. They even have prayers at their meetings and use prayer rugs during their meetings. That would be as much a religious exercise as if we had Pastor Curtis come speak to our group."

"Clay, I'm sorry, but you are clearly a religious group. And besides, the Muslim students tell me they think you Christians hate them and blame them for 9-11. If I let you meet, it could result in more hate speech, bullying and ultimately hateful behavior toward the Muslim students."

"Are you a Muslim, Mr. Turner? Or do you just hate Christians? It makes no sense!"

"You can't meet on school property and that's it. Now, get back to class!"

Principal Turner seldom attended church and had little use for pushy Christians. As the students left, they were stunned, hurt, and disappointed. All they wanted to do was meet and encourage each other in their Christian walk and offer the opportunity to non-Christians to come on a voluntary basis. The hope was that those nonbelievers could learn about Christ and what it meant to be a follower of Christ. They had been taught in civics class and in church that the Equal Access Act said they should be allowed to meet if the Muslim group could. As they met to discuss any options, they decided to form an organization called ERAC, Equal Religious Access for Christians. They decided to call Pastor Curtis for guidance.

The four students met with Pastor Curtis the following Monday afternoon. He led the group in prayer, thanking God for the witness of the four teenagers and praying for wisdom. Clay explained the situation with the school and Principal Turner. "Pastor Curtis, all we want to do is share Christ. Why can the Muslims meet at school, spread their religion, and we can't even meet? It's not fair!" one of the students said.

"I know it is not fair. Jesus said that we should not be surprised when we are persecuted for Him. He was persecuted, and we will be, too, for our faith. He said he was sending us out as sheep among wolves and that we will be mistreated, including by being delivered over to unfair courts to be tried. In that sense, life is not always fair as we view it, but sometimes those unfair situations give us an opportunity for others to see Christ in us. I think we need to think this through, pray about it and see how God would direct us to respond. In the meantime, I think you should let your parents know what is going on and I want you to not be discouraged. Continue to look for ways to share Christ with those around you. Remember, the Muslim students are not our enemies. The principal said they feel like we all blame them for 9-11. Let them know that is not true and that you love them. You don't have to agree with someone about their religious views in order to still love them. Demonstrate love for them. Even as you stand for trying to be treated fairly and allowed to meet, be sure you treat the Muslim students with love to try to encourage them to be followers of the God of love and his son, Jesus."

CHAPTER 10

PRESTON WAS IN HIS OFFICE trying to decide what he could do to encourage the students as they navigated how to stand firm on their demands to meet on school property, while also demonstrating love towards the Muslim students. Preston would address the issue in his upcoming Sunday sermon.

It just so happened that Pastor Curtis' sermon on the Sunday after meeting with the students was from John 14:6: "Jesus said to him, I am the way, the truth and the life. No one comes to the Father except through me," and John 3:36: "Whosoever believes in the Son has eternal life; whoever does not obey the Son shall not see life, but the wrath of God remains on him."

Preston got wound up preaching about the Biblical truth that trusting Jesus was the only way to Heaven, and condemning false religions. "One of the false religions is the Muslim religion. They don't believe in Jesus as the Messiah and they don't believe that faith in Him is the door to Heaven. Don't misunderstand me and hear me clearly: we are to love all of mankind, including Muslims. Jesus died for all of us, not just those who have accepted him as savior. But there is a major difference in loving someone as a person and agreeing with their theology. We must find a way to speak against theology that we believe is contrary to what the Bible teaches, but at the same time love the person. But the more radical elements of the Muslim faith teach their Muslim followers to kill infidels like us Christians.

"And the Muslim faith is being allowed to flourish in our school system and the Christian faith teachings are being shut down! Did you know that in our own school system—our own school system— Muslim students can meet in a school classroom, and teach about the Quran, bring in imams, pray on their prayer rugs, but four Christian students who are members of our church can't even meet together on school campus? A statement from Martin Luther appears to have been prophetic. 'I am afraid that the schools will prove the very gates of Hell, unless they diligently labor in explaining the Holy Scriptures and embracing them in the heart of the youth.' It is time to act. We must not be silent any longer in the face of this discriminatory and illegal practice. Don't misunderstand me. We are not saying the Muslims students should be prevented from meeting, just that Christian students should be allowed to meet also. Therefore, I am calling on all church members and other members of our community to call the school board members, the superintendent and Principal Turner to protest allowing these Muslim meetings on school campuses without allowing the same privilege to our Christian students. The approach currently being taken by the school district only opens the door to our students being sucked into a false religion that will lead them straight to Hell!"

The congregation gave Pastor Curtis a standing ovation at the conclusion of his comments. It was like they had been waiting to be unleashed and now their pastor had taken the gloves off.

No sooner than Preston had said the word "Amen" at the end of the service than the church phones began to light up! The volunteer manning the phones in the church office ran up to Preston and said, "Pastor, I don't know what you said, but we have had five calls in the last two minutes with three complaining about you protesting about the Muslim students meeting in the school and two wanted to know if they could sign a petition for a recall of the school board!"

"Oh, brother," Preston said. "This could be noisy and messy but maybe it will make a difference!"

The next morning, Preston decided he needed a dose of his own medicine, so he decided to call Principal Turner.

"Pitfall High School" the receptionist answered.

"This is Preston Curtis, and I would like to speak to Principal Turner please."

"Oh, Pastor Curtis, our phone has been ringing off the wall with people saying you told them to call Principal Turner to complain about the Muslim students meeting. I don't know if he is available, but I will check."

"Please do," Preston replied, "but I also need to set something straight. My complaint was not about the Muslim students meeting, it was about the Christian students not being allowed to meet when the Muslim students do get to meet. I am not trying to stop the Muslim students from meeting, I just want the Christian students to be able to meet, too."

"Okay, I'll check and see if Principal Turner is available." After about five minutes which seemed more like twenty minutes, the receptionist got back on the phone and said, "I'm sorry, but Principal Turner is not available now. Would you like to leave a number?"

"Certainly," said Preston. Oddly, Principal Turner never called Preston back even after two more attempts and messages.

Preston also decided to call the entire seven members of the school board. Only two of them would take his call. "Well, Pastor Curtis," said the school board president, "I understand you have said we have to give in to your wishes or you are going to try to get us all kicked off the school board."

"Sorry it is being presented as a threat. That was certainly not my intention. It just seems clear to me, and our students have been advised by a lawyer, that the law says if one religious group gets to meet at the school, other religious groups can as well. Somehow it appears to me the principal and superintendent have kind of lost their way on this one, and I was hoping the school board, as our elected representatives, would help straighten it out."

"Pastor Curtis, I appreciate what you are saying, but with your sermons and all the negative publicity, if we try to change directions now, we will embarrass and undermine the principal and superintendent. It is hard for us to publicly take positions telling them to change because this has become such a public uproar since your sermons, so some of us are talking privately to the superintendent to try to get it changed. But I wouldn't hold out a lot of hope. You and your church members have kind of put the principal and superintendent in a corner, and any action they take now is a lose-lose situation."

"Why lose-lose?" Preston asked. "Why isn't it simply do the right and legal thing? Their out would be that the law requires the district to let Christian groups meet if another religious group like the Muslim students get to meet. It sounds more like a win-win situation rather than a lose-lose. I was hoping the ultimate decision would be based on what is the right thing to do, not what was politically best for either the principal or the superintendent."

"Well, sometimes things aren't that easy," replied the board president. "But we will see where this goes. Thanks for the call."

As Preston hung up, he felt like he was wasting his time and that the school district would not change its position.

⁂

The week following Pastor Curtis' sermon, the school board had two closed-door meetings with their attorney to discuss the situation and how to respond.

"If we keep the current position of letting the Muslim students meet but not the Christian students, several of the school board members will likely be recalled or removed from office at the next election," the superintendent said. "And there are rumors a lawsuit will likely be filed against the district, which will cost money and keep this stirred up. On the other hand, if you agree to meet the Christian students' and parents' demands, then you will look like you are caving in to the Christians, and that would infuriate the Muslim community. Who knows the political implications for re-election of board members if that happens?"

The blowback from Preston's comments in his sermon had rippled through the community and reached national ears. A local Muslim cleric said he was seeking permission from the Islamic Supreme Council of America to issue a *fatwa* against Pastor Curtis. A *fatwa* is a formal ruling under Islamic law, usually issued by an imam, that calls for the death of an enemy.

Local media also started probing and inflaming the dispute, interviewing civic leaders and students in the high school, who began to take sides. One Muslim student told the local newspaper that he felt bullied and threatened by Pastor Curtis and by the students who attended his church.

"Pastor Curtis is teaching people to hate me simply because I am a Muslim."

About two weeks later, when Pastor Curtis was asked by a newspaper reporter for a comment, he said he did not hate Muslims because Jesus taught Christians to love all people. The next morning, Preston was anxious to read the newspaper article in the hope that his position would be clarified. Instead, his heart sank as he was quoted as saying: "the Bible is clear. Anyone who does not trust Jesus as their savior is going to Hell, and any religion that teaches anything different is a false religion."

I can't believe it! he thought. *I laid out how Christians love*

Muslims and don't hate them! Not a word about that! I really believed that reporter would be accurate and trustworthy! Lesson learned— from now on, my only media comments will be in writing!

CHAPTER 11

UNKNOWN TO PRESTON, AT THE same time as his difficulties were mounting his attorney friend RT Glassman was involved in a case of religious liberty of his own. His first real-life adventure into the constitutional implications of religious leaders and religious liberty came at the hands of his own pastor in Texas. By the time Preston's issue came up, RT's pastor at Mercy Baptist Church found himself in some legal hot water. One of his church members, Nancy Urbanik, wanted to help sponsor a pro-life march on the anniversary date of the Roe vs. Wade decision by the US Supreme Court that legalized abortion. She wanted to call attention to the sanctity of life from the time of inception, and to celebrate life. The march would also emphasize the importance of adoption and would include signs with words like "Adoption NOT Abortion."

Nancy worked in the church-sponsored crisis pregnancy center to help women figure out how to proceed with an unwanted pregnancy without resorting to abortion. The crisis pregnancy center not only provided sonograms, but also additional support such as an alternative residence, medicines including maternity vitamins, clothes, other medical care, and counseling. Nancy had applied for a permit to demonstrate but was denied. The city manager said the march would be too controversial. However, the city had previously permitted a march by the pro-choice group, Planned Parenthood.

"This is wrong," Nancy told her pastor. "The city manager won't approve for us to have a peaceful march to support the sanctity of life for the unborn. He turned down our request for a permit to march and won't even schedule an appointment for me to talk to him. But he did approve a pro-abortion march last year. What else can I do? I've prayed and prayed but the door still seems to be closed."

"Nancy," he replied, "I agree with you. This does not sound right or fair. There are both pro-life and pro-choice marches across the country on the anniversary date of Roe vs. Wade. The fact that the city manager approved a pro-abortion march but now denies a march to celebrate life makes this even more egregious. Let me do some checking and see what I can do."

Pastor Stone happened to be preaching through the book of Psalms, and the Sunday following his meeting with Nancy, he came to Psalm 139:13, 15 which says, "You made all the delicate inner parts of my body and knit me together in my mother's womb . . . . You watched me as I was being formed in utter seclusion, as I was woven together in the dark of the womb."

"Let me tell you," Pastor Stone said, "every life has value. Every baby, both born and unborn, is loved by God and deserves to be allowed to grow and become all God intended for him or her to become." There was a standing ovation from the congregation. He continued. "Abortion is the killing of babies and is a sin against God who teaches us in the Bible that he 'formed the baby' while in the mother's womb. There are over three thousand abortions daily—yes, I said *daily*—in the United States alone. Sin always progresses in a downward, dark direction, and the sin of abortion has been no different. When the debate on abortion started it was about protecting women who were the victims of rape and incest, and then it progressed to putting a stopwatch on a baby: if they were in the first three months of life, it was okay to abort them. It was an unlucky baby whose mother went to the abortion clinic two months and twenty-nine days after conception. Then we moved to the question of *viability* and some doctors said they are not *viable* until after the sixth month, which we now know is both medically and factually inaccurate. Now, did you hear this? The Virginia governor apparently supports a law that would allow a doctor and mother to decide after the baby is born whether the baby lives or dies. Do you understand? Now the sin of killing innocent babies has progressed to the point where a mother and her doctor could be able to let a living baby die! Did you know in Texas your teenage child can get a judge's order for an abortion without you as the parent even knowing about it? Heaven help us! Just this week a member of our church sought to get a permit for a peaceful pro-life march to celebrate life and to call attention to the sinful practice of killing babies through abortion. The reason given by our city manager for turning down the request is that the peaceful march would be too controversial. This is the same city manager who had approved the year before a pro-abortion march. This is also the same person whose wife works for Planned Parenthood that supports abortions. This is wrong. God celebrated life and as a culture, we cannot condone what God has condemned. Our city council should immediately pass an ordinance authorizing any march that celebrates life and encourages protection of the unborn. They should include in the ordinance that no pro-abortion march permit should ever be granted. We need to let our city councilors know how we feel and how we expect them to govern. Get on the phone today; send emails today; write letters today. Our babies need protection, and we need to send the message that God loves babies—even the unborn babies—and so do we."

Again, there was a standing ovation in the congregation. RT was supportive of his pastor's position, but he thought, *this is going to get ugly.* Sure enough, the storm began. There were petitions to fire the city manager, and daily protests at city hall. The letters to the editor section of the local newspaper was filled daily with screeds against the city manager's position to deny the permit. The mayor and council passed a resolution that said there shall not be a ban on any march that supported the right to life for any unborn child, and stated that any peaceful march that supported the right to life for all unborn children should be granted. The ability of pro-abortion advocates to receive a permit to march was not addressed. The net effect of the requested ordinance was to take the decision out of the city manager's hands when it came to approval of pro-life marches. The city manager was furious. Through a surrogate, he contacted the Dallas Chapter of the ACLU and told them what had happened. A *pro bono* lawyer for the ACLU found fifteen pro-abortion plaintiffs to sue the city to have the ordinance declared unconstitutional under the First and Fourteenth Amendments to the US Constitution.

The case was assigned to the most liberal federal judge in the Dallas Division of the Northern District of Texas. Judge Jessie Brighton was regularly reversed by the conservative Fifth Circuit for his socially liberal rulings.

While sitting in his office preparing for a deposition, RT's legal assistant, Janice, stuck her head into his door. "Your pastor is on the phone and he says he needs to talk to you immediately."

As RT answered the phone, his pastor got right to the point. "RT, I've got a problem. I have been served with a subpoena to give a deposition in that lawsuit about the ordinance allowing pro-life marches."

"Of course, I'll be glad to help," RT said. "Scan it and send it to me so I can review it." Thus, began RT's journey back into constitutional law.

RT was not so worried about his pastor giving a deposition, but he did want to keep the pastor and the church from becoming parties in the suit. The city had separate legal counsel defending the city ordinance.

In evaluating the risk to Pastor Clayton and his church, RT weighed the legal strengths and weaknesses of the lawsuit. As he researched, he concluded that while abortion was the main issue of the march, it was not the primary legal issue.

There were three legal issues, as he saw it: (1) Is it discriminatory for the city manager to approve a pro-abortion march and deny a pro-life march? (2) Is there a free speech issue for Pastor Clayton to be able to speak his convictions; and finally, (3) Is there a religious liberty constitutional protection for Pastor Clayton's preaching his religious convictions from the Bible about abortion?"

As he pondered those issues and reviewed the lawsuit petition filed by the ACLU attorney, he concluded the only action requested at that point was to declare the ordinance unconstitutional, and there was no basis of liability expressed in the lawsuit against either the pastor or the church.

"I think we are OK for now, but I've got to keep an eye on the depositions and pleadings filed to be sure nothing changes to create any risk for either Pastor Clayton or the church," RT told his aide.

On the day of his deposition, the ACLU lawyer asked Pastor Clayton about his convictions and Biblical interpretation:

Lawyer: "Do you believe the Bible says life begins at conception and that abortion in every situation is a sin?"

Pastor: "Yes."

Lawyer: "Don't you realize that preaching that way causes people listening to you to hate some pregnant women, including some who may have been objects of rape and incest?"

Pastor: "My message is not one of hate. God loves both the mother and the baby, but he hates the sin of killing babies. I and my church love the mother, including those who have had abortions, but I believe I have a responsibility to preach the truth from God's Word: that the only way to truly live a life with the right relationship with God is God's way."

Lawyer: "Your position is that there should never, under any circumstance, be an abortion. Is that correct?"

Pastor: "Yes, except in the case where you have to save the life of the mother and the parents are put in the impossible situation of being able to save either the mother or the baby, but they are unable to save both. I believe we should help women who find themselves in difficult positions, but those babies are precious lives that God loves, and we need to protect them."

Lawyer: "So, if a woman is brutally raped and she gets pregnant, you think that is okay and she just needs to get over it and have the rapist's baby?"

RT was getting nervous and moved to the edge of his seat, prepared to object.

Pastor: "Of course it is not okay. That man should be prosecuted to the full extent of the law and all kinds of support needs to be given to that poor woman. *Getting over it* is not the same thing as believing that every life is important and a gift from God. Counseling, help with doctor expenses, help with maternity vitamins, the option of adoption, on and on with support for her. But it is not the baby's fault in the way he/she was conceived. That is still a precious life to God that needs to be spared."

With that answer, RT was able to relax and thought, *Okay, that answer does not give a basis for liability against either the pastor or the church.*

Lawyer: "Do you think that prohibiting and banning all abortions will keep young ladies from again resorting to using clothes hangers and other death-inflicting tools to end pregnancies?"

RT had had enough. "I am going to object to this line of questioning. This lawsuit is not about this pastor's conviction on abortion. It is about the legality of the city ordinance. The objection is that these questions are not relevant to the legal questions to be presented to the judge, and therefore, I am going to instruct the witness not to answer your last question." The ACLU lawyer changed his line of questioning.

Lawyer: "Did you encourage your church members to attack the mayor and city council members until they granted anti-abortion marches?"

Pastor: "I never used the word 'attack.' I simply urged them to contact the mayor and city council and let their voices be heard, but only in a peaceful way, to encourage action to protect unborn babies that are unable to speak or protect themselves. I would never encourage an attack, as you have phrased it, but only an expression of a wrong that needs to be corrected. Nothing is more vulnerable and unable to protect itself than an unborn baby."

As only lawyers can do, the questions droned on about the pastor's sermons on abortion and pro-life. Since the sermon had been on TV and was a matter of public record, there was very little RT could do except be sure the proper rules applicable to a deposition were followed.

The questions then shifted to the pastor's efforts to push the city council to pass this ordinance.

Lawyer: "Did you state from your pulpit, and I quote, 'If the city council does not pass an ordinance and allow pro-life marches, we will hold the city council responsible for their vote come election time?'"

Pastor: "Yes, I did."

Lawyer: "Were you quoted accurately in the local newspaper: 'Although the City Council wants to run away from this issue, we will not allow it'?'"

Pastor: "Yes."

Lawyer: "Did you meet with the mayor to discuss action allowing anti-abortion marches?"

Pastor: "Allowing pro-life marches, yes."

Lawyer: "How many times?"

Pastor: "Once for lunch and probably about six other times over the following eight months."

Lawyer: "In every one of those discussions, did you request the mayor take actions to allow pro-life marches?"

"I object to this question because the mayor is a member of the pastor's church and under the pastor-penitent privilege, the actual conversations would be protected."

Lawyer: "Without disclosing the actual contents of your conversations with the mayor, would it be fair to say that on each occasion the subject of the marches and refusal to allow anti-abortion marches to occur was discussed?"

Pastor: "Pro-life marches, yes."

By the end of the deposition, the pastor and RT were both very tired, but RT felt the pastor and the church were protected and would have no liability, nor should they be brought into the lawsuit against the city.

At the court hearing to declare the ordinance unconstitutional, the pastor was subpoenaed to appear and give testimony. RT was again present to be sure the rules were followed and that nothing would occur that could create legal problems for either the church or the pastor. During the course of the hearing, the pastor was essentially asked the same questions from his deposition, and he gave the same answers. Since neither he nor the church was a party to the lawsuit, even though the judge allowed RT to be at counsel table during the testimony, there was very little he could do except watch and be prepared to object if the lawyer got out of line.

At the hearing, the city attorney did a good job of presenting the case for those seeking to march to protect the unborn. One witness was called who said her one regret in life was that as a teenager she had gotten an abortion. She said the decision "haunts me to this day."

The woman speculated about who her child would be today. She explained that she and the father were not married and that he pressured her into the abortion. "I regret that we took that step. I want to be able to peacefully march and use my voice as one who has experienced the devastating effect of abortion."

The city manager testified that he had turned down the permit because he feared violence. He had no good answer as to why the pro-abortion march he had previously approved had a lesser chance of violence than the pro-life march.

By the end of the hearing, there was no question what this judge thought about the city council's resolution. One month later, he rendered an opinion finding the city ordinance unconstitutional.

"This case involves the censorship of freedom of speech and discrimination against those who support a woman's right to choose," the judge wrote. But he also ruled that the ordinance violated the pro-abortion plaintiffs' "rights to speech and peacefully protest."

RT found the seemingly divided ruling confusing. How could allowing pro-life marches while not prohibiting pro-abortion marches be unconstitutional and violate the right to speech and peacefully protest? After reading the opinion, RT went back and reread the US Constitution and was reminded how judges insert and delete words from the Constitution to fit and support their decisions. Ultimately, Judge Brighton said the ordinance constituted a "heckler's veto" and was unconstitutional, without citing any real case authority to support his opinion except Roe v. Wade. Finally, the judge found that the government was usurping the mother's right to choose what was appropriate for her. Again, RT was puzzled because the city ordinance did not ban abortion. Neither did the ordinance ban pro-abortion marches. While giving surface recognition that the government has an interest in protecting children, Judge Brighton stated that the breadth of the ordinance was unacceptable.

"If citizens believe abortion is a woman's right, they should have the right to choose without being attacked by a pastor, the city council or protestors," the judge wrote.

After the decision was released, RT asked the mayor and city attorney whether the decision would be appealed. The city attorney said, "I believe the Fifth Circuit would reverse this decision in five minutes, but I can't publicly say that because I was hired by the same city manager who wouldn't approve the permit for the march. I have to be careful or I could lose my job."

The mayor also weighed in. "As you know, the city manager likes the judge's decision declaring the ordinance unconstitutional, and he has been lobbying several council members by saying he will approve the next request for a permit to allow a pro-life march, so in his opinion, the ordinance is not necessary. Also, there are taxpayer dollars that would have to be spent on outside legal fees to file an appeal. Finally, several of the council members are getting a lot of pressure from a group of voters threatening to run opponents against them in the next election if the council appeals the judge's decision. Truthfully, I don't think the council has the desire to continue the fight. I don't think we will appeal the decision, but you can tell Nancy to request another pro-life march permit, and the city manager says he will approve it. It's over."

RT decided he needed to talk to his client about the likelihood that Judge Brighton's decision would not be appealed. "Pastor Clayton, I talked to both the city attorney and the mayor, and I don't think the city will appeal Judge Brighton's decision."

"Does that mean the city manager can deny the pro-life march again, and approve an anti-abortion march? How is that right or fair?"

"It's neither right nor fair," RT responded. "You need to tell Nancy to file another request for the pro-life march and see if the city manager approves it. This is not a good long-term solution, but it will get us past this immediate issue."

"Ok, I will do that, but back to the bigger and longer-term picture: does this case mean that, going forward, if I preach from the Bible about an issue, whether it is about abortion, gay marriage or any other Biblical issue that is not viewed as politically correct, that I will get subpoenaed again?"

"The judge didn't address the question about what truths a pastor can or cannot preach from the Bible, but I can tell you, I have the alarm bells ringing in my head about that issue. It is scary to me, but I don't think judges like Brighton will be too worried about constitutional protection of religious liberty or the freedom of a pastor to preach the Bible from the pulpit. In a different context, I can imagine a scenario where a pastor might be attacked for preaching truth; but that fight has been pushed to another day. You stood up for truth to protect unborn babies and free speech, and on a positive note, we should be able to have the pro-life march that you were pushing to have. My guess is that because of the controversy created by the city manager denying the permit and the subsequent lawsuit, that the pro-life march will be the biggest one ever. So, in the end, you got the results you wanted. Hopefully, the city manager will keep his word."

After hanging up the phone, RT was worried. While he tried to put a good face on it for his pastor, he wondered, *what if the next time the attack is directly against the pastor and the church?* What would happen if the pastor was preaching that homosexuality was wrong from a Biblical perspective, or if a gay person was denied membership in the church and sued the pastor and the church? Would the principles of free speech and religious liberties under the Constitution provide protection? In the case of the permit for the pro-life march, his pastor had only been a witness. But what would happen if his pastor was sued next time?

I have no idea what would happen, he thought, but he felt pretty sure if Brighton or another judge with the same judicial philosophy presided, the outcome might not be pretty.

Multiple times during the course of this trial, RT was reminded of that day in law school where the professor asked him about the Supreme Court declaring the Mormon religious practice of polygamy illegal. He suddenly remembered that event as if it had been only yesterday, hearing his professor discussing restrictions on religious liberties. He remembered how some liberal courts twist the Constitution to serve their own purposes or perspective.

I'm just a small-town lawyer, he thought. *I am very confident that the case with my pastor and the pro-life march will be the last time I will ever be involved in such legal issues. Those kinds of cases will probably come out of some liberal state like California, New York or Oregon.*

RT generally believed that following the law leads to logical conclusions. But there was nothing logical about the judge's decision.

I can't escape the conclusion that this time they just attacked the ordinance, he thought. *But what if they ultimately turned the attack on the pastor and the words of his sermon? Would the Constitution protect the pastor and the freedom to preach the Bible?* His legal mind said such actions should be protected, but his practical mind feared that the world of political correctness was marching forward like the Legion of Doom.

CHAPTER 12

ON THE NIGHT OF THE anonymous phone call about the DA filing charges against him, Preston got out of bed for the second time that night and decided to do some online research about other pastors being harassed for preaching the Bible. He also wanted to check on his lawyer buddy, RT, to see if he had handled anything like Preston's anticipated case. Preston read in a seminary update article about Texas Pastor Clayton being subpoenaed as a witness in a case because of a sermon he preached that God was pro-life and loved even the unborn. He saw that RT had appeared in court as the attorney for the pastor. He was proud of RT and happy that his lawyer friend had some experience representing a pastor in a case involving his sermons. *The religious liberty attack on preachers has started,* he thought. The fact that his friend had been the lawyer for the Texas pastor gave Preston renewed hope that RT could provide the assistance he needed from his friend.

Preston's own legal quandary continued to weigh heavily on him. The ERAC students whom he had counseled continued to express to him their frustration about the principal's refusal to let the Christian students meet on campus. But they wanted to follow their Pastor Preston's encouragement to show love to the Muslim students.

As they brainstormed how to demonstrate love, one of the ERAC members, Sherryl Forrester, reminded the group that she had been best friends since elementary school with one of the Muslim students, Aadila Shahan. Aadila's family was from Saudi Arabia and had moved to Oregon before Aadila was born. Her parents had become US citizens. Aadila had grown up as a Muslim. She and her parents knew Sherryl was a Christian and Sherryl's parents knew Aadila and her parents were Muslims, but their different religions never entered into the relationship. Sherryl's parents had encouraged her to pray for Aadila and her family.

Sherryl and Aadila grew up playing together with dolls, playing soccer, singing, and talking about boys. They seemed inseparable and thought of themselves more like sisters than friends. They had both just been elected cheerleaders at their high school and were looking forward to their senior year together.

When the subject was brought up about the meetings of the Muslims United and the inability of the Christians to meet, Aadila's first response was "You don't understand," refusing to discuss it with her best friend. Sherryl kept pushing about the unfairness of it with Aadila.

"Sherryl, you don't understand what it is like to be a Muslim in this 'Christian' country. Everybody blames every Muslim for 9-11 and thinks we all want to kill the 'infidels.' You yourself have never done this, but other people have called me many bad names just because my family is Muslim. My father has been denied jobs and my mother has been denied membership in some women's organizations simply because we are Muslim. We have to stick together as a group, or we will die. We Muslim students need a place to meet and encourage each other. You Christians are everywhere. You don't need a classroom to meet in. Why do you need a room in school? We don't have a lot of other places to meet as students, other than at school. If we tried to meet on school grounds outside of the building, we fear we will be insulted or worse. You don't understand what it is like."

"I'm sorry," said Sherryl. "You are right, I don't understand. You are just my best friend and I don't want this to come between us. Please don't take us trying to meet in school as being against you or other Muslims. We don't have a problem with you meeting with other Muslims. I totally respect your desire to meet and I don't want to interfere or stop you from being able to meet as a group. I love you. Jesus teaches us to love you. Please don't think all of us Christians blame you for 9-11, or that we think you want to kill us. We want the same thing you want. We just think the law says that if one religious group meets at school, other religious groups can meet there, too."

They did the pinky promise they had done as kids, hugged and said this issue would not divide them. But, as they left, they both worried that things were about to blow up, and that their deep bond would be frayed.

CHAPTER 13

ON THE SUNDAY FOLLOWING THE newspaper article, Muslim supporters marched outside Grace Bible Church carrying signs saying, "Christians Hate Muslims," and "No More Bullying," and "Lock Him Up." The church was under attack like never before. Lines were being drawn by church members and community residents, with some saying, "Pastor Curtis was just preaching the truth of the Bible," and others were saying: "He's preaching hate!"

Pastors of other churches that had once been friendly to Preston went silent, either because they didn't believe the Bible was meant to be interpreted this way or because they were too cowardly to be on the receiving end of attacks.

The controversy was also taking its toll on the high school students and their parents. Aadila's father told her, "Aadila, I know you and Sherryl have been friends since elementary school. But she and her family attend that church that hates Muslims and keeps saying we are going to Hell. For some reason, Sherryl and her family must agree with that pastor, because they continue to attend that church. Therefore, you may not associate with or show any friendship to Sherryl."

"But Papa, Sherryl is my best friend. She doesn't hate us, and you know that! Don't do this terrible thing! She has continued to be my friend and stand up for me against kids who make snide or snarky comments about Muslims."

"That's enough Aadila! I have spoken. We cannot be friends with people who support such intolerance and hatred."

Despite Aadila tearfully begging her father to change his position, he insisted. She sent a text to Sherryl explaining what had happened and then blocked Sherryl's number from her phone. When Sherryl saw Aadila the next day at school, Aadila said, "You don't understand. My father has spoken, and we can't be friends anymore. Please leave me alone or you will make my life very hard."

Christ's call to be peacemakers and even to "love your enemies" told Sherryl she couldn't give up. She went home that night and told her dad what had happened and what Aadila's father had said and done. She said she had lost her best friend.

"Daddy, isn't there something we can do?"

"Sherryl, let's keep praying for them. I am trying to decide if it will be ok for me to call Aadila's dad. Let me see if I can talk to him to try to help him understand that we support and love them."

They prayed together and asked God to give wisdom and to help them be able to communicate the love of Christ, not only to Aadila and her family, but to other Muslims as well.

Sherryl's dad, Robert, finally decided to give Aadila's dad, Umran, a call to discuss the situation. Umran was very cool.

"Umran, our relationship and our daughters' relationship goes back to their early days in elementary school. My daughter has been very hurt by all of this as I am sure Aadila has been. Our family loves Aadila and your family and I believe your family loves Sherryl and our family. We would hate to see that relationship end. Don't let this issue create a barrier between either our girls or us. We have known you are Muslims over the years, and you have known we are Christians, and yet we have never let that be an issue between us. We don't want these events to create a divide. Our daughters are hurting, and I would like to find a way for them to continue to be friends and for you and me to also be friends."

"What you say about our girls and our relationships is true," Umran responded. "But tell me why you belong to that church where the pastor says hateful things about our faith and your daughter is involved in a group at school that is attacking the Muslims in school?"

"Oh, Umran, I am so sorry that you have viewed all of us as Christians that way. Let me just say that the Bible I read and the Jesus I serve say I am to love all people of all faiths or of no faith—including Muslims. Neither Sherryl, nor I, nor our family hates you. We have nothing but love for you, Aadila and your family. The point the pastor was trying to make has gotten blown totally out of context. I think he was trying to say faith in Jesus is the way to Heaven, just like your imam would say belief and following Mohammed and the Quran is the way to Heaven. Certainly, there is a theological difference, but that does not make us haters or enemies. The media has fueled the fire of hatred to create headlines. Also, Sherryl and her group totally support Aadila and her Muslim friends meeting at school, but simply requested that she and her friends get to meet also. I am sure Sherryl would be willing to write something or speak up to say she does not want the Muslim group to have to stop meeting. I apologize for the hurt and offense you and your family have taken. I will stand up for you as a beloved friend and work to heal the hurts."

"You have no idea how much pressure my family and I feel from the other members of our mosque," Umran said. "There is a feeling that all Christians hate Muslims and blame all of us for 9-11, and that we want to kill all Christians and take over their country. My whole family has been on the receiving end of hateful actions by Christians. I want to protect my daughter from further harm. My Muslim brothers feel totally attacked by your pastor, your church and the ERAC students. However, I always act in the best interest of my daughter, and Sherryl has been a good friend. I will back off from not letting Aadila spend time with her for now, but I want your word that you will help me find ways to undo the harm and seek to restore relationships. If you and Sherryl will openly, verbally and in writing, support the right of Muslim students to continue to meet, and respect and allow for other faiths and beliefs to exist in school without attacking them, then Aadila and I will support the same privilege for the Christian students. I think we both also need to report—you to your pastor and me to my imam—that we are going to take actions to calm the waters, teach love, but not compromise our respective faiths. Can you agree?"

"I absolutely agree," said Robert. "If it's okay with you, I will have Sherryl call Aadila in about an hour to give you time to talk to her and then you and I can talk further at the girls' soccer game on Friday. Sherryl and I will prepare a statement tonight to send to the principal that her intent, and the intent of the ERAC students, is not to prevent the Muslims from meeting, and that they would simply ask the same consideration for the Christian students."

"Sounds good," said Umran.

As Robert hung up, he thought, *Now that is what Christians should be doing. That call should have happened sooner.*

After both talked to their daughters, there was an hour long talk-and-giggle time for the girls. At least one corner of the iceberg had begun to thaw.

CHAPTER 14

AT HOME, AS THE PRESSURE continued to build, Pastor Curtis had a discussion with his wife about the fact that she was afraid for him and their children.

"Preston, Sarah told me that at least ten people confronted her just today about her dad being either hateful or a bully, or that her daddy is a right-wing preacher nut. She comes home from school nearly every day crying and complaining. If we don't get a handle on this, I am worried about how she will ultimately respond. While she hasn't said it yet, it feels like resentment is growing in her simply because of who her daddy is. You need to spend some time with her."

"I know. I will talk to her, but I don't know how to stop all of this noise. I tried to talk to the media and got misquoted. I tried to call the principal and school board and was stonewalled, and finally, I have preached from the pulpit that we love the Muslim people, just not their theology." Preston paused. "How are the boys doing?"

"Well, the good news is that the boys don't seem to be impacted that much so far. Joshua is responding like a typical eleven-year-old boy. He thinks his dad being in the media all the time is cool. So I think the boys are fine, at least for now."

While Janie was a very committed Christian and believed what Preston was preaching, she was scared for him, her kids, the church, his job, and the incorrect perception that Preston was a hater or sought to do harm to anyone. She knew his heart and how hard he had worked to demonstrate that God was a loving God—even to the Muslims who now hated them—but she also knew that the situation was beginning to develop a life of its own and that things were spinning out of control.

"Preston, I know you are frustrated, and I don't know how you can do it, but you have got to do something to calm the situation down and correct these inaccurate assumptions and conclusions. I am worried about Sarah and I am afraid someone will try to harm you. I am afraid the church is going to split or that you will be fired!"

"But Janie, what am I supposed to do? I have done what I knew to do, and now people are waiting to see if I will change my theology because I am under attack for preaching the Bible. I have visited with the elders and they seem supportive of me. I have preached that we are to love Muslims, but they are a false religion according to the Bible, and I can't go weak-kneed just because I am under attack. Janie, we need to be strong for our family, the church and for each other." They prayed together and expressed their love for each other, but neither had a sense of peace about the situation.

CHAPTER 15

THE SWIRLING CONTROVERSY WAS TAKING an unwanted turn. Multnomah County District Attorney Mark Ryan was receiving phone calls complaining about Preston and woefully following media reports. There were threats of violence and rioting.

Not in my county, he thought.

At a staff meeting to discuss pending cases, Ryan asked one of his assistant DAs to research and report back on the definition of "hate speech" under Oregon law.

The assistant reported back that Oregon's statute defines hate speech as "speech that is intended to insult, intimidate, or cause prejudice against a person or people based upon their race, gender, age, sexual orientation, religion, political affiliation, occupation, disability or physical appearance."

An intentional violation of this statute could result in a sentence of up to two years in a state jail facility, plus a fine up to ten thousand dollars, or both. The statute had not yet been interpreted by the courts as to whether it restricted the freedom of either religion or speech.

"I can't find a single case where this statute has been used to prosecute a pastor," the assistant DA said. "If we can overcome the legal challenges on those grounds, at least on the surface it would appear there could be a basis to charge Pastor Curtis with the criminal charge of hate speech."

"Great," said Ryan. "Do the additional research needed, get the facts put together and then get back to me so we can re-evaluate before presenting to a grand jury to get an indictment."

One of the female assistant DAs, Stacy Randerson, said, "Mark, are you sure you want to try to prosecute a pastor? Is a war of words over theology between two religions and two churches a hill you want to die on? I have heard a lot of odd things from preachers over the years that are supposed to be from the Bible, like women shouldn't preach in church. There are denominations that prohibit such gender discrimination, while other religions say it is okay. It seems to me that theological differences should not be a basis for criminal prosecution. Usually those things have a way of resolving themselves. Frequently, they get resolved by the wild card pastor getting fired. Then you also have the legal considerations of fighting the constitutional protections of religious liberty. Finally, there are political implications to consider. I know you have been DA for a long time and have been successful in your campaigns, but I can envision scenarios that whichever way this prosecution goes, it could be political suicide.

"There is a lot of written material out there about how much damage radical Muslims have done to Americans, even notwithstanding 9-11," Stacy continued. "Is that the group you want to use as being hurt by this conservative pastor? He is simply preaching what many Christians believe, which is that Jesus is the only way to Heaven. I would encourage you to drop this one like a hot potato, because that is exactly what this is—a hot potato."

"Think about all of the other cases we have in this office," the assistant DA said. "Cases involving murder, rape, distribution of drugs, etcetera. Are you going to equate prosecuting one pastor on the same plane as prosecuting those cases? Or even on an elevated plane, since we are sure it will go all the way to the Supreme Court? My vote would be to run from this prosecution."

"Stacy, I hear you," said Ryan. "But the law is the law, and we don't get to pick either our victims or our criminals. If this man, whether a preacher or not, has violated a law that has been passed by the legislature that gives criminal penalties for violation, we have a duty to prosecute it."

Stacy shook her head in obvious disagreement but said nothing else.

When the statute was passed, everyone, including the Christian community, thought that not speaking in a manner that was hateful and mistreated or discriminated against other people was a good idea. No one had recognized that the insertion of the word "religion" into the statute could be interpreted as giving a prosecutor grounds to indict a pastor for simply preaching the Bible.

CHAPTER 16

STUDENT MEMBERS OF ERAC FELT like an underground prayer society. They were concerned for their safety and the backlash of other students. Sherryl told the group about what had happened between her and Aadila and their dads.

"We need to take the initiative to demonstrate that Christ is love, even to those who might act hatefully toward us. And we need to seek to continue to be friends with the Muslim students. We know that silence and withdrawal will only fuel more hateful thoughts and actions. Whatever plan we come up with must include us saying we don't mind the Muslim students meeting, but we want the same right, and we need to reach out to our Muslim friends saying we still love you and want to be your friends. I believe that is what Christ would want us to do as his hands, feet and voice."

"Okay, we need a plan," Clay said. "We don't want to be like Peter at Jesus' crucifixion when he denied Jesus three times. We need to be bold and take a stand. Pastor Curtis preached boldly because of the information we provided to him, so we need to speak up and defend Pastor Curtis, and also be a witness for Jesus."

It was decided that Clay would work on getting out the word to other students about ERAC and invite them to join their group. In addition to word of mouth, he used texts, Twitter, Facebook, Snapchat, email and blogging. Within three days he had forty students willing to join ERAC.

Cindy found a house right across the street from the high school that belonged to a widow who was sympathetic to their cause and said the students could meet anytime in her garage. Sherryl and Melinda began researching what the Equal Access Act provided for, and how other Christian student organizations in schools across the country had responded to similar denials of access.

1. They would organize groups that would carry their message in school at every opportunity, including making locker signs that would show up when the lockers were open, get wristbands with ERAC on them, and make statements in the classroom when the opportunity allowed that would demonstrate their Christian faith.

2. They developed electronic media groups that would send out regular reminders of their activities and specific messages they wanted to communicate, including the messages that they loved the Muslims and did not want their ability to meet to be altered. They warned the other students that there might be consequences for their conduct, like suspension, but they needed all to stand up for Jesus and to encourage each other as they went through this difficult process.

3. They would make signs and look for opportunities to display them. The signs would support Christians and oppose discrimination against Christians in favor of Muslims.

4. All of the ERAC members would reach out to their Muslim friends and extend Christian love and all four of the founding

members signed a statement that they wanted the Muslim students to be able to continue meeting, but they also wanted the same privilege.

———————◇———————

Clay decided the group could not let up pressure on the school district and its discriminatory practices. Every school day for three weeks he had a different student take an application to Principal Turner requesting approval for the ERAC group to meet in school. The first two were denied and the rest were ignored. Students also peppered the principal with complaints about the discriminatory practices against the Christian students and in favor of Muslim students. One day Principal Turner summoned Clay into his office.

"Clay, enough is enough. You are constantly stirring up trouble and harassing me and other administrators because you don't get your way. If you don't stop this activity immediately, you will be expelled from school for a breach of the student conduct code. The disorderly conduct and hateful speech violate our code."

"Mr. Turner, I am a Christian and my intent is not to stir up hate, but rather is to obtain the same equal access and treatment for Christians as you are giving to Muslims," Clay said firmly. "I cannot be silent as a Christian when I know that the school's practice of allowing one religious group of students to meet when denying the same right to another group of religious students violates both my conscience and the federal Equal Access Act."

"So, you refuse to stop your group with the activities viewed as hateful and disruptive?"

"Mr. Turner, I can't stop trying to do the right thing. We have not engaged in hateful or disruptive behaviors. I have always been taught that right is right and wrong is wrong and that I should take a stand for what is right. I believe what you are doing is wrong—both legally and on basic principles of fairness. Therefore, I just can't agree."

"Then you are expelled for five days from school. You will not be allowed to make up any test or homework that would have been required during that time."

"Mr. Turner, that is very unfair. You know that I am second in my class with my grade point average, and I am making a charge to be valedictorian. You punish me in this manner, and I will be dropped out of the top five GPAs."

"Your choice, Clay."

"I can't stop living my Christian faith!"

"I am not asking you to stop living your Christian faith. I am directing you to stop this hateful conduct directed toward Muslims. I don't see why you have to equate 'living your Christian faith' with stirring up hatred toward Muslims."

"Mr. Turner, I am trying to demonstrate the love of Christ toward Muslims, but also take a stand to see that the law is followed. I'm not stirring up hatred toward Muslims. I am trying to get equal treatment for Christians. None of this would have happened if you would have simply followed the Equal Access Law."

"It is too bad you feel the way you do. You are expelled for five days. Clean out your locker immediately and don't come back until day six."

Clay was crushed and wondered why God would allow this to happen. He needed the scholarships awarded to valedictorians or salutatorians in order to afford college because his family was poor.

His expulsion fueled the fire even more. Christian parents started bombarding the principal's office, the superintendent and school board members with calls and messages of protest and indignation. The superintendent didn't buckle, continuing to back his principal. Some of the Muslim students and parents were sympathetic and told Principal Turner to let the Christian students meet, but other Muslim students and parents were applauding the fact that the infidels were getting what they deserved. The majority of both the Muslim and Christian students and parents just wished the whole problem would go away.

Many of the parents of Muslim students feared they were being lumped in with the radical Muslims. They feared being ostracized or attacked for supporting the infidels. And fiery comments between the more radical and conservative elements of both groups became more and more frequent.

After Clay's expulsion, the original four ERAC members again decided to meet with Pastor Curtis. This time, they took their parents. Preston thought, *These kids are learning some hard lessons about trying to live a Christian life.*

"Pastor Curtis, why is this happening?" Melinda asked. "It's not fair that Clay has been expelled from school."

"Pastor Curtis, I think both the students and you need to stop talking about this for a while and let things cool off," Melinda's father suggested.

"Is that because you think the positions being taken are not Biblical, or not solid legally, or because you are afraid of the consequences?" asked Pastor Curtis.

"I don't want my daughter hurt. Muslims have a reputation of killing people they see as infidels. Melinda is trying to get good grades so she can get college scholarships, and she can't stand to be expelled like Clay. Plus, I think being quiet and letting everything blow over is standing for Christ. We need some common sense here."

"Melinda, you are right that it isn't fair," Preston said. "You need to submit to the leadership of your father. But I want the group to remember two things: Jesus said we would be hated for his sake; and He has promised inner peace and that he will never leave nor forsake us. So don't be discouraged."

Preston prayed for the group and dismissed them, knowing their divisions and uneasiness would only grow. He also decided he needed to speak out in favor of the students on Sunday.

The Sunday services wound up being anything but ordinary. Outside the church before the service, sign-carrying activists on both sides were shouting back and forth. One side carried signs reading "Equal Access For Christians," "Muslims Kill Christians,"

"Jesus ≠ Allah." On the other side the signs read "Infidels Burn In Hell," "Love Not Hate," and "Pastor Curtis Hates Muslims." As the groups grew rowdier, local police called in reinforcements from the county sheriff's office and adjoining police departments.

Inside the church things were not much calmer. Preston recognized the commitment of the four ERAC students and the unfairness of Clay being expelled.

"This conduct of hatred toward Christians and favoritism toward Muslims violates both the United States law and God's law. We are a nation founded on an almighty God with the right to teach the truth from God's word. The truth is, Jesus teaches us to love all people, including Muslims. Do you hear me? Love Muslims, but Muslims do not accept Jesus as Savior and because of that fact, the Bible teaches us they are condemned to Hell and eternal separation from God."

The words had no more come out of his mouth than some attendees jumped up and started yelling "Allah . . . Allah . . . Allah . . ." By the end of the day, six people were hospitalized— four Christians and two Muslims. Two had sustained serious injuries.

CHAPTER 17

WHEN CLAY'S DAD, REGGIE COOK, decided to fight his son's expulsion he called Murry Sinclair, a local civil rights attorney known for taking cases for free. After discussing everything with Mr. Cook, Sinclair said, "This should be a slam dunk. I can't believe the school district has totally ignored the law and lashed out at Clay this way. Come by the office this afternoon and we will have the papers prepared for you to sign so we can file the motion for a temporary restraining order against the school district."

The case landed before US District Judge Sullivan Chambless who had a reputation as a no-nonsense, bottom-line judge intolerant of shenanigans and shoddy lawyering. He was a Texan who had been appointed to the Oregon federal bench by President George W. Bush because he thought the Oregon judicial candidates were too liberal.

On the day of the hearing, Judge Chambless called the attorneys back into chambers. Cook's attorney was pitted against the school district's attorney, Rachael Young. Judge Chambless sat behind a massive oak desk and was surrounded by legal awards and baseball memorabilia. He was over six feet five inches and weighed over two-fifty, towering over the two lawyers when he stood to shake their hands.

"Okay, counselors. I have read the sworn and verified application for a temporary restraining order that has been filed by Mr. Sinclair on behalf of his client. Before we go out into the courtroom and spend a lot of time on evidence, I wanted to see if we could cut to the chase and get to the bottom line. Ms. Young, you represent the school district. I have several questions for you.

"Is it true that the school allows Muslim students to meet on school grounds, but has denied the Christian students the same right?

"Yes, Your Honor, but—"

"Ms. Young, I will ask the questions and you can contain your commentary and arguments. Is it also true that the principal was requested at least three times to grant the same meeting access to the Christian students as the Muslims had?"

"Yes, Your Honor."

"And is it also true that this matter was presented to the school superintendent and the school board, and they sustained the principal's decision to deny access?"

"Yes, Your Honor."

"Is it also true that because Mr. Cook peacefully pressed the matter to the principal, that he was suspended for five days, which could have the potential effect of killing his chances to be valedictorian or salutatorian?"

"Yes, Your Honor, he was suspended. I don't know what impact, if any, that will have on his class standing."

"I am not going to ask you to disclose attorney-client communications, but I am confident that, being the good lawyer that you are, you advised your client about the federal Equal Access Act and the United States Supreme Court case that upheld the Equal Access Act of 1984. So, would you like to explain to me why your client continues to take the position of denying the Christian students' equal access as required by federal law?"

"Your Honor, the principal's position is that the Muslim organization is merely a political group and not a religious group and because—"

"Let me stop you right there, Ms. Young. I was born at night but not last night. If the application is correct and the Muslim group brings in an imam, reads the Quran, has prayer rugs and conducts prayers, are you seriously going to try to tell me it was only a political group meeting?"

"Well, Your Honor, I was merely stating the principal's position, and that the school district felt it needed to support his position."

"So, you are telling me that the district's position is that it is more worried about hurting the principal's feelings than harming a student, particularly if that conduct is contrary to federal law and deprives a lawful group from meeting as other groups are meeting? That's a rhetorical question, so you don't have to answer it. But here is what I want to communicate: I feel no compulsion to support the principal for not complying with the Equal Access Law. Nor am I worried about hurting a principal's feelings when his conduct is unnecessarily harmful to students and his conduct is also contrary to federal law. We can go out into the courtroom and have a hearing and I will listen carefully and apply the facts to the law, but I want to explain to you, Ms. Young, that what has been outlined to me, to which you have acquiesced and agreed, appears to be a clear violation of the Equal Access Law.

"If we go out there and have a hearing and the facts are proven as they have been alleged and presented here, I anticipate I will find for the student and I will do so with very clear language about the intentional violation of federal law. Plus, I will award attorneys' fees to Mr. Sinclair, which I am sure will be very significant, perhaps as much as fifty thousand dollars before we get done. I will also continue the case to check on the harm done to the student Clay Cook and see if he desires to pursue personal damages for being deprived of the opportunity to be valedictorian or salutatorian and obtain significant college scholarships. I suspect if that happened, the student would seek redress from the district for the lost scholarships, and if there was a clear, intentional violation of law, I think most lawyers would like their chances of recovery. Have I made myself perfectly clear?"

"Yes, Your Honor."

"Then we are going to take a break for fifteen minutes and allow you to talk to your respective clients and see if an agreement can be reached to resolve this matter. If not, we will proceed to hear the evidence."

Attorney Young bolted from the judge's chamber and talked to the superintendent and the school board president. After only ten minutes, the attorneys sent a message to the judge that an agreement had been reached to settle the case.

Once everyone was in the courtroom, Mr. Sinclair announced to the judge that the parties had reached the following agreement: That the school district will be permanently enjoined from violating the Equal Access Act; Clay Cook and the ERAC organization would be allowed to meet on the school campus at comparable times and places to the Muslim organization; Clay would be reinstated and allowed to fully make up any work he may have missed; Mr. Sinclair would be paid five thousand dollars as attorneys' fees by the school district.

Once word of the ruling hit the community and school district, it only added fuel to the blazing fire. Principal Turner was called by the superintendent immediately following the hearing.

"Brad, you screwed up. You knew it at the time, and I knew it, but I tried to cover for you. Now, both you, me and the school board have egg on our face. Your actions have caused a lot of problems for all of us, including the loss of a lot of time and energy as well as the cost of attorney's fees. To say you are on thin ice is an understatement. I expect you to take those actions outlined by the judge in the order and implement them immediately, and I don't want to hear about any more problems over this issue. Have I made myself clear?"

"Perfectly clear."

The Muslim community thought the school district caved, but since an agreement had been entered that was backed up by a court order, there was no way the decision could be appealed.

The ERAC students wanted to celebrate in front of the school but decided not to out of respect for the Muslim students. Principal Turner delegated all responsibilities for coordinating ERAC meetings to an assistant principal.

"Fix it, and I don't want to hear about this issue ever again."

CHAPTER 18

THE DAY AFTER THE NEAR-RIOT at Grace Bible Church, some twenty miles away from the church, District Attorney Ryan was reviewing the police accounts of all of the events involving Grace Bible Church and the Muslim community. While his assistant DA Stacy had suggested this matter would die from natural causes, it seemed the fire kept burning brighter. He continued to be appalled at the notion that a pastor could stir up people to hate Muslims in the name of religion. He had previously asked one of his assistants to continue compiling all of the evidence surrounding Pastor Curtis' comments.

I can't imagine a jury thinking that when you essentially tell Muslims they are going to Hell that such words aren't hate speech, the DA thought.

Each Monday Ryan met with his criminal prosecutors to discuss which cases would be presented to the next meeting of the grand jury. Ryan wanted to be sure that his prosecutors had correctly evaluated every aspect of the case before obtaining an indictment, which they received virtually every time a case was presented because no opposing party or attorney was allowed to appear for the accused party. However, on this day, the tables were turned. His first assistant DA said, "Mark, why are you going to pursue this case? Really? You want to prosecute a pastor when we have a murder case, three sexual assault cases, ten robbery cases, four burglary cases and nine drug cases to present to the grand jury this week? This guy's crime was to read his Bible and say Muslims are going to Hell?"

Another assistant said, "And what about the constitutional issues of free speech and religious liberties? If you try a pastor, I bet the constitutional issues will be pursued all the way to the US Supreme Court. Plus, even if you convict the guy, he is bound to just get probation. He has no criminal record. So, what example have you really made? It will be a slap on the wrist."

Ryan stiffened, surprised by the pushback.

"Your officemate, Cindy, did a legal memo researching those exact issues. Cindy, you want to tell the group what you discovered?"

"Well," she began, "the Supreme Court says there are limits on religious liberty and those opinions go all the way back to the decision where the Court said that criminally prosecuting a Mormon for engaging in polygamy based upon his religious beliefs was an acceptable limitation on the rights of freedom of speech and religious liberty. Recently, there have been cases upholding intermediate appellate court decisions against perpetrators of hate for verbal hate speech against gays, with the appeal being based on responses that the speech was allowed as free speech by the Constitution. Secondly, a good argument can be made that the government is not prohibiting the free exercise of religion. It is simply saying that exercise must be conducted in a manner that does not harm someone else. In this case, the person harmed would be the Muslims who are the objects of the hateful speech. If Mark can prove actual harm to a Muslim or the Muslim body worshipping at the mosque involved in this dispute, I think there is a good chance we could win on appeal, even with the constitutional issues.

"Proving the pastor's actions fit within the statutory definition of hate speech is easy, since all of the sermons are available online and are pointedly directed at Muslims. I think we would be successful in the prosecution, and even on appeal. But the bigger question is whether we really want to use the time, energy, and financial resources of this office to prosecute this case instead of all the other cases we have? Plus, I want to emphasize the point previously raised by Stacy: isn't there a risk there could be a lot of blowback to you, Mark, in the next election? You know that sometimes cases can take on a life of their own, and one bad publicity case can draw an opponent in the next election."

"Look," DA Ryan said, "this is not about politics but about what is right. I don't care if you are a preacher or a street sweeper. The hate speech statute exists to keep people from attacking, hurting and causing harm. My folks took me to a church when I was a boy, and that preacher attacked everything and everybody. I never left church encouraged and decided I didn't need God or some preacher yelling at me. I think we need to make an example of this guy. I'll mull on it for a week or so, but unless my mind changes, I'm going to prosecute."

Stacy and the rest of the assistant DAs sat, stunned. Stacy returned to her office, troubled by the reality of a pastor about to be prosecuted just because of a personal vendetta against him. She stared out her window at the park on the lawn and thought, *What can I possibly do? He is the DA, and I can't go to the media, or publicly say anything or I'll be fired.* She closed the door to her office and reached for the phone to try to take the only action available.

"Reverend Curtis, you don't know me, but—"

CHAPTER 19

DA RYAN DOUBLED DOWN AND personally presented the case to prosecute Pastor Curtis to the grand jury.

"Ladies and gentlemen of the grand jury, I am going to conclude today's session by presenting a most unusual case that may make some of you uncomfortable. But you took an oath to apply the law equally to all people and we must prosecute cases in an even-handed manner that says no one is above the law.

"The Oregon legislature passed a statute that defines hate speech as speech intended to insult, intimidate, or cause prejudice against a person or people based upon their religion. That is exactly what we have in the case of Preston Curtis, the pastor of Grace Bible Church in Pitfall. I am going to present videos to you where he essentially said 'Muslims are going to Hell.' Not once, not twice, but at least five times that we know about. Additionally, he encouraged some high school students who were members of his church to intimidate the Muslim students at the high school trying to meet as a group on campus. As a result, there have been near riots, and at least one confrontation at a flagpole rally on the high school campus where one Muslim student got her arm broken. We simply cannot allow this type of conduct—even by a preacher—to go unchallenged."

Ryan played selected portions of videos of Preston's sermons where he proclaimed that Muslims were going to Hell. Since neither Preston nor his lawyer was permitted to be in the grand jury room, the jurors did not see the context of the sermons nor hear the Biblical basis for the sermon.

Ryan called Imam Amar, who said that ever since Pastor Curtis had started preaching hate against Muslims, his people had been intimidated and verbally attacked. "One of our students was attending a flagpole rally, praying, and because of the attack by the Christian students she got a broken arm. We have had marches outside our church, our phone rings constantly with people spewing hatred toward us because we are Muslims. It's not right!"

Did any of these things happen before Preston Curtis started preaching that Muslims were going to Hell?" Ryan asked.

"No sir, only after. We would occasionally have a crank caller, but once he started preaching that we were going to Hell, that is when it all started."

After Imam Amar completed his testimony, one of the jurors said to Ryan, "This man Curtis was preaching, but I didn't hear him tell anybody to hurt anyone else or attack Muslims, or do anything else illegal. He was just preaching. Over the years, there have been some pretty fired-up preachers who preached a lot of verbal attacks on other religions or politicians, and I have heard that was just free speech. How is this any different? Are you going to start indicting all of the preachers who claim they are teaching the Bible, but offend someone?"

"Of course not," Ryan replied. "But this guy crossed the line and it caused people to be attacked and harmed. I think if we make an example of this guy, there is a chance this kind of thing will end."

An hour later, Preston was indicted, facing jail time and a stiff fine if convicted.

That evening his wife, Janie, came running into his home office and said, "Preston, you have got to come see this now. Hurry!" Preston had no idea what was going on, but quickly followed her into the den where the evening news was playing and he saw his face plastered on the TV screen and heard an announcer say, "the crime Pastor Preston Curtis is charged with, religious hate speech, carries a penalty of up to two years in prison and a maximum fine of up to ten thousand dollars. The indictment was unsealed today, and Curtis is expected to be arrested tomorrow." Janie implored her husband to call his old friend RT. "Now! Go call him now! They are going to arrest you tomorrow!"

CHAPTER 20

ONE OF RT'S LAW SCHOOL professors had told him to be wary of long-lost high school buddies and family members who just "need a little advice." That phrase usually translates into "free legal advice," and "lots of problems." RT had thought many times he should have listened to his professor's advice, but routinely ignored it.

It was ten-thirty at night when Preston called. RT was already asleep and must have sounded groggy.

"RT, this is Preston Curtis. Sorry to wake you up, but I've got a problem."

RT knew immediately "I" was going to mean "we." "Okay, Preston, tell me everything."

Preston started from the beginning.

"Wait a minute," RT said. "You're telling me that you got indicted for preaching Biblical teachings from the pulpit?"

"That's right, an announcement of the indictment was on the

news tonight," Preston said. "They said on the news that they are going to come arrest me tomorrow."

"Preston, this doesn't sound right. Your sermons should be protected under the US Constitutional provisions for religious liberty and free speech. But I am not licensed to practice law in Oregon, and it also sounds like a case with a lot of constitutional issues. That's not really my bailiwick, but I do know that the First Amendment prevents Congress and state legislatures from passing laws that prohibit the free exercise of religion. You need to hire you a local lawyer to handle it. Any judge should throw out the indictment if all they have is that you were preaching the Bible from your pulpit."

Preston took a deep breath and said in a soft, shaky voice that RT had never heard before, "I don't trust any lawyer but you. This is not the Bible Belt, and I am afraid for my wife and family that they are going to railroad me and put me in jail. Plus, I am pastor of a small church that doesn't pay much. I can't afford to hire a lawyer. Janie is scared to death, RT. Please help me."

"Oh man, Preston, I wish you had called me before the grand jury hearing. We could have tried to prevent the indictment from being issued. It will be really hard to try to persuade the DA to drop the charges now that the indictment has gone public." RT paused and said, "All right, old friend. I'm on my way."

RT hung up the phone and turned to his wife. "I am going to Oregon." Before returning to sleep, they prayed for Preston, his family and his church.

CHAPTER 21

THE NEXT MORNING, RT CALLED a lawyer in Portland to whom he was referred, hoping to convince the attorney to take Preston's case *pro bono.*

"I appreciate what you are doing, but I'm not going to defend some religious right-wing nut case for free." Calls to three other Portland attorneys ended about the same way.

RT next called the DA directly to discuss whether Preston could stay out of jail on an agreed personal recognizance bond until the case was either dismissed or tried. Such a bond doesn't cost anything.

"Mr. Ryan, my name is RT Glassman, and I am a Texas attorney and a friend of Preston Curtis whom you just indicted. I wanted to call and visit with you about the case for a minute if I could."

"Are you licensed to practice in Oregon?"

"No, sir. Preston's just a good friend of mine. We grew up together, so he called me and I thought I would file a motion to appear *pro hac vice,*" (which means a judge would approve an out-of-state attorney to appear in one case that had been filed in that particular court).

"I won't oppose your motion to appear and represent Mr. Curtis," Ryan said, "but I will oppose your motion for a PR bond. If Preston Curtis preaches again, he will keep the hate stirred up. The only way I will agree to a PR bond is if he agrees not to preach while the case is pending."

"So, you are telling me the only way you will agree to a PR bond is if Preston agrees to quit preaching until the trial?"

"That's right."

"Can you at least hold off on having him arrested until I see if I can get a bond hearing set and we can do the book-in, book-out process and bonding at the same time?"

"I don't like that approach because I don't want him to keep spewing his poison in our community," Ryan said. "But if we can do this before he preaches again next Sunday, I'll agree to the delay in arresting him, but I'll still be opposing the PR bond."

Two days later, Preston and Ryan appeared before Judge Hannah Jackson. The judge approved RT's motion to appear *pro hac vice*, with a stern warning that RT would be expected to fully comply with Oregon and not Texas law. Ryan then forcefully argued about the hate stirred up by Preston, and RT argued the pastor's speech fit under the umbrella of constitutionally protected religious liberties and freedom to preach the Bible.

"Judge," RT stated, "the First Amendment to the Constitution reads, 'Congress shall make no law respecting an establishment of religion or prohibiting the free exercise thereof; or abridging the freedom of speech.' Your Honor, these rights are guaranteed to all of us as United States citizens pursuant to the Fourteenth Amendment to the Constitution."

"Counselor, save your constitutional arguments for the trial. I will set the bond at ten thousand dollars and will approve a PR bond if the defendant will sign a document agreeing to not preach any sermon about any Scripture that could be interpreted to be hateful until after the trial. That means *no* topic that could be viewed as hateful. Am I clear?"

"Yes, Your Honor," RT replied. "May I have five minutes to visit with my client?"

After the judge granted the brief recess, RT looked over at Preston when they got into the hall and saw that he was shaking his head. "RT, I can't agree to that," Preston told him. "She's telling me I can't preach the Bible!"

"No, she's not," RT said. "She is saying don't preach any part of the Bible that can be viewed as hateful. You can preach about Jesus' love, the attitudes we learn from Jesus in the Beatitude chapter. Preach on creation, I don't care. Work with me here!"

"RT, when I preach, I have to be able to say the only way to Heaven is to trust Jesus. I can't choose to please this judge rather than God! Galatians 1:10 says, 'For am I now seeking the favor of men or of God? Or am I striving to please men? If I were still striving to please men, I would not be a bondservant of Christ.' No, I have to choose to obey Jesus rather than obey this judge."

"Preston," RT said, "I agree with you that salvation and where a person will spend eternity goes to the very heart of the gospel. But you have to understand that if you say no to this, they are going to take you to jail today where they will keep you until you or your family can post bond. With a bonding company that will cost fifteen hundred dollars."

"RT, I don't have that kind of money. I'm just a preacher at a small church."

"Preston, this judge thinks she is doing you a huge favor and she is going to be mad when you turn this down. Every decision regarding this case is going to be made by this same judge. This is not a good way to start. Think about Janie, your kids, the church. What would they want you to do?"

"RT, I appreciate what you are saying, but I just can't obey her rather than obey my calling from God as a pastor to proclaim truth from the Bible."

When they returned to the courtroom, RT tried to put the best face on this bad decision.

"Your Honor, my client appreciates what the Court has suggested, but he is afraid that no matter what he preaches that the DA will say he is continuing to use hate speech. He also doesn't believe he should have to let the DA preview his sermons to be sure no so-called hateful language is used. He believes he has not been preaching hate. That is not his intent. But he can't agree not to preach whatever sermon God may lay on his heart."

Judge Jackson's face turned red and RT thought, *We're both going to jail.*

The judge quickly ruled that there would be no PR bond issued, and that Preston would be jailed until he was able to post the $10,000 bond. As they put handcuffs on Preston and marched him off to jail, RT could hear his family and church members behind him, crying.

CHAPTER 22

A DAY AND A HALF later, RT was finally able to post Preston's bond. The church raised a thousand dollars and RT just paid the additional five hundred for his friend. Preston walked out of the jail with a big smile and a bounce in his step. RT stammered out, "You look good."

"It was awesome! When I first walked down the semi-dark hallway at the jail, I was humiliated because I was in handcuffs. There were a lot of catcalls and I was terrified. I thought of all of the despicable acts I had heard about that happened to people in jail. I knew I was weak physically and would be no match for someone wishing to harm me. Then when I realized I had been placed in a cell with a man sleeping off being drunk, I was able to relax. I began praying about whether I had in fact been hateful in my speech or whether I was simply preaching God's truth. I know God loves Muslims, and I began to pray that I could communicate God's love for them, even as I recommitted myself to standing firm on the truth of God's word.

"Then I started weeping as I thought about how my family was being subjected to verbal assaults daily, and my kids were having to deal with their dad being called a 'Muslim hater' and 'criminal.' They were confused and hurting because of my preaching. I asked God *Why?* many, many times. I was praying David's prayer from the Psalms where he waited patiently for the Lord, and the Lord heard his prayer and lifted him up from the pit of destruction.

"Finally, after I had prayed and cried myself out, I was overcome by a sense of peace. It was then I began to see God work, even through the bad circumstances of being in jail. You wouldn't believe how I got to share about God's love just in one night while I was in jail! At first, I just started singing 'Jesus Loves Me!' Those around me went quiet as I started singing. After that song I sang 'Amazing Grace,' and I heard a few prisoners start singing with me. Finally, I just started sharing about Jesus' love for us no matter what we had done, even if what we had done caused us to be in jail. It was unbelievable! People around my jail cell wanted to talk and tell me about their sadness and problems. Every sad story I was told opened a door to for me to share about God's love! I remembered how Paul responded when he was thrown into jail for sharing his faith, and so I just started praying and singing out loud. Finally, other people started singing and praying. I bet there were ten of us praying and singing late into the night. I believe God is still in control and He can take a bad situation like being thrown into the pit called *jail* and use it for his good."

As they walked away, RT said, "Man, you *are* crazy! Maybe an insanity defense will work."

CHAPTER 23

WHEN PASTOR CURTIS RETURNED HOME, he found chaos. His wife grabbed him and was overcome with emotion as she kissed him and asked, "Are you okay? I have been so worried!"

"I'm fine. I'm fine," he said. "Nothing happened to me other than being locked up, and I'll share everything with you later, but right now it looks like I need to talk to the kids."

His daughter, Sarah, looked at him, turned away, and without saying anything, went into her bedroom and slammed the door. His son Caleb ran up and hugged his leg, while brother Joshua simply stared at him. He decided he needed to divide and conquer, and address each child separately.

After Janie turned Preston loose, he dropped to a knee and asked Caleb, "How are you doing buddy?"

"Okay," he said. "Are you really going to jail?"

Preston choked a bit. "Caleb, all I know is that some people don't like for me to preach from the Bible or about Jesus, and they are trying to stop me from doing that. You understand that I have to do what God called me to do rather than what some people want me to do, right?"

"I'm scared, Daddy!" The boy started crying while Preston embraced him. "It's going to be okay, buddy."

After Caleb settled down, Preston spoke to Joshua.

"Dad, it's not fair. Why did you go to jail just for preaching?"

Preston could only repeat the mantra he had thought a thousand times: "Joshua, life is not always fair. The Bible teaches us that Jesus was not treated fairly by the government, and Paul was put into prison for preaching. This is nothing new, but it is new for preachers in this country to be put in jail just for preaching the Bible. But I have to be prepared to accept the consequences, if it comes to that."

"But what will happen to Mom, Sarah, Caleb and me if you get thrown in jail?"

"Joshua, I don't want you to worry about that. We will figure it out and God will provide for us."

Preston next stood outside Sarah's door and knocked. He knew this would be the most difficult conversation.

"Go away Dad. I don't want to talk about it!"

Preston kept knocking, and finally Sarah jerked the door open and said, "What?"

"Honey, we need to talk. I can tell you are angry, and I want to know what happened to make you so angry."

"What happened?" she yelled. "What didn't happen? You ruined my life! Since you got arrested, my friends won't answer my texts or talk to me. No one will sit with me at lunch. The teachers give me the stinkeye, and the boy who asked me to go to homecoming told me today he wasn't going to be able to go after all. He made up some excuse about being busy. My cell phone rings nonstop with people telling me that my dad teaches people to hate. And you have the nerve to ask what happened?"

She burst into tears, hugged herself and turned away. When Preston tried to hug her, she kept pulling away.

"Honey, I am so sorry. You know that I would never intentionally do anything to hurt you. You, of all people, know that I am not a hater. I preach the love of God and try to lead people to turn to Jesus. This is so unfair to you, and I am so sorry."

"Dad, can't you just make it go away? Quit preaching, or can we all move someplace else? I heard the judge told you that if you wouldn't talk about the Muslims going to Hell you would not have gone to jail. Why didn't you agree to that? She didn't say you couldn't preach! If you won't stop preaching that way, can't we just move someplace else that doesn't care what you are preaching?"

"I would gladly move someplace else," Preston said, "but God hasn't released me as pastor here, and I view this as a test of whether I will serve God or give in to political correctness. But I am going to do everything I possibly can, without compromising my oath as a pastor, to try to protect you and the rest of the family."

"So, you would rather see your family get destroyed and your kids constantly ridiculed than to leave this place or to change the sermons so nobody could say you are not preaching hate?"

"Sarah, it's not that simple."

"It is to me," said Sarah. "Please leave my room."

Preston started to speak but Sarah said, "You either leave my room now, or I am walking out the front door and I don't know if I will ever come back."

Preston started walking out the door and said over his shoulder, "Sarah, just know that I love you and would never want to see you hurt." The last words he heard as he walked away were, "Then fix it."

Preston was wrung out, but he knew he next needed to talk to Janie. Janie was quiet and looked tired. Her eyes were baggy and swollen. Preston knew she had been through a lot the last few days, having borne the brunt of everything from the church and the kids.

All he could say was, "I am so sorry, and I want you to know I love you and the kids, and I would never want to do anything to hurt you."

She started speaking slowly. "Preston, I know you love us, but you have no idea how bad it has been. You have just gotten a glimpse by talking to the kids, but that is not the complete picture. We are all worried about you being sent to prison. Every night I listen to new tales of mistreatment by other kids in their school. Then I worry about how we will pay the bills. How can I take care of the kids by myself if you are in prison? We are living in a house that is owned by the church, and if they fire you, which I have heard mentioned, will we be moving somewhere new without you and without a source of income? Why is God allowing this to happen? My faith at this moment is weak."

Preston knew that no church answer would be satisfying, so he just held her, and she cried.

Finally, he said, "Janie, I don't think I have ever been as confused, frustrated and tired as I am this minute. You and I both prayed and believed God called us here as pastor, but now I have half of the community calling me a hater. The church appears to have some members who doubt me. I have a daughter who now hates me, and a DA who wants to send me to prison. I'm not sure, even if I left the church, that the DA would drop the charges. And, in the face of this attack being about my preaching directly from the Bible, I wonder if this is a time God wants me to stand, even in the face of the persecution, even if that means being sent to prison with my family facing harsh, harmful and unfair treatment. I would love to find the burning bush God used to speak to Moses so I could feel comfortable with the answers and directions. Do you think I should just resign at the church and agree to move away from Oregon?"

Janie regained her composure. "I don't know what we should do, but this situation may be just like the situation for Esther. God may have you here for such a time as this. I don't want to go through this, and I am scared to death. But I think, for now, we need to pray for you, me, our kids, the church, for wisdom, and for RT. Maybe after we try to sleep on it tonight, God will give us more clarity tomorrow. We need to stay in prayer, and let our kids and people in our church and community know that God loves them, and we do, too."

"I love you," Preston said. "I do need to tell you about what happened last night while I was in the jail. It gave me hope in the middle of hopelessness." He explained to her the same thing he had told RT about sharing the gospel and singing praise hymns.

"Wow!" Janie said. "I was so scared for you, but it sounds like a lot of prayers were answered. Your experience in jail makes me happy, but also very uncomfortable. I didn't want you hurt, but I don't know about God using you in jail because I am afraid that will tell you that you have to stay and fight it out!"

They kissed and laid their heads on their pillows to see if sleep would be possible.

The next day Janie got a phone call.

"Ms. Curtis, my name is Linda Townsend, and I am an investigator with the Portland Child Protective Services Department. I would like to come interview you concerning a complaint that has been filed against your husband claiming he has engaged in emotional child abuse, based upon his hate speech."

"What?" Janie cried. "You have got to be kidding me! Who would do such a thing?"

"I'm sorry," Townsend said, "but all of that information is confidential according to the law. I can't tell you who filed the complaint, but I promise I will do a thorough investigation. Can I come over now?"

"Now?" Janie said, "I need to talk to my husband about this first."

"Ms. Curtis, I would advise you not to talk to your husband before we visit. Right now there is no complaint filed against you, but if you hinder our investigation or act complicit in supporting your husband's hate speech, our only recourse may be to remove your children from the home until we can be assured that the emotional child abuse has ceased and the children are properly protected."

"Ms. Townsend," Janie said, "I appreciate all that CPS does to protect neglected and abused children, but my children are neither neglected nor abused. Everyone who knows Preston and I ensure that our children are well provided for, protected and loved."

"There are other types of abuse," said Townsend. "Those sermons where your husband sows seeds of hatred toward Muslims or other religious groups is very serious and can be harmful to the emotional wellbeing of children. We take that very seriously."

"This can't be happening," Janie replied despondently. "I've got to think about what I should do based upon your call. I am going to call my attorney."

"I understand this is upsetting, Ms. Curtis, but I will be there in two hours and I suggest you not do anything that gives me the impression that you are impeding my investigation." With that, she hung up.

After ending the call with the CPS investigator, Janie leaned against the wall and slid down to a seated position with both hands covering her face. *What am I going to do?* she thought.

She called the one person she hoped could help, the lawyer who had stood with them through everything so far. When RT answered the phone, she broke down sobbing.

"RT, they are coming after our kids! The CPS lady just called and told me a complaint has been filed alleging child abuse because of Preston's sermons, and she is on the way over to talk to me about this so-called abuse. She told me I can't talk to Preston. All I knew to do was call you, but she said she would be here in two hours."

"Janie, when she shows up, just tell her on the advice of your attorney you are not answering any questions. Give her my name and phone number. In the meantime, give me her phone number and I will call her and try to talk to her. For now, if Preston asks about it, you can tell him CPS called but you were told not to talk to him. He can call me and, as his attorney, I can talk to him about the CPS situation."

Janie hung up and thought about driving to the school to grab her kids and drive away, anywhere to get away from all the craziness. She calmed herself and drove home to wait for Ms. Townsend to arrive.

CHAPTER 24

AFTER TALKING TO JANIE ABOUT the CPS call, RT muttered a prayer for God to protect Preston and Janie's children, and to give him wisdom as he sought to help them navigate through this latest swamp hole. RT then leaned back in his office chair and shut his eyes to try to get some perspective. He was stressed out and extremely tired, going back and forth from Texas to Oregon and spending money for airfare and having little time for paying clients. His legal assistant was stressed to her limits because she had been working on discovery documents, client conferences and communications with courts, opposing counsel and clients—normally, all roles for the lawyer.

"RT, I can't keep doing things like this," his assistant said. "I am so far over my head and I don't know what to tell clients."

"I know it has been hard," RT said. "I have put you in an untenable position where you have essentially been required to practice law without a license. You have done a great job and you are so qualified. I would never be able to survive without you. I kept thinking things were going to let up, but it seems that things keep getting worse instead of better."

"I understand, but really, there was no other choice for me except to try to take care of things while you were out. But you do know that your partner has been muttering about you generating no income, so you aren't going to get a draw this month unless things turn around."

"All right," RT said. "How about this game plan: we will talk every morning either in person if I am here, or on the phone if I am out of town. I will just block off thirty minutes each morning for us to discuss any pending matters. You have your questions lined up so we can cover them quickly, but in a meaningful way to help you. We will try that approach for a while, and if that isn't enough time, then we will reexamine it. I will also plan on spending at least one hour a day responding to emails, calling clients and addressing questions you have. I may not be able to respond immediately, but I will respond before I go to bed. If you tell a client I will call them that day, be sure to tell them it may be late at night before I can call them. Is that a good start and will that give you enough help for now?"

"That works," his assistant said, somewhat relieved. As she left his office, RT thought, *my bank account is dwindling, my family is on my back about being gone and working all the time and my clients are upset and threatening to find a new attorney. And yet, here I am, representing a good friend with no money and yet enough legal issues to keep a multi-lawyer law firm fully employed!*

Every day, RT kept thinking the worst of the storm with Preston's legal issues had passed, but every day was like playing whack-a-mole at the local Chuck E Cheese!! You whack one mole and two more pop up! "Lord," he prayed, "I need your wisdom, strength and guidance to deal with this latest crisis with CPS."

CHAPTER 25

RT SPOKE TO MS. TOWNSEND with CPS. "Ms. Townsend, my name is RT Glassman, and I am Janie Curtis' attorney. She told me that you are headed to her house shortly, but I wanted to call and tell you that I want to be present when you visit with her, but I am in Texas right now. We need to put this off for a few days until I will be back in Oregon."

"Mr. Glassman, you need to understand that under Oregon law I have the right to immediately go and enter premises where we believe a child may be in danger. The complaint is that Mr. Curtis is emotionally harming these children, and by not allowing me to visit with Mrs. Curtis, the only information I have is the hate speech sermons by Mr. Curtis. I also have no assurances the children will not be subjected to more emotional child abuse, either at church or in the home. My recommendation to my supervisor will likely be that because I have been denied the opportunity to visit with your client, I cannot get assurance that future abuse will not occur, and therefore we should place the children in foster care until I can be assured the children will be protected."

"You have got to be kidding me," RT said. "First of all, I have not denied you access to Mrs. Curtis. I just need to be present and need to coordinate travel arrangements with everything else going on. Secondly, this so-called abuse is just taking words from the Bible. You mean we have now moved in the realm where CPS will say if pastors and parents teach their kids the Bible, they are guilty of emotional child abuse? Don't you folks have enough real child abusers that you need to be spending your time on?"

"Mr. Glassman, you need to understand that all child abuse is taken very seriously by CPS, and your client is teaching his children hateful attitudes directed at Muslims in the name of religion. That is no joking matter, and it must be taken very seriously by the Curtis family and by you."

"Ms. Townsend, trust me, we all take this very seriously, but we are having a hard time understanding how teaching Biblical principles could possibly be put in the same category as people beating, starving, or literally doing physical or emotional harm to their kids. Pastor Curtis and his wife love their children. I will be back in Oregon on Monday of next week and if you can hold off until then, I will let you visit with either or both in my presence. Can we handle it that way?"

"Okay," she said, "but they need to understand I am taking this very seriously and if I hear of other hateful speech while the kids are present, I will not hesitate to act."

"Ms. Townsend," RT said, "believe me, we have no doubt what you are saying right now, and we get what you mean." As he hung up the phone, he thought, *yes ma'am, we totally understand the threats you are making.* RT had a distant memory from a Sunday school class about some Bible verse that states, "they called what is right, wrong, and what is wrong they called right." *I think I finally understand that verse, but if Ms. Townsend knew I was thinking that she would probably have CPS come and take my kids, too.*

With the attack on Preston's family under control—at least for the moment—RT was able to concentrate more fully on the criminal case against Preston. He had initially thought, before doing legal research, that it should be easy to get charges against Preston dismissed. It appeared that all the complaints included in the indictment were related to Preston's speech from the pulpit. But he still needed to review the specifics of the claimed "hate speech" contained in the indictment. As for the allegations of child abuse, they were, in RT's view, nothing short of absurd, and without legal foundation.

He discerned that the DA's complaint was centered around two statements that Preston preached that he claimed were Biblical positions—that trusting Jesus is the only way to Heaven, and anyone not trusting Jesus will go to Hell, including Muslims.

RT first explored whether the Bible says Jesus is the only way to Heaven. He looked at the verses Preston used in his sermons to support that point:

- John 3:16: "For God so loved the world, that he gave his only Son, that whoever believes in him should not perish but have eternal life."
- John 3:18: "Whoever believes in him is not condemned, but whoever does not believe is condemned already, because he has not believed in the name of the only son of God."
- John 14:6: Jesus answered, "I am the way and the truth and the life. No one comes to the Father except through me."

RT thought those Biblical verses supported the claim Preston made in his sermons. The phrases "condemned already, because he has not believed," and "no one comes to the Father except through me" made it clear that Jesus was the only way to get to Heaven. Also, the phrases "have eternal life" and "comes to the Father" refer to being in Heaven. Next, he looked at the verses that Preston relied upon to say, "anyone not trusting Jesus as savior, including Muslims, were going to Hell." He looked up those verses:

- John 3:18, again.
- Acts 4:12: One translation said: "No one else can save us. Indeed, we can be saved only by the power of the one named Jesus and not by any other person." Another translation said, "Salvation is found in no one else, for there is no other name under Heaven given to mankind by which we must be saved."

Clear enough, RT thought. Now he needed to see what the Muslims believed, or what was taught to Islamic believers about Jesus and how to get to Heaven.

- Muhammad is believed to be God's prophet.
- Jesus is a prophet, but is not divine.
- Quran 5:35 says, "O you who believe! Be careful of (your duty to) Allah and seek means of nearness to Him and strive hard in His way that you may be successful." Muslims believe their entry into Heaven is based on belief in Muhammad and their deeds.
- Quran 2:82: "But those who have faith and work righteousness, they are the Companions of the Garden. Therein shall they abide forever."
- One quote from the Prophet Muhammad said in His hadith: "Whoever believes in Allah and His Messenger (PBUH) and establishes the prayer and fasts in the month of Ramadan, it is incumbent upon Allah that He enters him in Jannah."

RT could find no reference in any Muslim material that trusting Jesus was the way to Heaven, or *Jannah* as the Muslims called it. He concluded that while different religions taught salvation through other means than Jesus, the Bible did teach—from Jesus' own words—that faith in Jesus as Savior was the only way to Heaven and that Islamic-Muslim followers did not believe the way to Heaven was the same as Preston had preached. RT concluded that Preston's Biblical assertion that Muslims, and anyone else not trusting Jesus as Savior, was going to Hell appeared to be appropriate and defensible. Those conclusions could mean only one thing—a constitutional crisis was brewing, one of free speech and religious liberty.

A pastor's speech from the pulpit should be protected by the US Constitution, and any judge with any objectivity toward enforcement of valued constitutional provisions and interpretations should be able to recognize that, RT concluded. However, his confidence began to erode as he started doing the legal research:

- One Ninth US Circuit Court opinion defined hate speech as "speech that is intended to insult, intimidate or cause prejudice against a person or group of people based upon religion. . . ." In that case, a person (not a preacher) had been evangelizing and the speech that was found to be hateful was that a third party's religious beliefs were wrong, and they were going to Hell. The similarity to the complaints in Preston's case was chilling.
- A Canadian Supreme Court opinion affirmed the hate crime conviction of a Christian activist passing out anti-gay pamphlets that said the Bible taught homosexuality was a sin.
- The Obama administration, which appointed many of the judges in the Ninth Circuit Court where this case would be heard, sponsored a resolution at the UN Human Rights Council that called on nations to criminalize "any advocacy of national, racial or religious hatred that constitutes incitement to discrimination, hostility or violence."
- A Maine middle school student put some ham, considered unclean by Muslims, on a school cafeteria table occupied

by Muslim students. As punishment, the school suspended the student, and the principal sent a referral letter both to the local district attorney and to the Maine attorney general seeking prosecution as a "hate/bias crime."

- One particular indication of a troubling trend was a case involving a Canadian pastor who was concerned about Muslin favoritism in a local high school. The pastor began passing out pamphlets protesting the favoritism and promoting the Christian faith. He was charged and convicted of "willfully promoting hatred," and was sentenced to 340 hours of community service at the Islamic Society of North America. The Canadian courts ruled that Canada's human rights hate speech laws are a "constitutionally valid limit on freedom of expression and religious liberty."

RT found no recent US Supreme Court opinion exactly on point to say that Pastor Curtis' speech and conduct was protected. *Oh man*, he thought. Preston's freedom would ride on the decision of five of nine elderly people, each appointed to the US Supreme Court in a very highly partisan political process. RT was not feeling confident, given the recent apparent hostilities of the Court to long-standing legal views on religious rights, such as those relating to the issue of gay marriage or the display of religious symbols like the Ten Commandments.

CHAPTER 26

THE ELDERS HELD A SECRET meeting at Grace Bible Church the day after the indictment, and one of the elders said, "Chaos has begun to spread in the church. I have been getting a lot of calls from concerned church members wondering what the elders were going to do. Some people are panicked about the pastor being indicted and arrested. Don't we as the elders need to do something?"

After much discussion, Chairman Martin said, "It sounds like we have a consensus that we shouldn't do anything right now, and that we just monitor everything to be sure we don't need to take some action."

One week after Preston was released from jail on bond, there was another secret meeting of the five church elders. When Chairman Martin was asked why Pastor Curtis was not present, he simply said, "We need the ability to speak frankly about the problems the Pastor has caused. We have a big problem because of his sermons about Muslims. Here is a summary of what we are dealing with since he started preaching about the Muslims going to Hell:

- Our church attendance is down by twenty percent.
- Offerings are off by twenty-five percent, and we will blow through our reserves in six months at this rate.
- The church receptionist told me yesterday that one week after Pastor Curtis' indictment, she still averages fifteen negative calls a day to the church.
- I constantly get reports from church members that their kids are being attacked at school just because they go to the church where the pastor is teaching them to hate Muslims.
- Every week our janitorial staff has to clean hateful graffiti off the outside church walls before Sunday worship.

"I believe Pastor Curtis' leadership is in shambles. There have been comments by some members that he is distracted, and some church members are no longer listening to him. To save the church I believe we have to dismiss him as pastor."

The other members sat silently, neither agreeing with nor challenging Chairman Martin. To some it seemed the Chairman was moving too quickly. The chairman sensed dissent in their silence.

"We have got to do something to protect the church," said Chairman Martin.

The senior elder, eighty-year-old Paul Reed, stood and said, "The only thing I have heard you say Pastor Curtis has done wrong is preach directly the teachings of the Bible. Is anyone aware of any other crime he has committed? So, if I hear you correctly, rather than have Pastor Curtis' back for proclaiming the truth of the Bible, you want to throw him under the bus of political correctness? Let's say we suspend or fire him: do you think the next pastor would believe we expect him to preach truth and that we would have his back? I believe this group of elders needs to strongly support the pastor and help him, his family and the church make it through this crisis, not tuck tail and run. No hasty action. There will be time to respond once the dust settles."

When he sat, the room was silent. Finally, another elder suggested they spend time in prayer before moving forward. After an hour of intense prayer for divine wisdom and additional discussion, the chairman asked Elder Reed to prepare a plan of action for the pastor and church that the elders could review in a week and present to the church on the following Sunday.

Elder Reed nodded his consent but was troubled by the approach and attitude of Chairman Martin, and disappointed that the pastor was not provided an opportunity to defend himself before the board.

CHAPTER 27

BY THE TIME OF THE interview with CPS Investigator Townsend, RT had come to his senses. *Glassman*, he thought, *you are an idiot and guilty of malpractice as a lawyer if you let Preston talk to Townsend before the criminal case is resolved! She will be the DA's first witness in the criminal hate crime trial, and she will be a sympathetic witness protecting his children from this hater! There is no way you can let Preston talk to this woman!*

RT was concerned about how Townsend would react to his refusal to let her talk to Preston, but the risk of Preston talking to her, with the criminal action pending, was too great. Plus, he had a plan on how to deal with the CPS issue.

He spoke to Preston and Janie. "Preston, you cannot meet with the CPS investigator because it is a no-win for you. No matter how you explain yourself, she is going to say that your message is one of hate, and what you tell her is not protected like attorney-client discussions. I anticipate she will be a sympathetic witness for the

DA to put on the stand and say how she had to protect your children from this hateful person."

They both acknowledged that they heard what he was saying, but they were fearful about how Ms. Townsend would react.

"I am afraid she will immediately take our kids away if Preston doesn't show up, too!" Janie said. "And why? What have we done wrong?"

Preston was even more forceful. "RT, let me talk to her. She doesn't know me. I can convince her that I am not a hater, and that I love my kids and would never do anything to harm them."

After about thirty minutes of back-and-forth, RT told Preston he wanted to play out a mock scenario and ask him a couple of questions that Ms. Townsend would likely ask him. Preston agreed.

RT asked Preston, "Pastor Curtis, do you believe Muslims are going to Hell?"

Preston answered, "Ms. Townsend, the Bible teaches that Jesus is the only way to Heaven, so when Muslims, or anyone else who doesn't accept Jesus, dies, then yes, I believe they would be going to Hell."

"Have your children heard you say Muslims are going to Hell?" RT asked.

"They have heard me say people who don't believe in Jesus as their Savior are going to hell, according to the Bible," answered Preston.

"So, they have heard you say, and they know you believe, that Muslims are going to Hell, is that right?"

"They have heard me teach the Bible," he answered

"They heard you teach specifically your personal view, that Muslims, who don't trust Jesus, are going to Hell?"

Preston said, "Yes, ma'am."

"Mr. Curtis, are you going to continue to preach that Muslims who don't trust Jesus are going to Hell?"

Preston looked at RT and responded. "I am going to continue teaching and preaching the Bible, yes, ma'am,"

RT continued. "Do your children attend church when you preach about Muslims going to Hell?"

"They attend our church services when I preach, yes, ma'am."

RT pressed. "So, as I understand it, you have taught that Muslims are going to Hell, your children have heard you preach that conclusion on more than one occasion, and you intend to continue to preach that 'truth' in the future, right?"

"I am going to continue to teach the truth of the Bible, including the fact that Muslims—and anyone else—who doesn't trust Jesus as savior, is going to Hell. Yes, ma'am."

"Now Preston," RT said, "what conclusions do you think Ms. Townsend is going to reach after those questions?"

Before he could answer, Janie spoke. "She's going to say that you teach people to hate Muslims, including our kids, and if she doesn't stop it, you are going to continue to teach that to our kids. Preston, I love you and you are persuasive, but she will twist everything you say. I think RT is right about this one as much as you not talking to her scares me to death!"

RT asked Preston, "Can you see that the instant the DA sees the statement you made to Ms. Townsend about Muslims going to Hell, and that you are going to continue with the same or similar statements, that he will be chomping at the bit to put her on the witness stand? Nothing you tell Ms. Townsend is privileged or protected, so she can testify about anything you tell her, including the conclusions she draws from what you say. Just imagine the first witness in the criminal case is the CPS lady who says you are abusing your kids, and she had to take the kids out of the home to protect them. What kind of tone do you think that will set for the trial?"

"What can we do?" Janie sobbed. "We can't have them take our children away. That would just kill us and them. First, they say they want to put my husband in jail, and now they are trying to take my kids away from me!"

"I am going to call Ms. Townsend on our way to see her, and

I'll explain why I can't let Preston talk to her. Then you and I will go talk to her."

"RT," Preston said, "I would rather go to jail than have the kids put in foster care. That just can't happen. Keeping them with Janie has to be our first priority."

"My goal is that neither of those two things happen," RT said. "I am going to do all that is within my power to protect you and your family."

To calm them, RT quoted Proverbs 3: 5-6: "Trust in the Lord with all of your heart, lean not on your own understanding; in all your ways acknowledge Him and He will direct your path." RT prayed over Preston and Janie and asked the Lord to give wisdom, calmness, peace and direction. He also prayed that Ms. Townsend would act appropriately and not take action to remove their kids. Finally, he prayed for their kids to be spared from ridicule at school.

After the meeting, RT mulled a possible solution, one he knew that neither Preston nor Janie would like. But it seemed to be the only way he could envision protection for the kids from CPS and also allow him to focus on Preston's defense.

RT called Ms. Townsend, and she pounced.

"Mr. Glassman, you told me you would bring both of them for me to interview. Since you refuse, I believe I should just turn the findings I have over to my supervisor and see if she wants to take actions to protect the children."

"What are you talking about?" RT said. "What findings? You haven't talked to either parent or the kids, you haven't visited their schoolteachers, you haven't visited with any neighbors or friends— nothing! How could there possibly be any findings? Look, I know I said Preston would talk to you, but with the criminal case still pending, and with what he tells you not being privileged, I just can't take that chance. But Ms. Curtis and I will be at your office within fifteen minutes. You can see for yourself that she is a caring mother who loves her children and would not let anything, or anyone, harm them."

She agreed to hold off until they could meet with her.

What a life! RT thought. *It seems like everybody around me is either crying all the time when they talk to me, or they are mad at me. This must be what they call living the dream!*

As soon as they walked into Ms. Townsend's office, the attack began.

"Ms. Curtis, you have to understand that your husband's hateful speech that is directed to Muslims is taken very seriously by me as being emotionally harmful to your children. His refusal to come talk to me makes me think either you don't believe I will remove your children from your home because of his conduct, or he knows he can't defend his hateful speech but he has no intention to stop."

"Ms. Townsend, Janie and Preston both take your claims seriously, and Janie is here because she takes this seriously and does not believe Preston has done anything to deserve the threat of having their children taken away," RT said. "She has appeared voluntarily and is willing to cooperate. But, as I told you, based upon my advice as his attorney, and my advice alone, Preston Curtis cannot be talking to anyone about the criminal case. He wanted to meet with you, but I would not be doing my job if I let him show up and start talking about the facts involved in the criminal case. Ms. Curtis is here voluntarily because she loves her kids, wants the best for them, and believes there is absolutely no reason to consider removing her children from the home. Janie, why don't you tell Ms. Townsend about your kids, what they do, your home, and let her know all the reasons that they are well taken care of and are happy healthy kids."

Janie spent the next fifteen minutes describing her kids in detail, their ages, their activities, school grades, their friends and even their hobbies. Then she turned her attention to her husband.

"Preston loves our kids deeply. He takes time to go over homework; he talks to them when he gets home; we always eat dinner together; he plays games with the kids; he has taught our two boys how to play baseball; he makes sure our kids have plenty to eat, a good place to live and he teaches them good values, like honesty, integrity and respect. He has never done anything to physically harm them, nor does he emotionally harm them by berating them or talking down to them . . . and he never would."

"Tell me about how he disciplines the children," said Ms. Townsend.

"During the day, I am usually the disciplinarian, but Preston assists when he is home. We have a similar philosophy, which is that we tell our kids what we expect. We may verbally correct them and if necessary, we put them in timeout, limit privileges like the use of their computer, or we may ground them. We don't spank them, though we might have on occasion when they were younger. There has never been a problem in the area of discipline."

"Ms. Curtis," said Ms. Townsend, "tell me about the kids hearing their daddy preach about Muslims going to Hell. Do they hear those sermons and does Mr. Curtis talk about that in the home?"

"Ms. Townsend, those comments are a single sentence in a few sermons when he's trying to emphasize the importance of people trusting Jesus and that nobody—no matter the religion, whether Baptists, Methodists, or Muslims—gets to Heaven without trusting Jesus. That perspective comes straight from the Bible, where Jesus says no one gets to Heaven except through Him. This has all gotten blown way out of proportion. Preston has never mentioned anything about Muslims in our home to the kids when I have been present. All he talks about is encouraging our kids in their Christian faith. He speaks of love for other people, love for our friends, love for our family, and he even says we are to love the Muslims, even if they are misguided in the area of theology.

"We have fun. We go hiking, biking and camping. He takes them to music lessons. He teaches our kids to love the unlovely by leading out for us, as a family, to feed the homeless on Thanksgiving. That's the example he sets and that is what he teaches our kids, Ms. Townsend. Your call, where you said you wanted to talk to me about our kids possibly being abused, and even this meeting, scare me to death. The trauma of removing our kids would be far worse for them than anything my husband has ever said from the pulpit."

"Ms. Curtis," replied Ms. Townsend, "you do seem like a loving and caring mother. I am going to depend on you to protect your children from being taught to hate. I am going to maintain an open file and will call on you at home—sometimes unexpectedly—and will monitor events concerning your husband. If his public hateful comments continue, and your children continue to be exposed to them, I am reserving the right to take additional action."

"Ms. Townsend," said RT, "this family deserves to be recognized as Family of the Year and should not be threatened with removal of the kids from the home. You can see there is no basis for CPS to be involved. You should just take no action, close your file, and let these people live their lives."

"As I said, I'm not closing my file, but I am not recommending any action at this time. We will remain in contact."

As they drove away from the CPS office, RT could see that Janie was shaking from the whole experience. He, too, was rattled.

"Janie," he said, "you did great and I think for now the crisis has passed, but we are going to have to deal with this situation long term because I don't think she is going away."

"RT, I think I am more worried now for my kids than before we came. She really believes Preston poses a threat to our kids, and I'm going to be worried, every time Preston preaches, that she might come pick up the kids and put them in foster care."

She leaned her head back and closed her eyes for the rest of the ride. When they got to the Curtis home, she turned and said, "Thank you, RT, for being there today and for being such a good friend to Preston. I don't know what we would do without you fighting for us."

Later that night, RT went back to Preston and Janie's house to talk about the CPS visit and Ms. Townsend. To protect the discussion as attorney-client privileged communication, RT had told Janie not to talk to Preston about any specifics of the discussion without the lawyer there. RT began the discussion.

"I have been involved with a lot of CPS workers over the years. They have a hard job trying to protect kids from abuse, but occasionally, I have seen workers with a 'little god' syndrome. They feel a need to show everyone they are in charge. They think only their view or opinion is important, and they will be quick to pull the trigger and remove the kids if you don't do what they say. In my opinion, Ms. Townsend fits that bill. I think she is going to remain an active thorn in your side. The first time she gets word of a sermon she doesn't like, she will be knocking on your door."

"We can't let that happen," Janie said. "What can we do?"

RT knew that Preston was not going to change the message of his sermons. He had already told the judge that was not an option.

"Guys," he said, "I am worried. I already told you I don't trust Ms. Townsend, and I don't know her supervisor or the other CPS workers. I have no idea what she is going to do. I have one possible suggestion, and nobody is going to like it, but I believe it is the only way to have confidence that Janie and the kids can remain together. Janie, your parents still live in Archer County, Texas just outside of Wichita Falls. You need to move and take the kids to live with your parents until the criminal case is over. Archer County is in the Bible Belt and neither the CPS workers nor any judge located in Texas would think preaching the Bible is a crime or child abuse. Even if Townsend tries to refer the CPS investigation down there, I am confident it will go nowhere."

"What?" Janie blurted. "Pull my kids away from their school, their friends, their church, their father and move to Texas? I can't leave Preston to fight this by himself. He needs us to support and encourage him. Plus, it will look like we are just running away. I can't do that."

"I hear you," RT said, "But if you stay, I can't promise you that one day Ms. Townsend won't show up with an *ex parte* court order that gives her the right to remove the kids and put them in foster care. Plus, I am having to spend a lot of time with this issue, and you guys are spending a lot of time and emotional energy on this CPS action rather than on the criminal case. I believe we can eventually win the CPS case, but I have a law practice in Texas, and between Preston's criminal case and my law practice, I can't spend time fighting both the criminal case and the CPS battle. If you are going to stay here with the kids, you have got to get an Oregon lawyer familiar with CPS cases to handle that case."

Preston and Janie went off by themselves to talk about their options. They returned and Preston said, "You are right, RT. As much as it pains me, this seems like the best plan to make sure that Janie and the kids stay together, no matter what happens to me. Plus, she will have the support of her parents and your wife while she is there. Janie and the kids will move to Texas."

Two days later, after Janie and the kids were on the road and in Texas, and RT was driving to the airport to return to Texas, he called Ms. Townsend and relayed to her that Janie and the kids had moved to Texas to live with her parents.

"I can't believe the Curtis family ran away like that. Ms. Curtis' action tells me there is a serious problem. I am going to have our attorney prepare a petition for removal of their children today!"

"Save your time, Ms. Townsend," RT replied. "Janie and the kids are already in Texas. Texas now has jurisdiction over the children. Plus, they did not run away. You said Janie had to protect their kids, and the only negative you raised about their parenting approach was they heard their dad preaching hate. That is no longer a problem because they aren't here to listen to his sermons. I'll give you their address in Texas where the kids are staying, and if you feel the need, you can have the Texas CPS check on them. You and I both know that in Texas no prosecutor or CPS worker is going to get too excited about a preacher dad who simply preaches the Bible."

After more back and forth, she finally settled down, and then RT asked her if she would close her investigation.

"No, but I think I will suspend it. I will also have the Texas CPS monitor to be sure the kids continue living there. If I find out they move back together with Mr. Curtis without telling me, or that the kids are listening to hateful sermons from their father, the investigation will be reactivated."

CHAPTER 28

ONE EVENING, AFTER HE HAD been working on Preston's criminal case, RT decided to spend some time with his old friend to encourage him. When Preston answered the door, he looked at RT and said, "This must not be good. Every time you show up like this, it is to tell me something bad is about to happen."

"Nope, not this time." RT smiled and handed him a pizza box. "I knew Janie and the kids not being here was eating on you, and I wanted to come by and eat pizza, just like when we were growing up. This is a personal visit. We can talk about anything but your legal issues."

"I can hardly think about anything except the case, and Janie and the kids not being here, and whether the next time I see my kids it will be from prison. I am glad to be able to think about something else for a few minutes. We haven't talked much about what you have been doing. I read where you defended your pastor when he was subpoenaed for preaching about being pro-life, and going after a city manager. Before we went to college you were unsure what profession you wanted to go into, but you wanted to try to help people, too. I know sometimes there are situations where I walk away feeling good because I helped someone who needed my help. Are there some of your cases that stand out to you, where you felt like you really helped your clients?"

"Oh, man," RT said. "I love adoptions. I call it 'happy law' because it is the only time everyone in the courtroom is happy. And I think about how lucky that child is to be chosen by those parents who are willing to take on the role of loving and raising that child. It also reminds me that God views us as his adopted children, and that He has chosen me as His child and loves me more than any earthly parent could. There is one case that comes to mind that has nothing to do with what you are facing, but it was one that made me feel really good about being a lawyer."

"Tell me about it," Preston said.

RT laid his head against the back of the couch and sighed. "One day, there was a scheduled appointment with a young lady named Lorinda Hunter, who went by Lori. As she came into my office, I could see shadows under her eyes and some worry lines on her forehead. She had been referred to me by a mutual friend from church. When I asked her what I could do for her, she began to cry. She said her husband had been killed three weeks earlier in an oilfield accident. She was a stay-at-home mom with two daughters. Her husband's boss said the insurance company wanted to discuss payments to her from the company's worker's compensation insurance carrier. She knew nothing about it, and friends wisely told her not to sign anything.

"I hate to admit it, Preston, but on the one hand, for just a minute, the lawyer in me took over and I thought about the potential big bucks that a wrongful death lawsuit might generate. But on the other hand, as a husband, father and Christian, my heart was breaking as I thought about how my wife, Kathy, might respond in a similar situation, and what I would want a lawyer to do for her in that moment. I asked her to tell me about her husband, Keith, and their family. She told me they had been high school sweethearts and married before her sophomore year in college, and they had two daughters who were five and three. Lori and Keith apparently did everything together and had been married seven years before he was killed. They had a home garden, and would go for walks with the kids, and help look after his mother who was a widow. They attended church regularly, and one Sunday a month they would work in the nursery during the church service. Keith was a strong Christian, and he would teach the kids Bible stories and pray over them each night when they tucked them in bed."

RT stopped, took a deep breath. "My heart was already breaking, and then she told me how her girls would cry at night and say they 'want Daddy' or they 'miss Daddy.' As she started crying, she said she was not strong like Keith had been, and she didn't know how she was going to make it. She hadn't finished college and she had no real marketable job skills. About that time, I looked over at my legal assistant, and she was boohooing like a baby. As I looked back at Lori and thought about her situation, I told her it was not fair, and I wanted to talk about the legal aspects of her situation. But, instead, I asked her to let me pray for her. She agreed.

"I don't know where this came from, but I claimed in my prayer the promises set out in Jeremiah: 'for I know the plans I have for you, declares the Lord, plans to prosper you and not to harm you, plans to give you hope and a future.' That prayer seemed to be an encouragement to her.

"It was a long and difficult case, as we learned about Keith's accident. Keith had a couple of buddies who talked to me privately and they told me that one of the oilfield tanks that was to go out into the field was being lifted and moved in their yard so it could be hauled. Keith was helping guide it to the trailer when something broke, and the tank swung and hit him in the head and killed him instantly. His friends said that the cable and connection on one side of the lift broke, and that this was the second time in three months something like that had happened, but it was the first time somebody had been hurt. Because the tank hit Keith in the head, neither Lori nor either of her kids could see him, which made closure more difficult for them. Ultimately, after many months of depositions, hearings and negotiations, we were able to settle the case right before trial. When I met with Lori and laid out the final offer to her, I felt very satisfied that even though no one and no amount of money could ever replace Keith, I knew I had helped them be able to look forward and not have to worry about their finances. They could just worry about the next chapter of life. On top of my legal fees, I was able to obtain a settlement that provided Lori with a half million in cash, a five-thousand-a-month annuity, four installments of one hundred thousand dollars paid out every five years, and seventy-five thousand a year for each of the girls for four years after they reach the age of eighteen, and then two thousand a month each for ten years.

"Lori was ecstatic and relieved, partly because of the financial relief, but also because she would not have to endure a trial. When we got through with our discussion, she gave me what was probably the biggest hug I have ever gotten, except from my wife Kathy, and she told me that she was so thankful for my prayer and that she had been holding onto the verse in Jeremiah I had prayed over her.

"Preston, I can't begin to tell you how good I felt as I walked back to my office after meeting with Lori. God had fulfilled my desire to become a lawyer, just as we had talked many years ago, and I had been able to truly help someone. At the same time, God used me as a Christian influence while I was making a good living for my family".

"RT, that is awesome. Lori will remember what you did for her until her dying day. Who would have thought, when we were leaving high school, that you would be able to do so much good? I am really proud of you!"

"How about you, Preston? What do you enjoy about ministry?" asked RT.

"Well, I certainly can't help a hurting family get a bunch of money like you did, that's for sure," Preston laughed. "But I commonly see people when they are at their worst moments. A child has died, there is a bad cancer diagnosis, or a job has been lost. I hate those circumstances, but in those moments, I get to not only comfort them, but share Christ and the hope he can give them. I had a little ten-year boy whose dad died, and I was there for him during the funeral, and we now meet once a week where I can visit and try to mentor him. The spiritual growth and understanding I have seen in him is phenomenal! I almost talk to him as much as I do my own kids. When those kinds of moments happen, I wouldn't trade what I do for anything in the world."

"All right, Preston, that is where you need to keep your mind as we go through this trial. Remember those moments, what you have enjoyed, and the difference you have made in the lives of people. Those things are more important than any amount of money or any other accomplishment."

After RT left, Preston went to bed and was able to sleep for the first time since he had been indicted.

CHAPTER 29

FOR THE THREE WEEKS SINCE he had gotten out of the jail, there had seemingly been no opportunity for Pastor Curtis to visit with the elders of the church. There had been some one-on-one conversations with individual elders, but it had been hard for Preston to get a feel for his status, which added to his anxiety. Finally, he was able to schedule a meeting with the elders. Instead of Chairman Martin speaking, Elder Reed addressed his pastor.

"Pastor," he said, "I, for one, am fully committed to you and intend to weather this storm with you. I am going to support you publicly, privately and within the church. I totally support your convictions about the truthfulness and integrity of the Bible. You have preached nothing but truth. This is having an impact on you personally, your family and the church. How are you and your family doing?"

"It has been tough," Preston said. "It was like a tornado or hurricane, or actually more like a tsunami had suddenly hit my entire life. As we sit here, my wife and kids are in Texas. CPS has been threatening to put my kids in foster care, and I am facing the possibility of two years in prison. There are questions in the church about whether I should remain as pastor. Every time I turn around it seems I am dodging another arrow. Janie and the kids were my biggest supporters and watching them drive off without me was one of the hardest things I have ever done. I have to be very transparent with you as the elders of the church. I am hurting right now."

"How are Janie and the kids doing?" asked Elder Reed.

"They are confused and hurting. They don't understand why my preaching has created this mess. They don't understand why they have to leave and go live with grandparents while I am still here. They don't understand why a good God would allow this to happen when all we try to do is serve Him. So, in a word, I would say confused. Janie is having to carry the heavy load right now."

"Pastor, are you emotionally and physically able to continue as our pastor?" asked Reed.

"Paul, were it not for the support of the elders, the church, and this ministry, I am not sure I could keep going. I appreciate your support and any wisdom and guidance you can provide. But I also want to say that God is good, and when I think what Jesus and his disciples went through, and what many Christians go through around the world, and compare that to what I am going through, I am a blessed and fortunate man. I find time each day to stop and thank God for the way he has blessed me. Even with all that is happening now, God has given me a sense of peace that He is still on His throne and He can be trusted."

Elder Reed led the others in an intense time of prayer for Pastor Curtis, his family and the church.

After the prayer time, Elder Reed said, "Pastor, we think we need to come up with a plan to protect and support you and your family. All of us as elders, including you also, have a responsibility to protect the church. Most in the church support you, but we would be less than candid if we didn't say there are some issues with some members. Offerings and church attendance are down overall about twenty percent, and the local TV station that broadcasts our church services has been making some veiled threats about canceling the broadcast of our Sunday morning worship service if you keep preaching them. We think we need to have a plan going forward and be able to communicate that plan to the whole church. We think it needs to be bold, aggressive but positive. At the same time, we need for you to be able to preach the truth of the Bible, and we don't want to tuck our tails between our legs and hide."

Elder Reed enumerated the suggested steps the elders would take:

1. "The liberal media is controlling the message. I have personally committed to give twenty-five thousand dollars for radio, TV and billboard spots to focus on the positive things going on at the church and the positives of your ministry.

2. "Over the next six weeks we have scheduled twelve events in the church and community. These events will include a couple of concerts with contemporary or gospel music. We have one community-wide event, and we are awaiting final approval from Franklin Graham to come, at his own expense by the way, to preach about the love of Jesus.

3. "Ms. Drake has agreed that, in addition to any meetings now allowed at school, the ERAC students could continue to meet weekly at her house. She is playing a Beth Moore video Bible series about spiritual warfare. Ms. Drake is paying personally to advertise the study series by buying an ad in the local newspaper and flyers the students can pass out.

4. "Three Sundays from now, we are going to have a special day of offering for the church and we are calling it 'Fuel the Fire Sunday.' We heard that theme from a church in Texas, but thought it accurately reflected our goal. The main emphasis will be that the gospel started with a spark that spread to the entire world. We want to have a special offering that reinforces the need to fuel the fire of the gospel in our community and keep our base strong so we can continue to minister.

5. "We believe nothing spiritual happens without prayer. So, we are starting a prayer chain to pray 24/7 over the next thirty days for you, for our church, our students and even for the Muslims who believe we are attacking them. Some of the details still need to be worked out, but we have some men and women in the church who are prayer warriors and they will head up that effort.

6. "We are going to add some private security on Sunday morning to try to help ease some of the tensions from those trying to stir up trouble.

7. "And, finally, while we are not saying this as a 'you must do this,' we want to encourage you to start preaching through the book of James in the Bible. There are great practical passages on living out our faith and about God's love and mercy. We want you to continue to preach that the way to Heaven is by faith in Jesus, but until we get past this crisis, we would suggest you not call any false religions by name or focus on them— particularly Muslims. We don't want to hinder you in any way from relying upon and proclaiming God's truth, but as a matter of timing and discretion we would encourage you to not say the word *Muslim* for a while.

"How do all these practical steps sound to you?"

Pastor Curtis was silent for what seemed like several minutes. He was praying and focusing on what he had just heard. Finally, he said, "I want to thank you, as the elders of the church, for the strength and leadership you have shown and the wise counsel you have provided me. But there is an elephant in the room I think we need to address before moving forward. Do you as the elders, and does the church, and more importantly does God, want me to remain as pastor of this church while I'm going through this criminal trial? I have been told that the reality is that I may have to choose between preaching God's truth—all of it—or going to prison. If I lose this trial, I understand that forever it would be said that the pastor of this church stirred up hatred and was sentenced to prison. It is a given that I love this church and community. But I must be obedient to God above all else, and you have been placed in leadership roles by God and the church, with the responsibility for the church."

By the time he finished speaking, he was overcome by emotion. "I have to confess, the pressure of all of this is overwhelming. Again, when I watched Janie and the kids drive off, I thought I couldn't make it. I am holding onto 2 Corinthians 12:9 which says: 'My grace is sufficient for you, for power is perfected in weakness.' I can tell you that I pray the power will be perfected in me, because I sure feel the weakness."

The elders looked at one another. It was quiet for a moment. Finally, Elder Reed spoke. "We do believe it is God's will for you to remain as pastor. In many ways, the integrity of the Bible, this church and perhaps religious liberty in this country is on trial—not just you or our church. As Esther was told in the Old Testament, we believe you have been called and placed as our pastor 'for a time such as this.' Can I say it would be unanimous among the church members for you to remain as pastor? No. But we believe this is the direction God wants us to lead the church."

Pastor Curtis thanked them for their encouragement and support.

"I am totally onboard with the plan you have outlined and think those are all great steps." Preston closed the meeting in prayer. He made a mental note that it was very unusual that Chairman Martin neither led the meeting nor spoke during the entire meeting.

CHAPTER 30

THE FOLLOWING SUNDAY, PRESTON STOOD behind the pulpit with mixed feelings. He could not look into his wife's smiling face and supportive eyes while he preached because she was in Texas. There was a news camera zeroing in on him from the back of the church, and there were rumors of a plan to disrupt the services. When he looked around, he recognized both uniformed and plainclothes security. So many things had changed over the past few weeks, a long list of unexpected and undesired changes. As he stepped to the pulpit, all he could do was silently pray, *Lord, use me today. Speak truth through me. May your spirit provide the insight and power. Touch our hearts today*. His timidity was erased by the power of the Spirit of God as he stepped up to preach.

He had decided to follow the direction of the elders and begin preaching in the book of James. He chuckled a couple of times during the week as he wondered if all of them had read the book of James, because it played right into the direction he wanted his sermon series to go.

As he began the sermon, he read James 1: 2-4: "Consider it joy, my brethren, when you encounter various trials, knowing that the testing of your faith produces endurance. And let endurance have its perfect result so that you may be perfect and complete, lacking in nothing."

As he finished reading the Bible verses, he looked up at the congregation and sarcastically said, "These last few weeks have been just like any other week." As he smiled and gave a halfhearted laugh, he heard some light chuckles throughout the sanctuary.

"This church has been under attack, my family has moved to Texas, and I am facing the great uncertainty of potentially going to jail. I will confess that the possible outcome of this trial where I am accused of a crime is scary. But James was writing this book to Christians who were facing persecution because of their faith. In this country we have been historically blessed with religious freedom and the freedom to speak the truth of God's word. But that is all changing now. So, while this is new to us, it is not new to God and it was not new to those Christians that James was addressing."

Preston knew he needed to step carefully with his next words: "The attacks and challenges can come in many shapes and forms. For me, the attack has been that I—and we—hate Muslims. While you and I know that is not true, that theme has been promoted publicly. I want to restate the message from God's word. God loves us—each one of us—no matter our race, creed, gender or religion. To be clear, neither God, nor me, nor our church hates Muslims. We see them as part of God's creation, and we want to communicate that message in word and in deed. God desires for each one of us—including each and every Muslim—to spend eternity in Heaven. So, we need to daily be sure that those in our church, our community and throughout the world understand that God loves them and that our message is one of love. Every day we need to know what each one of us must do so we can accept that love and spend eternity with God."

Pastor Curtis continued to explain the certainty of personal trials, the presence of God during those trials, and the ultimate positive consequences of those trials.

"Part of our challenge is to use the opportunities presented by these tests. We must allow others to see Jesus in us and to be able to claim the victory for Him, no matter the outcome of the actual trials we are facing. Be strong in the Lord. Again, I say, be strong in the Lord."

After the conclusion of the service when the cameras were turned off, Pastor Curtis said, "I wanted to be able to visit with you, just as a church family, for a moment. Around our house I would call this a family meeting. I wanted to speak to you as my church family that has been impacted by all of the events of the past few weeks. I started to share these comments with the TV audience but decided this needed to be a personal and private time for just our church family, to hopefully encourage you and prepare you for the coming days. I want to thank you and the elders so much for the support, encouragement, and prayers you have provided for me, my family and this church. We are okay. God is good. The elders have set out a plan for addressing various issues. That plan will be laid out to you in the coming days. I also want to reaffirm to you that we are not a people that hate others. Nor do we teach hate. We should continue to show the love of Christ, no matter what others may say about us. The Bible teaches us that if we get hit in the face on one cheek, we are to turn and let them hit us on the other cheek. We are also taught that we are to forgive seventy times seven or forgive an infinite number of times. Please continue to love and show love, particularly show love to those who are attacking us. Be sure everyone understands we love—and do not hate—Muslims. Muslims are not our enemies, but Satan is. The only way we can overcome Satan in situations like this is if our love can overwhelm and overcome the hate.

"Be intentional and creative in finding ways to love the people in our community. Already I have been encouraged as I have heard testimonies of how you have turned the other cheek to those who have acted in a hateful manner toward you, and have also heard stories of how some people anticipated that a member of this church would be snobbish and hateful, only to have you be positive, loving, and caring in both your words and actions. So, thank you, and keep it up! At the same time, we must not compromise the teachings of Jesus in the Bible: that no one gets to the Father in Heaven except through Jesus. Our message is one of correction, direction, love and hope. To abandon that message when we face struggles would mean our faith is only real when things are going well. Only when these trials come, and the chips are down, will those around us and those watching us see that our faith is real. So, be encouraged. We need to endure this challenge in faith, knowing that God has a greater purpose that he wants to accomplish. Janie and I love you, and I am thankful God has given me the privilege of being your pastor. God bless you."

The headlines in the local newspaper the next day stated, "Local Pastor Continues Approach of Hate." Preston immediately called his lawyer.

"RT, did you see the newspaper headlines this morning?"

"Yes, I did. And I thought we agreed that you wouldn't say anything about Muslims period until this case is over. You know the DA and likely the judge will be monitoring the media and your conduct prior to the trial. What happened?"

"Nothing happened. That's just it. I only mentioned Muslims once during the sermon and a couple of times after the sermon, but only said God loves Muslims and wants them in Heaven for eternity. I never said anyone was going to Hell or that they were wrong. I emphasized that we need to love Muslims over and over. I have no idea where the newspaper got this information. From my perspective, it was just made up. I don't know the reporter and never spoke to her."

"Okay," RT said. "Get as many of the elders to prepare individual responses in their own words of what you said, and a response to the accuracy of what was in the newspaper. I need to have something to give to the judge to try to keep her from forfeiting your bond and putting you back in jail."

"I will call them right now," said Preston.

After RT hung up, he was concerned about how the media coverage would impact the trial. He feared his job of finding a fair and impartial jury for the upcoming trial had just gotten harder.

Back at his law office in Texas, everyone was drowning from work overload. RT called his partner.

"Hank, I am sorry about all of the things you are having to deal with. Hopefully, this case won't be much longer here in Oregon."

"RT, I am overloaded and I'm not going to be able to pay the overhead by myself very much longer," said Hank. "I am sometimes afraid to ask your paralegal what she is doing. We both know she doesn't have a law license, but she is being forced to act like she does. We could get into a lot of trouble with the Texas Disciplinary Committee for lawyers. We need you back here handling paying clients' cases."

"I know and I truly am sorry. Preston is my friend, and I can't just leave him hanging. He has no money to pay for a lawyer, and I couldn't find a lawyer in Oregon who was willing to help him. If there was any way for me to get out of it and not leave him hanging, you know I would do that. I have worked out a plan with my legal assistant to provide her more help and supervision."

Two days later, back at his home in Texas, RT's wife Kathy was sympathetic but was also feeling the strain of him being gone. She had reminded him on a couple of occasions that every time he got home, he practically had to reintroduce himself to his kids.

"RT, I was at the grocery store today and my debit card was declined," Kathy said. "I put the groceries on the credit card and when I got home, I looked at our bank account and we did not get paid this pay period. What happened?"

When he checked at the office, his partner had not paid his draw because he said RT's revenue was down below the draw amount. RT transferred money from his savings account to cover his expenses.

As he sat in his office trying to organize his thoughts, he was interrupted by a message that Judge Kirkland was on the phone. Judge Kirkland was a local district judge who took the phrase "rocket docket" to a new level.

"Good morning, Judge," RT said.

"We are going to pick your jury tomorrow morning at nine in the Williams vs. Osborne car wreck case, so we will see you then."

"But Judge," RT protested, "I have been out of town a lot and have not been able to get that case ready for trial. Plus, we only filed an answer about thirty days ago, and haven't finished all of the discovery. I need a continuance."

"Sorry, RT," he said, "no can do. The Texas Supreme Court wants us to push our dockets and it is just a simple car wreck. You have tried a ton of those types of cases, so it won't be a problem. See you tomorrow."

After hanging up, RT wondered when and why judges forgot what it was like to be a practicing attorney. He also wondered what he had done in his previous life that was piling on in his present one. God's word said he would not be given more than he could bear, but at the moment he felt the boat was getting full of water and his bailing bucket was too small. His to-do list was long: prepare *voir dire* to pick the jury; prepare cross-examination questions for the cheating plaintiff; prepare his client to testify; research legal issues; prepare a written motion for continuance. With all of those things to do, he established his priority—settle. By midnight he collapsed into bed, but in fact, he actually *had* been able to get the case settled (almost miraculously, and for a surprisingly good amount). Now Judge Kirkland would have to pull the chain of some other lawyer. But the judge had accomplished his purpose: removing the case from his docket. In the meantime, RT had to get back to Oregon.

CHAPTER 31

PRETRIAL HEARINGS IN CRIMINAL CASES are usually just a formality. Defense attorneys get an opportunity to see the state's evidence and witnesses, enter a plea, and then negotiate for a plea deal. This pretrial was different. RT had filed a motion to dismiss the case, claiming the arrest and indictment violated his client's First and Fourteenth Amendment rights to free speech and freedom of religion.

"All statements by Mr. Curtis were made in the context of a religious setting—the church—and in his role as pastor of the church," RT said to the judge. "Those statements have to be constitutionally protected. Additionally, I recently heard an applicable and appropriate statement from a Texas deputy assistant attorney general that said, 'There's no constitutional right to not be offended. There is a constitutional right to speech.' Speech that is offensive to one person or to one group of people has long been declared to be covered by constitutional protections. Offensive speech can certainly not be declared to be criminal speech."

"May it please the court," the DA responded, "we all know there are exceptions to the right to freedom of speech that have long been recognized. You can't yell fire in a crowded theater, and crimes against individuals based upon race and religion have been part of the definition of 'hate crimes' for many years. If someone threatens the president of the United States by speech only, that is a criminal offense. We can't excuse, overlook, or permit criminal offenses to continue in the name of religious freedom or freedom of speech.

"In this case, as a result of the so-called sermons of Pastor Curtis, there were hateful actions directed toward Muslims at the local high school and even outside his own church. We have those sermons videotaped and, in addition, we have video evidence of violent protests outside his church. We also have statements from Muslims who have been on the receiving end of hateful slurs and conduct as a result of this man. He has expressed no remorse, no willingness to cease such conduct, and his church continues to give him the platform to allow this conduct to continue. Your honor saw at the bond hearing his astonishing refusal to agree to cease such conduct as a condition of a personal recognizance bond. We live in an enlightened age, thank goodness, where even preachers are limited in how far they can go with hateful statements in the name of religion. This frivolous motion should be dismissed."

RT moved to the podium. "Your Honor, under the US Constitution there is a great difference between yelling 'fire' in a crowded theater that might result in people being trampled to death, and a pastor preaching what he believes the Bible says from the pulpit in the church. In this case, there was no sermon advocating injury or harm to any person or group, there was no violent action by this man nor violent action encouraged by him. He simply preached on teachings from the Bible, which have been believed by Christians for hundreds, if not thousands, of years. The US Constitution is very clear. The First Amendment prevents any law which prohibits the free exercise of religion. If you make criminal speech that simply reflects principles from the Bible that have been widely accepted for years, as is clearly Pastor Curtis' conduct in this case based upon his religious convictions, this statute is clearly contrary to that constitutional prohibition. The Fourteenth Amendment provides that no state shall make a law that abridges the privileges or immunities of citizens of the United States. This Oregon statute violates those constitutional protections. This Court remembers from a number of years ago a preacher by the name of Dr. Martin Luther King. As a result of his preaching, words that some thought were offensive at the time, even if they were not, and marches he led sometimes resulted in riots and criminal acts that were not sanctioned by him. Dr. King was justified in his right to preach, his right to speak and his right to fight for what he believed to be Biblical doctrine. I am not comparing my client to Dr. King, except from the perspective of what would have been the result if the courts of this great nation said Dr. King was a criminal and could no longer preach because he stirred up people in a manner that occasionally had violent results. Dr. King did not advocate violent conduct, just as my client does not advocate violent conduct. Both men used religious platforms to preach and teach what they believed the Bible taught. I would encourage this Court to dismiss this case. We have provided the Court with a legal brief containing citations of cases about both religious liberty and freedom of speech."

While he was speaking, it appeared the judge's face was turning red and she was giving RT the stink eye. So the Texas lawyer decided to close with a bang.

"Surely, Your Honor does not want to be known as the judge who declares preachers in America can no longer preach the Bible, and that the Bible is a document of hate."

As RT started to sit, the DA jumped up and started to speak, but the judge motioned to him to sit and directed her ire at RT.

"Mr. Glassman, your ridiculous attempt to put this defendant on equal footing with the late, great Dr. Martin Luther King is not even worthy of a response. There was never anything in Dr. King's preaching to equate with saying an entire religious group was going to Hell. Your motion is denied, and I would suggest you get prepared for trial. The jury trial is set for two weeks from today."

"Your Honor," RT said, "we move for a continuance. The defendant can't possibly be ready for trial in two weeks. There is still such a thing as due process in this country."

RT was on a roll of offending the judge, but he wanted to make a record for appeal since she was already set to rule against him.

"We haven't been provided the information from the DA, including any Brady or exculpatory materials. Nor have we been able to contact the witnesses and prepare for trial." Usually, delay is in the best interest of a criminal defendant. Sometimes, the fire dies down and witnesses may get lost, and RT was not about to voluntarily give up that advantage.

"Mr. Glassman," Judge Jackson said, "here in Oregon we have something called the Speedy Trial Act. You lawyers in Texas may not have to deal with such things, but we believe it is important to move these cases quickly for the benefit of the victims, the defendants, and the public. Is the DA's office ready for trial in two weeks?"

"We are ready, Your Honor," the prosecutor said.

"Very well," said the judge. "I'll see you in two weeks. The motion for continuance is denied."

"Your honor," RT said, "we would request the court suspend the trial and further action to give us the opportunity to appeal this important constitutional principle."

"Motion denied," said Judge Jackson.

Preston went pale. The potential of going to jail looked like it was turning into a reality. The hostility of the judge was unexpected.

As they were leaving the courtroom, the bailiff handed RT a note and said, "Some lady that I think is with the DA's office gave this to me a while ago, and asked me to give it to you after your hearing."

RT opened the note and there were seven words that sent a chill down his back: 'You have a traitor in your camp.' RT handed the note to Preston and said, "You better do some searching."

"I have no idea who this could be, or what it could be referring to," Preston replied.

"My guess is it is someone in your church, but you need to be careful who you talk to, and begin looking for a mole. I have no idea what this could mean or what is being disclosed, but this cannot be good."

After Preston left the hearing, he returned to his dark, quiet, empty house. The silence of his family being in Texas was deafening. He collapsed into his recliner to pray, but all he could do was stare at the ceiling and replay the court proceedings over and over in his head, and reflect on the note RT had given him.

I am going to prison and now I have someone I trust who is apparently betraying me, he thought. *I'm no Jesus, but someone sure appears to be Judas.*

He got out of his chair and lay face down on the floor and prayed, begging God to help him, help his family, and remove this terrifying criminal disaster. Once his emotions were spent, he read Scripture and prayed for more than an hour. His spirit had been refreshed and he finally resolved that everything around him was totally out of his control and in God's hands, so he began working on the next Sunday's sermon.

CHAPTER 32

AADILA'S FATHER, UMRAN, HAD BEEN encouraged by his conversation with Sherryl's father. He had also talked to several of his Muslim friends and they thought calmer heads should prevail, and both Muslims and Christians should work together to try to bring peace. Umran thought the first step should be to go to the mosque and talk to Imam Amar. He was trying to teach by example, so he took Aadila with him. By the time they arrived at the mosque, the imam had gathered four of his most ardent supporters for a meeting.

Imam Amar did not know that Aadila and her father were coming to speak to him about pursuing a path of reconciliation with Grace Bible Church. But just as Umran and Aadila were about to turn a corner to go to the imam's office area, they overheard the imam.

"Brothers, Allah has presented us with an excellent opportunity to strike a blow to the infidels at the Grace Bible Church in our community, a blow that may ultimately strike all infidels in the United States. This is an opportunity for Muslims to be given the benefit of being recognized by the courts as a privileged class, like minorities or females. If we get that protection, we will be untouchable. That designation will come at the expense of the Christians who don't have such protection. *Insh' Allah* (God willing)! Anytime there is discrimination or hate speech directed at us, we will be able to claim harm as a protected class. Can you imagine the benefit that gives us, compared to the Christian infidels? We have got to help their preacher get convicted of this hate crime without anybody seeing our involvement. We must act now!"

"Subhanallah,(glory to Allah)" said the men.

One of the men, Ahmed Hasnain, who had been in Syria and taught by Islamic radicals, spoke up.

"Imam, let's eliminate this infidel who would dare oppose Allah. That step would remove the threat."

"Ahmed," said the imam, "that would make the infidel a martyr. It would make us the criminal instead of Curtis. It could also turn the goodwill we now have against us. No, we need to act as the offended party, the victim, and show how hateful this conduct is, and by doing so, fan the flames of this hate crime. Once the preacher is convicted and the appellate courts affirm this finding, our Muslim faith will be able to spread like wildfire and there will be nothing those Christian infidels can do to stop us. We will be protected by the courts! Isn't it beautiful the opportunity Allah has provided us?"

"Ahmed," said the men in unison.

"Now," continued Imam Amar, "we need to develop a plan to turn up the heat on this infidel and his hateful conduct. I want us to work on four different strategies: we need offended Muslim students to regularly come forward to the media about how the hateful speech and conduct has hurt them; we need a Muslim march the day before the trial that will go outside the courthouse where the trial will occur; we need to contact the DA and offer our support with hurt people who are prominent members of this community; and I am going to contact the Islamic Society of North America to challenge them to get similar religious hate speech laws passed in every state and on the federal level. When the courts rule in our favor in the case of this infidel preacher and say preaching against the Muslim faith is criminal hate speech, we will be poised to shut down and prosecute every Christian preacher in America. Praise Allah!"

The men could not contain their excitement as they each took areas of responsibility as outlined by the imam.

As he listened, Umran was shocked and appalled. Never in a million years could he imagine his imam plotting out the course of conduct against the Christians that he had just heard. Unfortunately, his daughter Aadila was with him and she had also heard the conversation. She looked up at him with fearful and troubled eyes and simply said, "Daddy!"

Umran was preparing to quietly and quickly leave the office area when Imam Amar and other men walked out and saw them. The imam said, "Umran, Aadila, what a pleasant surprise. Come in." The other men leaving the meeting looked at Umran suspiciously.

After they were seated, Imam Amar said, "Umran, what brings you to my office today?"

"Imam, I couldn't help but hear part of your conversation. Aadila and I are friends with one of the girls in the ERAC group and her parents. Her friend's dad and I talked about trying to find ways to resolve the situation, or at least ease some of the tensions. However, I heard that you and others intend to fuel the fire of controversy and plan a course of conduct that is intended to make the situation worse. That seems very inconsistent with what you have taught and what I believe the Quran teaches about how we are to live. I am stunned, disappointed, and I don't know what to say. While that pastor may be saying things you and I believe are hateful, are we to try to rectify the situation or do we take pleasure in it? The father of Aadila's friend is a good man, and he said he would be willing to try to get his pastor to meet with you and seek to cool the situation. How am I to now go back and say not only do you not want to resolve the situation, but you want to go on the offensive, attack and make it worse?"

"Umran," said Imam Amar, "you have to understand the situation I am in. We have lived in this community for fifteen years as second-class citizens to the Christians. You know as well as I do that people have lost jobs, been called names, been harassed, and even injured by so-called Christians. I also have a diverse population and some members quote Sura 9:5 that says 'slay the pagans' or Sura 66:9 that says 'for hypocrites (unbelievers), Hell shall be their home, evil their fate.' While we don't initiate action against the pagans, because they started it, we must defend Allah and our faith. All of the actions outlined are non-violent but will help protect Muslims, not only in our community but throughout America. This situation gives us the opportunity to advance our faith for Allah by gaining media and national acceptance while getting the courts to put constitutional protections in place to protect us from future attacks. I will do nothing, nor will I permit anyone else to do anything, that would intentionally cause physical harm to any of the infidels. But you need to understand: if we were in a Muslim country and you acted contrary to our faith on the teachings of Mohammed as communicated by the imam, the result could be death. Some of our believers still believe that principle should be applicable in America. Therefore, I am commanding you to be silent about what you heard, and understand that Allah has presented us this opportunity that we cannot pass up."

Aadila started to say something but her dad shook his head at her and said, "Thank you" as they left.

After they got in the hall, Aadila said, "Papa, we have to do something. We can't let these things happen to Sherryl and her family."

"Not now," Umran said. "Wait until we leave, and we will talk about it."

Umran had never been caught in such a bind because of his religion. He had been taught the Quran since he was a child. He was familiar with the teachings in the Quran that the imam quoted, but during his life he had been taught that in America, those specific quotes did not apply. He had never heard the imam address those teachings as he just outlined it. He had followed the teachings of Mohammed, but he had never been given a direct order from an imam that conflicted so strongly with both his conscience and his understandings of the principles from the Quran.

As they walked to their car, his uncertainty about what to say to his daughter grew. He had always taught her that she was to do the right thing. The command of Imam Amar was entirely against the conviction of his conscience. How could he guide his daughter to the right path when he didn't even know the right answer? Papa is supposed to know what to do and say. But both his mind and his heart were full of unanswered questions.

When they had settled into the car and begun to leave the mosque, Aadila said, "Papa, what are we going to do? I have listened to Imam Amar all my life and you and Mama have told me he is Allah's true messenger to us, but what he said sounds evil and may cause Sherryl and her friends to get hurt. All this time, I thought the Christians were the bad guys, but Sherryl kept saying she loves me and my friends, and now the imam is cooking up a plot that will hurt her, and he tells us to cover it up and keep silent. That doesn't seem right!"

"Aadila, I must tell you, I don't understand the imam's instructions and how that fits into our faith. But I do understand a veiled death threat if we don't go along with what he said. So we have to be very careful. Until your mama and I figure this out, please don't say anything to Sherryl or anyone else. I may be able to say something to Sherryl's dad and keep us protected from violating the imam's directive, but it is obvious that some students are involved in this plot with the imam, so we can't take a chance on one of the ERAC students slipping up and let the imam know we were not totally obedient."

"I'm scared, Papa," said Aadila.

"I know," he said. "Actually, I am, too, because I have never encountered anything like this, but we have always tried to do the right thing, and this should be no different. Let's get home and I will try to figure it out."

—————◦—————

When they got home, Umran told his wife about what had happened, and she was also shocked. She had heard complaints of radical Muslims who made threats, but she thought they were made against infidels who lived in another part of the world. Since the discussion with his wife about what to do next came to no satisfactory conclusion, Umran decided to compare what the Quran taught about love or hate with what the Christian Bible said about it. As he studied the Quran, he could not find any admonition to love nonbelievers. He only found passages like Sura 9:5 that talked about slaying the pagans and Sura 66:9 that says "for unbelievers in the Muslim faith that Hell shall be their home and evil their fate." Those were the excerpts the imam had quoted. But when he Googled Bible verses on loving or hating unbelievers, he found several interesting verses:

Matthew 5: 44 – quoted Jesus as saying: "But I say to you, love your enemies and pray for those who persecute you."

1 Peter 3: 8-9 – "To sum up, all of you be harmonious, sympathetic, brotherly, kindhearted and humble in spirit; not returning evil for evil or insult for insult, but giving a blessing instead; for you were called for the very purpose that you might inherit a blessing."

He also found this verse quoting Jesus in John 13:35: "By this all people will know that you are my disciples, if you have love for one another."

It appeared there were over a dozen verses in the Bible talking not only about God's love for people, but about how his followers were to love other people, including their enemies. In Umran's mind, he kept contrasting how Sherryl's dad had reached out to him to make peace and kept saying Christians loved Muslims, but on the other hand he remembered the plot cooked up by the imam. Finally, he decided to call Sherryl's dad and discuss the internal conflict. For now, he would not share either what he overheard or what the imam had said. He was convinced the imam would deal harshly with him if he learned that Umran had disregarded his directive of silence.

The imam was sitting in his office, wondering if Umran could be trusted, when his phone rang. As he picked it up, the caller said, "You don't know me, but I am on the inside of the Grace Bible Church and I don't like what that preacher is doing. I want to help put him away so we can get rid of him."

"Who is this?" asked the imam.

"No names," said the caller, "but do you want my information?"

"Of course," said the imam. The caller told of all the steps to be taken as outlined by the elders of the church and the ERAC students. He provided dates, activities, and names. He provided enough details and specifics that the imam was convinced he was the real deal.

After the imam hung up the phone, he couldn't keep from smiling to himself and thinking, *only in America could the Christians pass laws to silence Christians, then have Christians help put their Christian brothers in jail to protect the Muslims! Allah be praised.*

CHAPTER 33

ONE OF THE ACTIVITIES THAT Elder Reed had outlined was to rally local ministers around Pastor Curtis. He thought that surely the other ministers would support the teachings about salvation that came straight from the Bible.

Fifty ministers out of 250 member churches attended the specially called meeting of the Portland Ministerial Alliance. PMA was a nondenominational organization of ministers designed to present the gospel of Jesus in the Portland area. The chairman of the Alliance, who was pastor of the Smith Road Baptist Church, had included the purpose of the meeting in the notice to the group—"Discussion concerning support of Pastor Preston Curtis at Grace Bible Church."

The Alliance chairman recognized Elder Reed to speak, who then asked the group three questions:

"How many of you believe the Bible is true?" All fifty attendees raised their hand.

"How many of you believe the Bible teaches that salvation is by faith in Jesus alone?" Twenty-five hands went up. *Amazing,* thought Reed. *Only half of the ministerial alliance attendees believe salvation is by faith in Jesus alone.* Knowing that only twenty percent of the member churches were represented gave him little comfort.

"How many of you fear that, for simply preaching the Bible, you can be charged with a crime?" Again, all hands went up.

Reed continued. "I am here because my pastor, Preston Curtis, did nothing but preach the truth from the Bible, and he is about to go on trial for a crime called religious hate speech. As ministers of the gospel, you are called by God to preach the Bible. Pastor Curtis needs you to publicly stand up for his right to preach the Bible and for religious liberty. Today they're persecuting Pastor Curtis. Tomorrow it could be some of you."

Reed could hear mumbling in the group, and one minister said, "I could have supported him, but he was red-faced on TV and he seemed angry when he called out the Muslims as going to Hell. He could have just preached about the way to Heaven is by faith in Jesus, and not called out the Muslims. That is what stirred this thing up. I would never go as far as he did and stir up the Muslims."

Another minister said, "I just preach the love of Jesus and the need to love our brothers and sisters. I would never preach a sermon like that. It is so negative."

Pastor Reynolds of the First Baptist Church said, "You are missing the point. The point is not that one preacher may sound harsher than you would when you preach, but it's about whether we will have the freedom to preach the Bible. If we preach the Bible as we individually believe it, and one of us gets charged for religious hate speech, what will happen? Today, it is Preston Curtis, but it may truly be one of you tomorrow. There are a number of Biblical passages that could be interpreted as hateful by some people. Take the issues of homosexuality or abortion. We probably have different views on Biblical interpretation of those topics in this room, but if I preach one view and you preach another view, is that religious hate speech or is that the purpose and intent of religious liberty? Would you want the Alliance to stand up for you if you were charged with the crime of religious hate speech because of your preaching? We should all stand up for the religious liberty of being able to preach the Bible, even if we disagree with the tone, the manner of speaking, or even the interpretation of Scripture. We can't back down from Biblical preaching, whether it is your interpretation of the Bible or my interpretation, simply because of potential criticism. If we go down the path you are encouraging, before long we will each have to have our sermons reviewed and cleared by the district attorney. This case with Pastor Curtis is just the first step and if we don't stand up and try to stop it, we could be next."

"The Supreme Court will step in and stop this nonsense," said another pastor.

"Are you men willing to risk your freedom to preach on the interpretation of the constitutional right to religious freedom by nine judges dressed in black robes?" Pastor Reynolds admonished. "They have tilted to the left on moral and religious cases with typically one vote swinging the outcome of the case. Your faith in that system is greater than mine. I move that we come out forcefully against the action of the DA and in support of Pastor Curtis. We should preach against this abuse of power and encourage our church members to actively support Pastor Curtis with phone calls and letters to the DA and the media. We have known Pastor Curtis over the last few years, and we should not leave him dangling in the wind by himself."

There was a second to the motion and the vote was taken.

"We have a tie," Chairman Martin said. "I must break it. Pastor Reynolds, you made some great points and I will contact Pastor Curtis to encourage him, but I think he went too far in what he said, and I don't want to have the DA's attention drawn to me or my church. I vote no, so the motion fails."

Elder Reed muttered, "Heaven help us!" as he left the meeting.

CHAPTER 34

WHILE THE TENSION MOUNTED BETWEEN the Muslims and Christians, ERAC students had continued to meet. Their leader, Clay Cook, was growing increasingly suspicious that there was a mole within the group. It seemed like Muslims were always one step ahead of ERAC. When ERAC students planned events, such as a prayer time in a public venue, Muslims would show up first with their prayer rugs out and the women wearing their hijab, and the male students wearing a kufi. They kept quoting one of the five basic devotional pillars of Islam (*Shahada*), "There is no god but God, and Mohammed is the messenger of God."

Every morning one of the Muslim students would go to Principal Turner's office to complain about the activities of ERAC. And when the ERAC students planned a school rally to support Pastor Curtis, the Muslim students had arrived first and were conducting a rally with signs saying, "Love Not Hate," and "Christians Teach Hate."

If the ERAC students planned to try to talk to Principal Turner, who had continued to refuse to meet with the ERAC students because of the court ruling, the Muslims students would be waiting in his office when the ERAC students arrived.

One day at a meeting of ERAC leadership, Clay said, "How do the Muslim students seem to know every step we are going to take before we take it? How is that possible?" No one answered, deepening Clay's suspicions of a mole in the group. He later talked to the church elders about the potential of information being leaked, but no one provided a reasonable explanation or pointed a finger. Meanwhile, the imam just continued to smile each time Mr. Anonymous provided him with additional information about the ERAC.

Also struggling with the brewing conflict were parents of the students. The Christian and Muslim communities became more polarized as publicity about the conflict stirred emotions. Few felt that tension as much as Umran. Two days after the meeting with the imam, he decided he needed to visit with Sherryl's dad about the situation. After exchanging greetings, Robert said, "Umran, I have talked to Pastor Curtis and he would be very willing to visit with the imam to try to get things cooled off, and to communicate that neither he nor our church hate Muslims. Do you think the imam would agree to such a meeting?"

Umran struggled about how much to tell Robert, based on the not-so-veiled threats from the imam, so he finally said, "Robert, I don't think that is possible right now. He is very busy, and some of those attending his mosque might object and give him trouble. In the meantime, Aadila tells me that she and Sherryl are getting along great and that Sherryl has been standing up for Aadila with everybody, including her Christian friends. I appreciate the way she has treated Aadila."

Because the meeting with the imam was still ringing in his ears, Umran said, "Tell me what your Christian faith teaches about Jesus and love for other people. I feel like when I hear a preacher say

Muslims are going to Hell, the message is confusing when I then later hear you talk about Christians loving Muslims. Also, I observe how you and Sherryl have responded to me and Aadila, and it makes me curious to learn more."

For the next hour and a half, Robert shared from the Bible with Umran. Verses like John 3:16, "For God so loved the world that he gave his only son, that whosoever believed in him would have everlasting life," and, Matthew 5:44, where Jesus teaches Christians to love their enemies and to do good to those who curse you. Robert didn't press Umran, but thought this was simply a time to share. Umran pondered what Robert said, but because of his worry about the consequences to his family if he were to go against the imam, he chose not to share with the imam anything about the conversation. After Robert left, Umran was having a crisis of conscience as he struggled to determine the real Christian faith. Some Christians had demonstrated love to him and other Muslims. Others seemed to be hateful. Which brand of Christianity was the true religion?

CHAPTER 35

AS RT WALKED INTO THE courtroom, he and Preston could not help but feel overwhelmed by its majesty—the big sculpted wooden columns, the high ceilings with eye catching woodwork, and the elevated judge's bench made of beautiful oak with a dark finish that emphasized the grain in the wood. The majestic feeling quickly dissipated as they saw the DA sitting at council table with his three assistants and six boxes of documents. The bailiff announced, "All rise, court is now in session, the Honorable Hannah Jackson presiding."

"Be seated," Judge Jackson said. "Are both parties ready to proceed?"

The DA stood and announced proudly, "The state of Oregon is ready to proceed, Your Honor."

"Your Honor," RT said, "the defendant would renew our motion for continuance because two weeks has not given us enough time to review all of the evidence and talk to all of the witnesses. You can see the DA has six boxes of documents, and I have one accordion folder.

Moving the case this quickly denies the defendant of his constitutional due process rights."

"Overruled," said the judge firmly.

"Note our exception, Your Honor, we would then re-urge our motion to dismiss based on the constitutional rights set out in our motion regarding religious liberty and freedom of speech."

"Overruled," said Judge Jackson without hesitation.

Preston's wife had come back from Texas and was seated in the courtroom to support her husband. All of the church elders—except one—were seated with her. Several church members were also present. Sitting behind the DA appeared to be the entire membership of the Muslim mosque. The imam, his leaders and a large group of Muslim students were present, all wearing Muslim attire. Fifteen rows of people were dressed in black, compared to Preston's three rows of supporters. TV cameras were in the back of the courtroom and seemed to be focused on the large crowd of Muslim supporters.

The judge's goal for the morning was to empanel a jury, which meant lawyers from each side could ask potential jurors questions in a process known as *voir dire,* which means to "speak the truth." Most lawyers know prospective jurors say almost anything except the truth. Lawyers and their clients spend lots of time and money hiring experts to help them identify the kind of jurors who might be favorable to their case. With a shoestring budget and little time, RT had to essentially wing it. By contrast, the DA's team seemed confident.

The judge administered the oath to the jury panel to tell the truth, and then recognized the DA to question the panel. After covering some preliminaries, the DA asked, "How many of you have heard about this case involving Preston Curtis as pastor of the Grace Bible Church?" About half of the hands went up, and RT wondered where the rest of the group had been while all of the protests and claims had been going on. He suspected several were not being truthful. DA Ryan continued.

"How many of you are members of a local church, synagogue or mosque?" Eighty percent of the hands went up.

"How many attend your religious services two times or more a month?" ten hands out of the fifty people went up.

"How many of you have had your minister say that Muslims are going to Hell?" No hands went up.

"Have any of you ever attended a church that talked about Muslims, or Buddhists or other religious groups going to Hell?"

"Yeah, man," one man said loudly. "I visited one of those hellfire and brimstone churches one time and got away from there as soon as I could." His comments were greeted with snickers throughout the jury pool. The juror was excused by the judge.

The DA's final question was to try to keep RT from disqualifying any of the prospective jurors based on prejudice. "Can everybody here give Mr. Curtis a fair and impartial trial, without any bias or prejudice against him?" Of course, all of the hands went up.

In his most sanctimonious voice, with his bird-eating smile, the DA turned to the judge and said, "Your Honor, we believe all of these fine folks could be fair and impartial jurors and we see no need to try to disqualify any of them." As he returned to his chair, he winked at RT.

RT knew, persuading a jury that Preston's message was one of love and not hate, would be challenging.

"How many of you love your children?" RT asked. All hands went up.

"How many of you have ever disciplined your children?" Again, all hands went up.

"When you discipline your children, is it because you hate them or because you love them?"

"If you told your small child to not stick anything in an electric plug or to not drive drunk as they got older, would you be acting out of hate or out of love? What do you think, Mr. Sanderson?" The question was posed to one of the prospective jurors.

"Out of love," Sanderson answered.

"Was your child always happy and said, 'you sure do love me' when you disciplined him or her"?

"Of course not, usually they would be yelling back at me!" said Mr. Sanderson. Chuckles from the jury pool were met by a glare from the judge.

"Can all of you keep an open mind to Biblical teachings, that if God says to do certain things or to not do certain things, those directives could be out of love and not hate?" All hands went up and RT thought that was about the best he could do.

The jury that was selected only had one person who admitted to attending church at least one time a month. Preston leaned over and asked RT, "Is this a jury of my peers? There are no preachers and only one person who even attends church."

RT pointed to a paper and told him to write down any comments. He started scribbling like a madman, so RT told him to stop and suggested they would talk about it at the break. No need to communicate the panic to the jury.

Both opening statements were very predictable, with DA Ryan using the word "hate" at least a thousand times, and RT repeating words like "truth," "love," "free speech," and "religious liberty."

When it came time for the first witness, DA Ryan announced Bob Martin. When RT heard that name, he gave Preston a questioning look. Preston just shook his head and dropped his eyes. How could the chairman of the elders from Preston's church be the first witness? As he took the oath to "tell the truth, the whole truth and nothing but the truth, so help you God," RT was surprised and disappointed. It was now obvious who the traitor was. Preston tried to look at Elder Reed seated behind them, and Reed just shook his head as he wiped tears from his eyes.

"Mr. Martin, how do you know the defendant?" DA Ryan began.

"I am the chairman of the elders at Grace Bible Church where Mr. Curtis is pastor. I was chairman when he was hired and have been chairman for the seven years he has been there."

"How long have you been a member of that church?

"About forty years."

"Do you believe the Bible?"

"Yes."

"You are aware that your pastor has been charged with a hate crime for his sermons attacking Muslim beliefs, are you not?"

"I am aware of that. This has created a lot of problems for our church."

"What kind of problems?"

"Our attendance is down, our offerings are down, our members are embarrassed, we get hateful phone calls, we have protests at services, and when I tell people where I attend church I am embarrassed because they say things like, 'Oh, you belong to *that* church?' The church is divided, and the spirit is one of discouragement."

"You agreed to appear without being subpoenaed. Why?"

"Because Pastor Curtis is killing our church! We have never stood for hate, only for love!"

"Were you there when he preached that first sermon saying the Muslims were going to Hell?"

"I was."

"What did you think when you heard that?"

"I thought that was harsh and negative and does not communicate God's love."

"As the chairman of the Elders, did you take steps to address the problem?

"Well, the problem is I tried to talk to some of the other elders, to tell them Pastor Curtis was a problem and he needed to go, but none of them would listen to me."

"Was any action taken by the elders?"

"We told him to stop preaching like that and to preach from the book of James to try to get him off this subject. He would still periodically find a way to bring it back around to say a person was going to Hell if they didn't accept Jesus as God's son. Even if he didn't call out the Muslims, the principle was the same. We also tried to schedule some events to show some positive love for the community and prevent the harm this was causing."

"Did Mr. Curtis stop?"

"Some of his sermons toned down, but he would insert statements suggesting his belief that no members of religions other than Christians will go to Heaven, and then calling out Muslims by name. Privately, he continued to push the same theme."

"Do you believe he will stop preaching these 'hateful' sermons if he is found not guilty?"

"No sir, I do not."

"Pass the witness, Your Honor."

The judge decided it was time for the lunch break. As RT and Preston were walking out, Elder Paul Reed gave Preston a hug and said, "I'm sorry. I didn't know he was going to do that."

"Don't worry about it Paul," Preston said. "You can't control what he does. I am disappointed in him, but you and I both know he was not correct in his testimony. We need to just pray for him and the church, and try to be an encouragement."

RT told them to go ahead and enjoy lunch; he had lost his appetite.

When they returned after lunch, it was RT's turn to question Chairman Martin.

"Mr. Glassman, you may cross-examine this witness," said Judge Jackson.

"So, Mr. Martin, you are the Judas, the traitor of the group, isn't that correct?"

"Objection, Your Honor," said DA Ryan. Before the judge could rule, Martin yelled, "I am not the traitor . . . he is!"

"Mr. Glassman," said Judge Jackson, "that is enough of that. I sustain the objection. Rephrase your question."

"Gladly, Your Honor," RT said.

"Mr. Martin, did you reach out to either the DA or someone within the Muslim group?"

"I did. I called both the DA and the imam."

"Were those actions approved by the other elders?"

"No, sir."

"Did you report to either the DA, the imam, or any other Muslim about the plans being made by the elders, Pastor Curtis, the ERAC group, or the church?"

Martin just sat there in silence as he stared at RT.

"Mr. Martin, please answer the question."

"No, I did not."

"So, when the students who were members of your church planned a prayer at the flagpole, did you report that plan to either the DA's office, the imam, or to anyone else?"

"Yes."

"Who did you tell?"

"The imam."

"So, when you testified that you didn't report the plans to the DA or the imam, you lied to this jury, didn't you?"

He hesitatingly responded, "I was not accurate in my answer."

"I see. Well, some of us call that a lie, but moving on, did you tell the other elders you had done that?"

"No."

"Prior to when you began to report all of the students and church's activities to the imam, did you know the imam, had you met him or had any kind of relationship with him?"

"No."

"Then it is true, is it not Mr. Martin, that the first contact you had with the imam was initiated by you, and was to report activities of your own students, pastor and church to undermine and destroy the very people you had pledged loyalty to as an elder. Isn't that correct?"

DA Ryan stood up to object.

"I will withdraw the question, Your Honor; I think the jury has the correct picture," RT continued. "And when the students planned to hand out brochures advertising the church and the ministries of the church, did you tell either the DA or the imam about those activities in advance?"

"Yes."

"Did you tell the other elders what you were doing?"

"No."

"Did you tell Pastor Curtis?"

"No."

"Did you tell the DA and imam of other planned activities of the church prior to those activities?"

"Yes."

"Did either the DA or the imam elect or appoint you as an elder of the church?"

"No."

"How were you chosen?"

"The elders at the time made a recommendation to the church and the church approved my appointment as an elder. I was elected chairman by the other elders."

"So, these same elders that elected you are the same ones you were secretly reporting about to the DA and imam?"

"Yes."

"Mr. Martin, I could list seven or eight events where the Muslims were there, waiting at an event planned by either the students or the church—the student-led prayer event at a public park, the church picnic to promote the love of Jesus, the meeting to pass out flyers to the community about the church and Jesus, and so on. I could keep going if you like, but isn't it true that you told the imam, in advance, of each of those events?"

No response.

"Mr. Martin, isn't that true?"

"Yes."

"Did you tell any of the elders, at any point in time, you were giving information about those events to the imam?"

"No."

"None of them?"

"No."

"You attended every elder meeting while all of these events were unfolding and being planned, didn't you?"

"Yes."

"How many meetings did the elders have after Pastor Curtis preached the sermon at the center of this controversy?"

"Probably ten or twelve."

"And not once, at those ten or twelve meetings, did you tell the other elders you were feeding information to the imam?"

"Correct."

"Did you ever tell Pastor Curtis about any of your tactics of reporting the planned activities to the imam so his folks could outfox them?"

"No."

"Your Honor, I object to this entire line of questioning because Mr. Martin's conduct is not what is relevant: it is the defendant's conduct that is at issue," said DA Ryan.

"Your Honor, every witness who takes the witness stand puts their character for truthfulness at issue for the weight to be given to that testimony," RT countered. "A person acting one way with a group that trusts him is supposed to be trustworthy. Mr. Martin violated that trust and was undermining his board of elders and the church itself. The jury needs to be able to see that its chairman—and not its pastor—was being deceptive."

"Objection overruled," the judge ruled. "You may continue, Mr. Glassman."

"Did you ever tell your pastor—Pastor Curtis—that you were going behind his back and reporting this information to the imam?"

"No."

"Did you ever tell the church body that you were secretly reporting this information to the Muslim imam?"

"No."

"At these ten or twelve meetings of the elders, did you ever say, 'Let's fire Pastor Curtis'?"

"Not in those words."

"What words did you use?"

"Words like 'this is a problem,' or 'we need the problem to go away.'"

"Did the elders have the right to fire Pastor Curtis?"

"We could recommend that to the church."

"Did you ever make a motion at the elders' meeting that a recommendation be made to the church to fire Pastor Curtis?"

"No."

"Did you tell Pastor Curtis that you wanted him fired?"

"No."

"You would greet Pastor Curtis every Sunday and be friendly to him, even while you were privately telling the Muslim imam everything that was going on?"

"I would speak to him and be cordial."

"But not tell him what you were doing privately with the imam without his knowledge, or that of the elders or the church?"

"Correct."

"Do you believe the Bible?"

"Yes."

"How about the Bible verse found in Ephesians 4:25 that says 'Therefore, each of you must put off falsehood and speak truthfully to your neighbor, for we are all members of one body.' Do you believe that verse?"

"Yes."

"So, when you are being friendly to the elders, your pastor, your church, and yet going behind their back to report activities to the imam, is your conduct, from a Biblical perspective, more like Jesus or more like Judas?"

"Objection, Your Honor, this—",

Before the DA could finish, Judge Jackson said, "Objection sustained. Mr. Glassman, I am not going to warn you again."

"My apologies, Your Honor, I withdraw the question."

"Mr. Martin, do you believe John 3:16 that says, 'For God so loved the world, that He gave his only Son, that whosoever believes in Him should not perish but have eternal life?'"

"Yes."

"Do you also believe John 3:36 that says, 'Whoever believes in the Son has eternal life; whoever does not obey the Son shall not see life, but the wrath of God remains on him.'"

"Yes."

"The word 'son' in those verses refers to Jesus, correct?"

"Yes."

"Do you believe the words 'eternal life' in those verses have the same meaning as 'going to Heaven'?"

"Yes, I do."

"So, you agree with the Bible and Pastor Curtis that only people who believe in and accept Jesus as Savior will go to Heaven?"

"I believe the Bible and that people who trust in Jesus will go to Heaven, but that verse doesn't say 'Muslims are going to Hell,' nor does that verse say to slam the Muslims by saying they are going to Hell."

RT decided to shift his approach. "Mr. Martin, Grace Bible Church has Articles of Faith, does it not, that members say they agree with and support?"

"Correct. I helped draft them."

"You helped draft them? So, I would expect that as a drafter of the Articles and as a member and elder that you believe and support those Articles of Faith?"

"Absolutely."

"Does article four in those Articles of Faith say, 'There is no salvation apart from personal faith in Jesus Christ as Lord'?"

"I don't remember the article numbers, but yes, that statement is contained in the Articles of Faith."

"So, as a member of Grace Bible Church and as chairman of the elders of that church, you believe that the only way to salvation is by a personal faith in Jesus Christ, and if a person doesn't take that step they are going to Hell, correct?"

"Yes."

"Mr. Martin, you apparently have had a number of conversations with the imam. Did you ever ask him if he trusted Jesus as his Savior?"

"No."

"Do you personally know any Muslims who believe Jesus is the Savior, the Messiah?"

"No."

"Based on those Bible verses, and your own Articles of Faith that you helped write that you support even today, don't you agree that if the imam doesn't trust Jesus as Savior he is going to Hell?"

"I can't know a person's heart."

"I didn't ask you if you knew his heart. I asked if the imam did not accept Jesus, based on the verses we discussed and on your own beliefs you acknowledge in your Articles of Faith, isn't he going to Hell?"

"As I said, I can't judge his heart, but I believe that verse teaches Jesus is the way to Heaven."

"Let me state it in a different way. According to your understanding of the Bible and your Articles of Faith, do you believe the imam would be going to Heaven if he rejects Jesus Christ as Savior?"

"I can't know his heart."

"Okay, let me ask the question this way: how do you believe that the Bible teaches a person is saved and gets to have an eternity in Heaven?"

"By trusting in Jesus Christ as Savior."

"Then what happens to a person who dies and has not trusted Jesus Christ as Savior?"

"They don't go to Heaven."

"In other words, they go to Hell, according to the Bible and your interpretation of the Bible as set out in your Articles of Faith that you helped write and support as an elder in the church."

"Yes."

"So, you agree with Pastor Curtis, from a theological perspective, that people who don't trust Jesus as Savior are going to Hell?"

"I believe the Bible teaches a person is lost if you don't trust Jesus as Savior, but you don't have to say that someone, or some group, is going to Hell. That comes across as rude!"

"So, if someone thinks you are being rude because you say they will spend eternity in Hell if you don't trust Jesus, you can just walk away and let them go to Hell?"

"I have no answer to your question."

Since RT could not ethically punch Elder Martin in the nose, he just stared at him for several seconds and headed to his chair to sit down. "Pass the witness, Your Honor."

RT looked at Elder Reed and his head was down, and his eyes were closed. RT didn't know if he was asleep, dead, or praying, but based on his conversations with him, he suspected the latter.

CHAPTER 36

AFTER DA RYAN THREW CHAIRMAN Martin a couple of softball questions and mercifully allowed him to leave the witness stand, he began calling other witnesses, beginning with the TV station manager who authenticated the videotape of the offending sermons. The DA wanted to hammer home his point, so he insisted on the manager identifying five sermons with references to "Muslims going to Hell," and he played each individual excerpt to prove his point.

Ryan then called Principal Turner to testify.

"Did you visit with four high school students who wanted to have a Christian prayer group meeting on campus?"

"I did."

"What were their names?"

"Clay Cook, Cindy VanLoh, Sherryl Forrester, and Melinda Benson."

"Did they state whether they are members of Grace Bible Church where Mr. Preston Curtis is pastor?"

"Yes, they did."

"Did you explain to them why they could not meet?"

"Yes, I told them our school did not allow religious groups to meet on campus."

"How did they take that?"

"Not very well. They kept arguing that they were entitled to meet on school grounds because a Muslim group was doing so."

"Did you explain the difference between the two groups?"

"Yes, I explained the Muslims were a political group, and the Christians were a religious group, but they were not satisfied."

"How did they respond to your explanation?"

"They became hostile and asked if I was a Muslim, and I finally told them the discussion was over and to leave the office."

"Did they settle down?"

"They left the office, but they did not settle down. They came to my office other times. A couple of times they got into some verbal altercations with some Muslim students in my office, and I had to threaten expulsion to get them to leave my office. There were other confrontations between the Christian students and the Muslim students. It seemed like the Christian students wanted a confrontation. I did everything I could to try to settle things down, including conducting a meeting with their parents, and suspension of Clay Cook as one of the main instigators of the ERAC group. But they all kept being insistent that the ERAC students should be able to meet on school property if the Muslim students were going to be able to meet."

"And all of this started after the defendant, Mr. Curtis, started preaching that Muslims were going to Hell?"

"Yes, sir."

Finally, RT questioned Principal Turner.

"Mr. Turner, did you do any research about whether being Muslim means that you belong to a religious group?"

"No."

"Would it surprise you that Muslims are followers of the religion of Islam?"

"I don't know."

"Did you know that Muslims follow the teaching of the Quran, their version of a holy book like the Christian Bible, and are followers of the Prophet Mohammed?"

"I don't know."

"While Islam is the religion, did you know its followers are called Muslim?"

"No."

"If you had done research and found out that the Muslim students were part of the religious group of Islam, and discovered that these meetings included teachings of the Prophet Mohammed and the Quran, would that have made a difference in the decision about whether the Muslim group could meet, and the Christian group could not?"

"Probably not, because I consider the Muslim students a minority political group that felt oppressed by other students, and I thought they needed a place they felt safe to meet as a group."

"Would it have made any difference if you had known they had prayer rugs in the room and were praying in those rooms as part of their meetings?"

"No, because a lot of groups pray as part of their meeting."

"Do you have any research, or have you received any documents, that says Muslims are a political group and not a religious group?"

"No."

"You said Muslims are a political group, so, are you saying they are a political party like the Republicans, the Democrats, Libertarians, and so forth?"

"I don't know."

"Are you aware of any presidential candidate running on a Muslim platform adopted at a Muslim political convention that nominated that person for president of the United States?"

"Not that I am aware of."

"Isn't it true that you just didn't want the Christians to meet, but you did want the Muslims to meet?"

"I did not want Muslims to be shunned or treated as an object of hate. I was not considering the Muslims as a religion, but felt they deserved the right to meet without being harassed or treated hatefully."

"You were aware that federal law states that if you let one religious group meet in your schools, you had to let other religious groups meet as well."

"I was aware."

"And in spite of Muslims considering themselves to be religious followers of the Islamic faith, and virtually every publication refers to Muslims as part of the religious group of Islam, you said the Muslim students could meet at school, but the Christian students could not, didn't you?"

"Yes."

"Did you seek a legal opinion about whether the Equal Access law would require you to let the Christian students meet?"

"No, I didn't think I needed to."

"But the school district has an attorney employed in-house who is available to principals to answer legal questions, correct?"

"Yes."

"Had you ever consulted with the school district's legal counsel before on other issues?

"Yes. Many times."

"So, you knew that an attorney was available to you in this instance, when the students said you were violating the Equal Access law?"

"Yes."

"Did you ever consider that if you had just let these four students meet, that there likely would have never been an issue involving the Christians and the Muslims in your school? That you caused the problem by not following federal law, and refusing to let all religious groups—including Christians—meet in your school?"

"I don't believe the problem was caused by me. It was caused by the Christian students who demonstrated hate toward the Muslim students."

"Mr. Turner, are you a Muslim?"

"Objection, Your Honor. His personal religious beliefs are not relevant."

"Sustained," said the judge. "Move on, Mr. Glassman."

"Mr. Turner, ultimately the federal judge slapped you down and said you were wrong, didn't he?"

"Objection, Your Honor," DA Ryan barked. "No one was 'slapped down' as stated by Mr. Glassman. That is a total mischaracterization."

"Objection sustained."

"Mr. Turner, didn't the federal judge say you were wrong, and you should have let the ERAC students meet?"

"There was an agreed order that allowed them to meet."

"In any event, there was an order from a federal judge that said the ERAC students were entitled to meet just like the Muslim students, correct?"

"Yes."

"And this whole time, all the ERAC students asked of you was to permit them to meet like the Muslim students, wasn't it?"

"Yes."

"And you tried to make an example out of Clay Cook and suspend him, to intimidate other ERAC students, didn't you?"

"I thought Clay had gone too far, and that he and the ERAC students needed to stop."

"You knew that Clay's suspension would likely kill his chances of being valedictorian or salutatorian, didn't you?"

"No, not for sure."

"You didn't care about Clay Cook—whether he was valedictorian or salutatorian, or if he might get or lose any scholarships because of your action, did you?"

"I care for all of my students, but he was out of line."

"Oh, he was out of line for asking to meet in compliance with federal law, like the federal judge confirmed?"

"He was out of line in the way he responded to my decision."

"So, students have no right to disagree with you when you make decisions that violate federal law?"

"He needed to follow the procedures in place and not start doing things like asking me if I am a Muslim."

"Mr. Turner, isn't it true that the federal judge found you were the one out of line, and made the school district reinstate Clay and allow him to make up his work?"

"Yes."

"Did Clay in fact, graduate as either the valedictorian or salutatorian?"

"Yes, he was salutatorian. He was a half-point behind another student who was valedictorian."

"You almost cost him that position by your unlawful actions, didn't you?"

"No, Clay brought all of this on himself."

"Mr. Turner, isn't it true that if you had just quietly followed federal law and let the ERAC students meet, that none of this would have ever happened? No school rallies, no sermons against the Muslims being able to meet and not the Christians, no lawsuit against the District, and on and on . . . isn't that correct?"

"I don't think you can blame all of this on me."

"From a timing standpoint, isn't it true that when you told the students they couldn't meet, it was prior to Pastor Curtis preaching the first sermon about the students not being allowed to meet?"

"Correct, from a timing perspective."

"So, I repeat my question: if you had done the correct legal thing, as found by the federal judge, and let the Christian students meet, there would have been no sermon and we would not be here, would we?"

"The students and this pastor were out of line!" he shouted.

RT just shook his head in disbelief as he headed back to his seat.

"One last question, Mr. Turner. Has DA Ryan charged you with any criminal conduct for violating federal law and causing all of these problems?"

"No, he has not."

—————◆—————

The next witness was Muslim student Anna Ahmed. She was fully attired in her Muslim dress, including the hijab. After the preliminary identification and background, DA Ryan began his questioning.

"Ms. Ahmed, you are a student at the local high school, are you not?"

"Yes, I am."

"To cut to the chase, have you been on the receiving end of hateful comments or actions because of members of the Grace Bible Church where Preston Curtis is pastor?"

"I have."

"Could you please explain to the jury what you mean by that response."

"Well, it wasn't too bad at first. Some of the ERAC students would come up and tell me it wasn't fair that they couldn't meet like we could. But after the preacher said we were all going to Hell, it was literally like all hell broke loose. Please excuse my language, so sorry. I started being called 'raghead,' and there was a note stuck on my locker door saying, 'another Hell-bound Muslim.' The final insult was when we were gathering around the flagpole praising Allah, and the Christians said they were scheduled to be there for their own rally. I don't know how it got started, but there was pushing and shoving, and I got knocked down and broke my arm. I am afraid to go to school. I am afraid to go in the bathroom by myself. I worry about something bad happening to me."

"Pass the witness, Your Honor," said Ryan.

RT had just one question.

"Ms. Ahmad, who encouraged or told you about the rally around the flagpole?"

"We all knew about it because the Christians were talking about it, but the imam got a few of us together and suggested we get there before the Christian students arrived."

CHAPTER 37

AFTER FOUR LONG DAYS OF trial, the final witness for the state was Imam Amar. DA Ryan began the questioning.

"Please state your name."

"I am Imam Amar."

"Are you the leader of a local Muslim mosque?"

"I am."

"Are you familiar with the defendant in this case, Pastor Preston Curtis?"

"I am."

"How are you familiar with him?"

"He created havoc and hatred toward my people. We were living our lives like other Americans—working, raising families, and worshipping Allah—until he stirred up hatred toward us."

"What happened?"

"Students at the high school started coming to me very upset, saying other kids were verbalizing slurs toward them. They were being targeted for hateful statements, hateful signs on their lockers, that kind of thing. One of the girls got a broken arm at some point. I had people coming to me trying to figure out what action they could take—everything from violence to marches and all kinds of counteractions. I had to work hard to keep things peaceful on our end. We had protestors outside our church. Every aspect of our mosque was in turmoil."

"Had you or your mosque done anything to stir up such hatred?"

"No, I didn't even know about this church or this pastor until all of this started happening. In fact, I offered to meet with Mr. Curtis when all of this started and apparently, he chose not to even meet with me."

"Who did you tell you were willing to meet with Pastor Curtis?"

"Elder Martin, in our second phone call."

"Did you follow up with Mr. Martin and ask about your offer to meet and talk?"

"No. By that time I had learned that Elder Martin was the chairman of the board of elders and the one I anticipated was closest to Mr. Curtis. I felt I had done the right thing by offering to meet, and if he wanted to accept my offer I would have heard back."

As RT sat and listened to the imam saying he had offered to meet with Preston, he couldn't believe it. Surely Preston would have accepted that invitation.

The DA continued.

"Did these hateful events you have described happen just once or on multiple occasions?"

"On multiple occasions and in different contexts: our students at school; our students outside school; our mosque members walking into the mosque, and in conversations in the community. There were also hateful calls to our mosque offices."

"Pass the witness," said DA Ryan.

RT started his cross examination.

"Do you agree that the title 'imam' is a religious title?"

"An *imam* is a Muslim leader."

"And the Muslim religion is one that worships Allah, isn't that correct?"

"We worship Allah, yes."

"Isn't the mosque the place where Muslims worship?"

"Yes."

"Is your organization recognized as a charitable, religious organization by the Internal Revenue Service?"

"We are a 501(c)(iii) organization, yes."

"You believe Christians are going to Hell, don't you?"

"I can't judge someone's heart."

"You believe the Quran, correct?"

"Yes, of course."

"Doesn't 3.85 of Quran say, 'Whoso seeketh a religion other than the Surrender (to Allah) it will not be accepted from him and he will be a loser in the hereafter?'"

"Yes."

"'Loser *in the hereafter'* means not going to Heaven and instead, going to Hell, doesn't it?"

"According to the Quran, yes."

"Therefore, your Quran and faith causes you to believe that Christians, or those who believe and worship a god other than your Allah, are going to Hell, correct?"

"Yes."

"Have you been indicted and charged with hate crimes because you believe Christians are going to Hell?"

"No, but we have not broadcast those words nor tried to stir up hatred against Christians."

"At your mosque you study and teach the Quran, yes?"

"Yes."

"Your Quran is the Muslim equivalent of the Bible to the Christians, isn't it?"

"The Quran sets out the teachings of Mohammed. I view it as accurate and superior to the teachings of the Bible."

"Because you pray, worship, and teach as a Muslim, and have a 501 (c)(iii) exemption from taxes as a church, don't you agree that the Muslim faith is a religion?"

"That is not my decision or call as to how the law categorizes us."

"Don't you try to convert the infidels to your faith?"

"We are open to all people believing in Allah as the one true God, and Mohammed as his true prophet."

"You never personally reached out to Pastor Curtis about your belief that he was stirring up hatred, did you?"

"No, only through Elder Chairman Martin."

"So, even though you never directly tried to talk to Pastor Curtis, you did have a spy in the elder board that you talked to regularly, didn't you?"

"I am unaware about a 'spy,' but Mr. Martin reached out to me to tell me he was concerned about what his pastor was doing, and he and I spoke several times."

"How many times did you talk to Mr. Martin?"

"Probably more than five, but less than ten times."

"Did you communicate the contents of those conversations with Mr. Martin to members of your mosque, so they could anticipate and take action concerning those activities?"

"I think those conversations with members of my mosque would be protected and should not be disclosed."

"Are you trying to claim that because those conversations were somehow confessionals, that they would be protected under the priest-penitent privilege?

"Yes."

"You understand that privilege, if applicable at all to you, is only available to members of the clergy hearing confessional, correct?"

"I don't understand the legal technicalities, but I am claiming those conversations are confidential and should be protected."

"Your Honor," RT said, "the state of Oregon does not recognize the priest-penitent privilege and even if it did, what this man said to his mosque members would not be protected because that would not be a confession by the member. I did not ask what the member said to him, but what he said to the members. I would request this witness be instructed to answer the questions about what he heard from Mr. Martin that he then told to mosque members."

"Your Honor," said DA Ryan, "this line of testimony is not relevant as to whether this defendant engaged in hate speech."

"All of this hate activity," RT said, "was stirred up by Imam Amar and his mosque members, and not by Pastor Curtis. That makes it very relevant."

"The witness is instructed to answer the questions concerning what he told his mosque members that he learned from Mr. Martin."

"Imam Amar," RT continued, "did Mr. Martin tell you about the students from Pastor Curtis' church and the rally around the flagpole?"

"Yes."

"You passed that information on to members of your mosque, and because of that instruction, students from your mosque got to the flagpole prior to the students from Pastor Curtis' church, isn't that correct?"

"Our students had a right to be at the flagpole."

"That did not answer my question. You told members of your mosque about the Christian students plans to rally at the flagpole, knowing that your students would be there first and create a confrontation when the Christian students showed up at the flagpole, didn't you?"

"I passed along the information and our students were there. I had no way of knowing how the Christian students would respond, or that there would be confrontation. Our students had every right to be there and in fact, the Christian students were inviting other students—including Muslim students—to come to the flagpole event."

"Mr. Martin told you when Christian students would be at Ms. Drake's house for Bible study, so you could tell your students and they could create a scene there, too, correct?"

"I passed on the information Mr. Martin gave to me. The Christian students responded inappropriately."

"But, if your students had no prior notice of the meetings, they would not have been there and there would have been no confrontation, right?"

"That would call for me to speculate as to what would have happened."

"Mr. Amar, I can go through the contents of each of the five to ten conversations you had with Mr. Martin, but on each of those conversations you were told about plans that groups from Pastor Curtis' church had, and each time you passed that information on to someone in your mosque, didn't you?"

"I believe that is correct."

"We have already covered two of those events, but you knew in advance of the picnic planned by church members, and the outdoor baptismal service, and other events scheduled by church members from Pastor Curtis' church, didn't you?

"Yes."

"If you had not told your mosque members about these events so they could be there to stir things up, there would have been no conflict or hateful interactions, would there?"

"That is pure speculation. My mosque members never did anything improper or illegal. Any response was based on the hateful language of the defendant and his followers. If our members' attendance at those events was wrong, you need to take that up with Elder Martin. He kept telling us about those events, knowing and expecting members of our mosque to attend."

"I have no further questions for this witness, Your Honor."

RT returned to his seat at counsel table, still fuming about the unfairness of what his friend was having to endure. When they took a break, RT asked Preston, "Why wouldn't you meet with Imam Amar?"

"RT", he said, "I swear to you. I never heard about that until we got into court today. In fact, at one point, I told our Elder Chairman that I would like to meet with the imam to try to calm things down and tell him we didn't hate Muslims, and he said he would look into it. Since I never heard back from him, I assumed the imam was not interested."

"Wait a minute," RT said, "let me get this straight. Imam Amar told Martin that he wanted to meet with you, and you told Martin you wanted to meet with the imam, but neither one of you heard about the other person's desire? Am I getting this right?"

"It now appears that is correct," Preston said.

"Oh boy," RT said. "How did he get to be chairman? He's the kind of person that gives Christians a bad name."

—————◇—————

RT couldn't wait to get back into the courtroom. "Your Honor," he said, "in light of new information, I need to recall Elder Chairman Martin to the witness stand." After Martin took the witness stand and was reminded of his oath to tell the truth, RT jumped right in.

"Mr. Martin, Imam Amar asked you about meeting with Pastor Curtis, didn't he?"

"Yes, sir."

"But you never communicated that request to Pastor Curtis, did you?"

"No, sir."

"And Pastor Curtis told you that he would like to meet with the imam, didn't he?"

"Yes, sir."

"Did you ever communicate Pastor Curtis' desire to meet to the imam?"

"No, sir."

"So, even though both of these religious leaders caught in the controversy wanted to meet, and communicated that information to you, you took it upon yourself to remain silent and let the controversy continue to fester, even at the cost of students being harmed, the churches being harmed and your pastor being criminally charged, isn't that correct?"

"I suppose."

"You even fanned the flames by feeding information to Imam Amar, to the harm of your pastor, students in your church and the Muslim church, after the leaders of both groups trusted you and told you they wanted to meet, isn't that correct?"

"I did not communicate the request to meet to either party."

"Did you tell the elders of your church that the imam had offered to meet?"

"No."

"Did you tell any other member of your church that the imam had offered to meet, or that Pastor Curtis had offered to meet with the imam?"

"No."

"Isn't it true that the Bible teaches that an elder is a position of trust and is to be above reproach and to care for the church?"

"Yes, sir."

"Isn't it also true that, by you going behind the backs of your pastor, your fellow elders and your church members in such an underhanded, deceptive and secretive manner, you violated that trust?"

"I was protecting the church from this madman. None of the other elders were willing to act and put a stop to it. So, I was protecting the church."

"Unbelievable," RT said as he returned to his seat.

DA Ryan stood. "Mr. Martin, I only have one question. Why didn't you communicate the requests to meet?"

"Because I knew it would be wasted effort. Mr. Curtis would never agree to quit preaching that Muslims were going to Hell: he would say that by not preaching that message, he would compromise his ability to speak the truth of the Bible, and his willingness to stand for Christ, and his choice to accept the consequences."

CHAPTER 38

DURING THE COURSE OF THE trial, Sherryl's dad, Robert, and Aadila's dad, Umran, had been meeting in private. Both were concerned about the hostility and the trial.

"I am scared to death for me and my family because there has been a veiled death threat by Imam Amar if I disclose his intent and the intent of the leaders in the mosque," Umran said. "I can only imagine the response if I convert to Christianity. My wife will not understand, and the Muslim community will shun me and my family—or worse. You have taught me that Muslims are not your enemy, but that Satan is the enemy. After comparing the tenets of faith between the Muslims and Christians, I want to follow this Christ."

"Umran," said Robert, "that is outstanding. Would you like to make that commitment now?"

"Yes," he said.

Robert led Umran through a prayer confessing his sins and asking Jesus to forgive him. Umran acknowledged in his prayer that he wanted to follow Jesus and make him his savior. As soon as Umran finished his prayer, Robert gave him a big hug and smile. "You are now my brother in Christ!"

Umran felt a sense of peace and turned to Robert and said, "Your pastor's trial is nearly over. I want to testify for him and tell how Imam Amar had said the Muslims needed to strike a blow to all infidels and get the pastor convicted so Muslims would benefit. I could also tell how he planned to send students to disrupt the Christian students' activities and keep the controversy stirred up. I feel like I need to do the right thing. Aadila overheard that conversation with the imam, too, and she is looking at me to see how I will respond. I think the truth needs to come out!"

Robert was shocked by Umran's revelation and his offer to testify on behalf of Pastor Curtis. He thanked his new brother for the offer and told him that he would communicate his offer.

Robert called RT and communicated the information from Umran and his offer to testify. "That's terrific," RT said. "I need to talk to Preston and get his approval, and then I will get back to you."

RT called Preston and after discussing the potential impact on the trial, and the risks to Umran and his family, Preston said absolutely not. "The cost to Umran and his family would be too high. He needs time to grow in his Christian faith without this scrutiny and difficulty. He needs the love of Christ demonstrated to him, and to know and understand that Christians are different, and that our love is real and genuine. He needs to know we don't just use people for our personal benefit or gain. Plus, after talking to you and watching the trial, I don't think it will make a difference. Anyone listening would know the imam participated in stirring up the students and the controversy. Please have Robert convey my appreciation to Umran and my absolute joy that he has become a fellow believer."

While disappointed as his lawyer trying to prevent him from going to prison, RT had never been prouder of his friend.

CHAPTER 39

THEY WERE ALL EXHAUSTED FROM the trial, but the state had rested from presenting evidence, and they had come to the moment of truth. "Preston," RT said, "you cannot testify. The DA will tear you apart, and by taking the stand you will allow him to replay every video of your sermons and ask you about each of the statements you made. Everything I tried to do to protect you during the course of the trial will be undone. There can be no good outcome, and it could harm our case tremendously if you take the stand, both now, at trial, and later, if we need to subsequently appeal an adverse verdict."

"Only guilty people plead the Fifth Amendment and refuse to testify," Preston said. "They need to see I am not a hateful person and that I am motivated by love. I am the only one who can testify about my intentions and desire for God's love to reach all people. Nobody can do that but me."

They jockeyed back and forth, and Janie tried to encourage Preston to take RT's advice, but he refused. They spent several grueling hours that night trying to have him prepared to testify.

They took a break early in the evening so Preston and Janie could call their kids. "Daddy," Sarah said, "why don't you resign as pastor, tell them you won't preach there anymore and come back to where we are in Texas? PaPa said you wouldn't get in trouble for preaching the Bible in Texas, and we miss you. We are tired of living with PaPa and Mimmie, and we want to be with you and mom together as a family. We need you," she cried.

Preston and Janie were emotional but tried to console her. Before hanging up with the kids, Preston prayed for them that God would protect them, and that they could be strong and have good days. After hanging up, Preston and Janie hugged each other in silence. At that moment, RT knocked on the door and dragged Preston back into his office to spend the next three hours in preparation for his testimony.

***

Preston's first witness was Major Timothy with the local Salvation Army. He testified how Preston supported the Salvation Army and had led chapel once a month, helped them raise funds for meals and clothes, and spent time talking to the homeless. Major Timothy also testified that he never heard Pastor Curtis say anything hateful toward Muslims or anyone else, and just spoke of God's love.

DA Ryan only asked a few follow-up questions.

"Are you a member of Pastor Curtis' church?"

"I am."

"You don't want to see your pastor go to prison, do you?"

"No, I do not."

"And you would do anything to help keep him from prison, wouldn't you?"

"I wouldn't lie."

"Well, let's see how objective you are. Were you there when he said Muslims were going to Hell?"

"I was."

"Did you ever tell him he should not say that?"

"No."

"Never?"

"No, sir."

"You knew about all of the problems created in the high school and at your church, and not once did you tell Pastor Curtis to apologize or stop saying Muslims are going to Hell, did you?"

"No, sir."

"The reason you didn't tell Pastor Curtis to apologize or stop saying Muslims were going to Hell is because you agree with him, don't you?"

"I believe he preaches the truth from the Bible."

"Your organization, the Salvation Army, is non-denominational isn't it?"

"Yes, sir."

"It includes volunteers and donors of all faiths including Muslims, doesn't it?"

"I anticipate so, yes sir, but honestly, unless someone volunteers that information, I don't ask what church they attend."

"So, even though Muslims support your organization, pay your salary, provide money for food for those in need, you attend a church where the pastor says Muslims are going to Hell and you do nothing to rein him in, isn't that true?"

RT stood to object, but before he could say anything, DA Ryan said, "I will withdraw the question, Your Honor, and pass the witness." He then added, sarcastically, "I have no further questions for this very objective witness, Your Honor."

RT needed to use Clay Cook to establish a timeline concerning Preston's involvement with the students, so Clay was his next witness:

"Before you talked to Principal Turner for the first time, had you or any of the other ERAC student leaders spoken to Pastor Curtis about the problem of not being allowed to meet like the Muslim students?"

"No sir."

"Why did you talk to Principal Turner?"

"We had been made aware that the Muslim students were able to meet on campus as a group, and didn't understand why we couldn't meet as a Christian group."

"Who put you up to going to meet with the principal?"

"No one. I had spoken to my dad about the situation, but the group and I decided on our own to go visit Principal Turner. We thought surely there was some misunderstanding, and that we would be allowed to meet, but we were wrong."

"Was Principal Turner receptive to your request?"

"No sir. He was hostile and said he didn't have to let us meet and he wasn't going to let us meet."

"How did you respond?"

"Well, I was frustrated, and after we met with the principal, my dad talked to a lawyer who said that a federal law called the Equal Access Act required the school to treat all student-initiated religious groups equally. He said that because the Muslim students, a religious group, were being allowed to meet on school property, my group should also be allowed. So, I went back by myself and told Principal Turner what the lawyer had said and referenced the Equal Access Act."

"How did Principal Turner respond when you brought up the Equal Access Act?"

"At first he was just silent. Then his face got red and he stood up and said 'This discussion is over. You're not meeting. Period.' So, I left."

Clay testified that, after the first unsuccessful meeting with Principal Turner, the ERAC students went to Pastor Curtis for advice. Preston always encouraged them to demonstrate love for others even as they tried to stand for what was right. He further testified that none of the ERAC students ever started any conflict, but that the Muslim students always showed up at their events and seemed to be "itching" for a fight.

DA Ryan couldn't wait to get his claws into one of the instigators of the high school mess.

"Mr. Cook, you were the one who got the other three students to go to the principal and demand that he let you meet, weren't you?"

"I suggested to the other three students that we go meet with the principal."

"And after you did that, let's list some of the things you did." The DA wrote on a white board for the jury to see.

"First, you asked the principal to let your group meet, making your demand not once, not twice, not three times, but more than five times, didn't you?"

"Yes, sir."

DA Ryan wrote on the board, "Demand > 5 times."

"You took your group to meet with Pastor Curtis to tell them about your unfair treatment, didn't you?"

"Yes, sir."

DA Ryan wrote on the board "Told Pastor Curtis unfair."

"You planned the rally at the flagpole, which resulted in fights with Muslims, resulting in injuries to Muslim students, didn't you?"

"I encouraged attendance at the Flagpole Prayer Rally, but had nothing to do with anyone being injured."

DA Ryan wrote on the board, "Organized rally = injured Muslim students."

"And you handed out pamphlets inviting students to attend your Bible study, which resulted in confrontations again, didn't you?"

"I handed out invitations to our Bible studies but did not confront anyone."

DA Ryan wrote on the board. "Hand out pamphlets = fights."

"In one of your rages, you even accused the principal of being Muslim, like that was a big insult to him, didn't you?"

"It wasn't a rage, but yes, sir, I was—"

Before Clay could answer further, DA Ryan objected. "Your Honor, I object to everything this witness said after the words 'Yes sir' as being non-responsive."

"Sustained."

DA Ryan wrote on the board: "Accused principal of being Muslim."

"So, let's look at what has been listed on the board as to what you have been up to during this mess. It says:

> Demand > 5 times
> Told Pastor Curtis unfair
> Organized rally = injured Muslim students
> Hand out pamphlets = fights
> Accused principal of being Muslim

"So, it is true, is it not, that with all of these problems, from the confrontation at the flagpole, fights over prayer invitations, getting Pastor Curtis fired up, you accusing the principal of being a Muslim . . . all of this was started, kept alive, and fired up by you, wasn't it?"

"I think it was all started by the principal failing to comply with federal law and give us Christian students the same access and ability to meet that he gave the Muslim students, as the federal judge said he should do."

The DA's final point had been made. Clay Cook had played into his hands.

Elder Reed was the next witness. After the preliminaries, RT went to the heart of his testimony.

"Did you at any time hear Pastor Curtis preach or say anything that was not Biblical, or from the Bible?"

"No."

"You heard in the testimony that Mr. Martin, the chairman of the elders at your church was telling Imam Amar about all of the students' and church's plans, so the Muslims could show up to stir things up. Were you or the other elders, to your knowledge, aware that Elder Martin was doing that?"

"No."

"To your knowledge, did Mr. Martin inform the church of his activities?"

"No."

"Were you ever informed, as an elder of the church, that Chairman Martin had been told separately by both Pastor Curtis and Imam Amar that they were willing to meet with the other person to try to cool things down or resolve issues?"

"No."

"How would you have responded if you had been told of those conversations?"

"I would have quickly moved to encourage the meeting."

"Have the elders as a group told Pastor Curtis to stop preaching the Bible?"

"Absolutely not."

"You heard Mr. Martin testify that Pastor Curtis was 'tearing up' the church. Is that true?"

"Not at all. The church members love him, and he loves the members of our church."

"What do you mean by 'he loves the members of our church'?"

"He takes calls from church members day and night. He goes to the hospital. He calls the homebound. He officiates at weddings and funerals. He is always there and is caring and concerned for the members. His sermons stay true to the Bible. We could ask nothing more from the man."

"Have you heard him say anything that indicates he hates Muslims?"

"No, he proclaims God's love for all, and his desire is, based on the teaching of the Bible, that all would trust Jesus. He says that religions that don't view Jesus as Savior are misleading their members. But that is not hateful, it is just based on the teachings of Jesus and the Bible."

"Who stirred up this controversy?"

"Unfortunately, the school principal who denied access to the Christian students as required by law did that. Then the consequences were magnified because we had a Judas in our midst: Our own

Chairman Martin and Imam Amar conspired together and got the Muslim students, as well as other Muslims, to attend the church and school events to stir things up. They did a whole lot more to create controversy than Pastor Curtis did."

"To your knowledge, Pastor Curtis had nothing to do with the problems from any of those events?"

"Correct."

DA Ryan's cross examination did little to alter Elder Reed's conviction that Preston was not the instigator.

———————◇———————

Finally, it came to the time RT had been dreading during the entire trial. "Your Honor," he said, "the defense calls Pastor Preston Curtis to the stand."

"Mr. Glassman," said the judge, "have you fully advised your client of his Fifth Amendment privilege not to incriminate himself, and that he does not have to testify?"

"I have, Your Honor."

"Then you may proceed," she said with a frown. RT glanced over at the grinning DA.

After he identified himself and his position, RT decided to jump right in. "Pastor Curtis, do you hate Muslims?"

"Absolutely not!"

"Then why are you preaching about them going to Hell?"

"I believe the Bible, and it says no one gets to Heaven except by trusting Jesus as their savior. It doesn't matter if a person belongs to a particular religion or has no religious background at all. My goal is to see people trust Jesus as Savior—not promote hate. I want to wake them up to the fact that they are lost and will spend eternity in Hell apart from Jesus."

"You are charged with speaking with the intent to insult, intimidate or cause prejudice against a person based on their religion, in this case against Muslims. Did you do that?"

"I would never speak in a way intended to insult or cause harm or prejudice to anyone. I want people to see the love of Jesus through me, my preaching and my efforts to share the Bible."

After covering Curtis' background about his family, his roles in ministry, service to his church, the Salvation Army and his pro-life involvement, RT passed the witness.

DA Ryan pounced. "You preached that Muslims were going to Hell more than fifteen times, didn't you?"

"I don't remember the number."

"We have eighteen videos of the sermons you preached. Would you like for me to play each and every one of them for you and the jury?"

"No sir. I would anticipate you counted them correctly."

"You never preached by name that Baptists, Methodists or Presbyterians were going to Hell, did you?"

"I preached that anyone who did not trust Jesus faced an eternity in Hell, and I believe I referenced other religions and said no religion would save a person without their trusting Jesus."

"Mr. Curtis, I can play every one of those sermons if you would like, but wouldn't you agree that while you called out that Muslims were going to Hell in each of those sermons, not one time did you call out that Baptists, Methodists or Presbyterians were going to Hell?"

"I believe I did on occasion reference other religions, I really can't recall. But my intent was that you could be a member of a church, even one that is a Christian denomination, and if you are trusting membership in that church rather than having faith in Jesus, you could still not go to Heaven. It is not the religion that saves you, it is the relationship. Judas was a member of the early church and a member of Jesus' inner circle, and all indication from Scripture is that he did not go to Heaven when he killed himself."

"Well then, what about Jews or Buddhists or Hindus? Did you ever condemn them?"

"I can't say for sure, but I suspect there were times I did mention those specific religions."

"Mr. Curtis, did you have an invitation or altar call to trust Jesus at the end of each sermon?"

"Yes, sir."

"And as part of that invitation or altar call, you would always say the only way to an eternal life in Heaven is by having faith in Jesus, isn't that correct?"

"Yes, sir."

"By saying that Jesus is the only way, you are implying that others—like Muslims—are going to Hell, even if you don't use their name, aren't you?"

"I am only preaching the Bible! It teaches that the only way to Heaven is by trusting Jesus."

"And if this invitation, or altar call, as offered on the fifty Sundays you preached each year for seven years, that would be over three hundred and fifty times you have communicated that in our community, isn't that correct?"

"I give an invitation each Sunday I preach. I don't believe your characterization is accurate, but I do explain each Sunday that the way to be in Heaven is by faith in Jesus alone."

"You told the ERAC students to confront Principal Turner, didn't you?"

"No sir. When they came to see me, I simply encouraged them to talk to him about his reasons for not letting the Christian group meet, when he was letting the Muslims meet, because that refusal appeared to violate federal law."

"You know that at various events that the ERAC students attended there were some violent incidents involving Muslims, don't you?"

"My understanding is the ERAC students did not instigate any violence."

"Did you ever tell the ERAC students to stop what they were doing?"

"No, sir."

"Did you ever apologize to the Muslims in any of your sermons?"

"No, sir."

"Did you ever call Imam Amar to apologize to him?"

"No, sir. I offered to talk to him but never did talk to him."

"Can you tell this jury a single solitary thing you did to stop the ERAC students or to stop what happened to the Muslims as a result of your preaching the hateful 'word of God' that they were going to Hell?"

"I tried to encourage that Jesus loved all people, including those who reject him, and that we should communicate that love. The Muslims are not our enemies; they are loved by Jesus. I didn't tell anyone to stop speaking about Jesus or stop encouraging others to trust Jesus."

The haranguing continued until DA Ryan finally asked, "Mr. Curtis, for several hours we have gone through all you said, all you did, and all you failed to do. Will you just admit the truth: that you simply hate Muslims?"

There was silence as Preston just hung his head. Finally, the judge said, "Mr. Curtis you must answer the question."

Preston eventually raised his head, and with tears running down his cheeks, spoke. "No, sir, I don't hate Muslims. All I want to do is preach about Jesus and see people saved. It doesn't matter if someone is a Jew, Buddhist, Hindu, Muslim or any other religion. If they don't accept Jesus as savior, the Bible says they are going to Hell. It's about a relationship, not a religion. Anyone, and I mean anyone—be it Judge Jackson, you or anyone else who doesn't accept Jesus as savior—is going to Hell."

DA Ryan looked shocked, then paused and glanced at RT with a smile as he passed the witness. With that exchange, the evidence portion of the trial was concluded. The judge recessed the trial for the day to prepare the court's charge to the jury and closing arguments.

As they walked out of the courtroom, RT whispered to Preston, "I am praying that the judge didn't just interpret your comment as saying the person who will determine your punishment if you are found guilty is going to Hell."

Preston just shook his head. "That Ryan guy really got to me. I was just trying to make a point."

"Well," RT said, "I certainly think you did."

Preston, Janie and RT were exhausted—physically, emotionally and spiritually. The next day the jury would begin deliberations, but they had one more thing to do that day.

CHAPTER 40

ELDER REED HAD ARRANGED TWO events for the evening after the evidence was concluded. The first event was a meeting of the church elders. There, after a time of prayer, Elder Reed looked at Chairman Martin.

"Bob, you have sinned against this body of elders, this church, our pastor, and more importantly against the Lord and his work. We are extremely disappointed that you would violate the trust placed in you by the church and by the other elders. I was personally stunned when I heard in the courtroom for the first time what you were doing behind our backs. Before we take any action, we want to know you will take the necessary steps to repent and seek forgiveness."

"I will not repent," Chairman Martin huffed. "I was seeking to protect this church from that madman who made us a hateful laughingstock."

"Then you leave us no choice," said Elder Reed. "Is there a motion that Bob Martin be removed as an elder of Grace Bible Church?" The motion carried with only one dissenting vote—Chairman Martin.

"Bob," said Elder Reed, "we will pray for you, but you are relieved of your responsibilities as an elder of this church. You are excused from this meeting."

After Bob Martin left, Elder Reed was elected as chairman.

The second event was a prayer vigil for Pastor Curtis at the church. When Preston and Janie walked into the sanctuary, they were greeted by more than 200 people who stood and applauded. It was an emotional experience as the couple sat on a bench together, holding hands, as members came by and prayed over them with words of encouragement. After it concluded, Preston and Janie's spirits were lifted, at least for the night.

CHAPTER 41

TRIAL LAWYERS LIVE FOR THE closing arguments to a jury. It's a time to cut loose and hammer the opponent. DA Ryan bore in.

"'Hate' is such a strong word. Webster defines it as 'an intense or passionate dislike for someone.' How much more strongly can you express a passionate dislike than to tell someone they are going to Hell? Have you ever heard someone tell another person they are going to Hell, or to 'go to Hell' in a friendly, warm, loving, caring voice? Of course not! What this man did, supposedly a man of the cloth, one who preaches about God's love, grace and forgiveness, what he said about Muslims was 'GO TO HELL'!

"As a nation, and certainly as a state, we have moved beyond such rhetoric. As the judge gave you the law in the state of Oregon, our legislature, in recognizing that we should not be a state of hate, said that hate speech is speech that is 'intended to insult, intimidate, or cause prejudice against a person based upon their religion.' All of the events you have heard about—from the Muslim community ridiculed because they are going to Hell, to fired up ERAC students, to Muslim students being injured in confrontations—all began when this man of the cloth started proclaiming that Muslims are going to Hell! If that is not speech that is intended to intimidate or cause religious prejudice, I don't know what is!

"You heard from the defendant himself who knew exactly what he was saying when he admitted that more than fifteen times he said Muslims were going to Hell. And he intends to keep saying it if you, the jury, as the conscience of our community, do not stop him!

"Now, Mr. Glassman is going to try to create sympathy for the defendant with claims about religious liberty and preaching the Bible. But who will protect those without a voice, like the Muslims trying to live their lives quietly, and trying to worship in their mosque and mind their own business? This defendant is the only one in our county or state preaching and stirring up hatred against Muslims. You must stop him by finding him guilty!"

As he stood to give his closing, RT felt the weight of the world on his shoulders. Not only was constitutional freedom of religion at stake, but so was his friend's freedom. His legs felt heavy as he moved to the podium to begin his closing.

"If I thought there was one ounce of hatred in the body of Pastor Preston Curtis, I would not be standing here. What have you heard about this man? A loving husband, a caring father, a man who goes at all hours of the day and night when parishioners have a crisis, someone who helps serve meals at the Salvation Army and performs wedding and funerals. You also saw him be broken and full of tears on the witness stand as he expressed love for all people, including Muslims. Now tell me, is that the description of someone filled with hate? It seems to me that he should be given a humanitarian award rather than the threat of prison. I am not from this community, but if your community is like the community I am from, criminal trials are reserved for people who commit assaults, murders, rapes or are drug dealers. The state, and DA Ryan, want you to put Preston Curtis on the same plane and in the same place as criminals guilty of those very offenses simply because he is a Christian and wants to preach from the Bible. Our nation was founded on Christian principles. Over ninety-eight percent of the colonists were Protestants, and an additional two percent were Catholics. The Declaration of Independence says, 'We hold these truths to be self-evident, that all men are created equal, that they are endowed by their creator with certain unalienable rights: that among those are life, liberty and the pursuit of happiness.' It further references 'nature's God,' and appeals to the Supreme Judge of the World, and notes the signers' 'reliance on the protection of divine Providence.'

"George Washington, the founding father of this nation, said in a letter to Virginia Baptists, 'Every man, conducting himself as a good citizen, and being accountable to God alone for his religious opinions, ought to be protected in worshipping the Deity according to the dictates of his own conscience.' This perspective of religious liberty was carried forward into the First Amendment to the United States Constitution which states, 'Congress shall make no law respecting the establishment of religion or prohibiting the free exercise thereof.'

"Of course, that provision also applies in Oregon. So, what is Pastor Curtis accused of? Preaching the word of God from the pulpit of a church, directly from the Bible. And what does that Bible say? There is one way to Heaven and that is through faith in Jesus Christ.

"This trial is a direct threat to our Constitution and a direct violation and affront to the wording that there shall be no law prohibiting the free exercise of religion. Now, you may not believe the way Pastor Curtis believes, but that is not the point. Our founding fathers and even our own Constitution protects the right of pastors to preach the Bible. Have we, as a country, gotten so 'politically correct' that we want district attorneys, judges and even juries to censor sermons? Heaven forbid! It's a slippery slope. The message from this jury should be to tell DA's to leave our pastors alone. Focus on the real criminals in our community. Protect us from the murderers and rapists. Don't spend our precious money and resources trying to imprison pastors preaching from the Bible and doing good in our community.

"You are the only safety net to protect our pastors and people like Preston Curtis from overzealous prosecutors like DA Ryan. Ladies and gentlemen of the jury, you must find Pastor Curtis not guilty if you wish to protect all pastors, all religions, and even our nation. May God bless you in your journey."

CHAPTER 42

THE NEXT MORNING, THE JUDGE read instructions to the jury. Over RT's objections, the judge had refused to give the jury instructions about freedom of speech or freedom of religion. She also refused to instruct the jury about the effect of a person's good-faith belief that his actions were lawful. RT had never been in a trial where the judge so obviously and intentionally ignored the law. The train of conviction was barreling down the track, about to run over his friend.

The one juror who attended church was not elected jury foreperson. Once assembled in the jury room, the foreperson said, "I think it is clear he is guilty. Let's take a vote and see where we are."

The first vote was nine guilty and three not guilty.

"How can you three vote not guilty?" the foreman pressed. "Didn't you hear the evidence about what this man said, and all of the bad things that happened because he said the Muslims were going to Hell?"

The one juror who attended church said, "if Pastor Curtis is guilty, then every preacher in this country that preaches the Bible can be found guilty of hate speech. I can't find him guilty of that. Plus, I think the principal of the high school and the Muslim imam did more to stir up hate than the pastor. Why aren't they on trial? I'll tell you why, because the pastor is a Christian and it is now politically correct to attack Christians."

They argued back and forth for two hours and then voted again. The second vote was ten to two for guilty.

By four that afternoon, the 'guilty' group had worn out one holdout, so the vote was eleven to one in favor of guilt. The foreperson sent a note to the judge saying they were deadlocked and could not reach a unanimous verdict. Then the judge gave the jury a 'dynamite' charge, over RT's objection, that the jurors needed to be reasonable, seek to get along, and reach a verdict. "If this jury fails to reach a verdict, then everybody's time and expense will have been wasted." The jury was excused for the night, but the message from the judge was clear—reach a unanimous verdict, and I am not dismissing you until you do!

The next morning the jury deliberated for three more hours and finally announced they had reached a verdict. As they entered the jury box, RT could see that the lone churchgoer was crying, and he knew they were sunk. He turned and said, "Preston, they are going to find you guilty. You need to keep your composure and not display emotion." Preston looked back at RT in shock.

The judge turned to the foreperson and said, "Has the jury reached a verdict?"

"We have, Your Honor. On the one count of hate speech, we find the defendant guilty." Both sobs and cheers erupted in the courtroom. All RT could think was, *How could this possibly be happening in America?*

⁕

It was the longest night that Preston and Janie had ever faced. They called Janie's parents and they cried. Their kids cried. For three hours a stream of church members visited, and they cried. Finally, Preston decided to turn out the lights.

"I am scared," Janie said. "What am I and the kids going to do if this judge sends you to prison? How will we pay our bills? Will you be safe? How can I take care of the kids? How can I protect them from mean people? Why would God allow this? All you were doing was preaching the Bible! Why? How can that be hate speech?"

Preston shared that they had to trust the Lord and be strong.

"How can I be strong when it seems my world is collapsing, and it doesn't feel like my prayers are getting any higher than the ceiling?" Finally, she collapsed into Preston's arms and they prayed and spent a restless evening knowing that it was very likely Preston would be sentenced to prison the next day.

RT could not sleep that night either, because he felt he had let his client and friend down. He felt sure that Preston was now headed to prison because of a bad statute, a bad jury, a bad judge, and a political environment that created a hateful and hostile environment for religious liberty. RT prayed for Preston, Janie and their kids.

When RT called his wife Kathy, she was concerned not only for Preston and Janie, but also for RT.

"Are you going to be okay?" she asked. "You did everything you could possibly do to protect Preston."

CHAPTER 43

BY STATUTE, SENTENCING WAS TO be determined by the judge rather than the jury.

DA Ryan began.

"Your Honor, the state of Oregon would reoffer the evidence presented at trial."

"Subject to the same objections and rulings of the court, that evidence is deemed to be readmitted for purposes of sentencing."

The DA then rested as to sentencing without calling any additional witnesses.

RT's first witness was Preston's wife, Janie, and he wanted to start off with a bang. "Janie, how can you live with and stay married to such a hateful person?" He could see her face turning red in anger, but he needed to stir her passion.

"How could you say that? Preston is kind and caring. He is a loving husband, father and pastor. He has stayed all night at the hospital with church members, he has cried at funerals, he never turns down an opportunity to witness for Christ, he helps our children do homework, attends their recitals and soccer games, leads us to volunteer at places like the homeless shelter, pro-life sonogram clinics, and he goes on mission trips. All of that is on top of preparing sermons each week by studying the Bible and praying for guidance. He is not a hateful person."

"Janie, what kind of effect will it have on your family if Preston is sentenced to prison?"

"It will break our hearts," she said, crying. "Our kids don't understand it. They cry and wonder what will happen to their daddy. Kids at school are cruel and call their daddy a criminal and a hatemonger. Preston going to prison will ruin us financially. We have no other source of income besides his salary from the church. We were told last night that the church will begin the process of calling a new pastor, so soon we will lose that salary.

"The media has been following me and our kids. They even came to my parents' home in Texas. The kids and I will have to move in permanently with my parents until Preston gets out of prison, and we can get back on our feet again. We don't know if Preston will ever be able to pastor a church again, whether he goes to prison or not."

"How have you been getting by during this process?

"By the grace of God and taking each day one day at a time. We also hold onto Bible verses like 'my grace is sufficient,' and 'I can do all things through Christ who strengthens me.'

"What would you like to tell Judge Jackson about your husband, about whether she should send him to prison?"

"Preston is very loving and very caring. All he has done is serve God and try to point others to Jesus. He spends long days in ministry. He goes to hospitals to visit the sick, he holds hands of family members in grief; he has never, ever hurt another person or done anything to harm another person. He is a minister in the truest sense.

"This is all a bad nightmare that I can't believe. How in America can a pastor preach straight from the Bible and be sent to prison for doing that? We hear of those kinds of things happening in places like China, Africa and Iran, but here in America? I never thought it would happen. Preston risks being sent to prison with rapists, murderers and drug dealers simply for preaching directly from the Bible. I worry about how he can stand up to criminals like that, and what he would be like once he gets out. It seems to me that sending him to prison cannot be right, fair, or reflect how our country was founded as a Christian nation. I would ask the judge to be fair, not sentence Preston to prison, and consider all of the good things he has done and the religious, biblical and Christian foundation and heritage of this country."

"I pass the witness," RT told the judge.

The DA asked Janie just two questions. "Ms. Curtis, you have heard your husband preach from his pulpit that Muslims are going to Hell, haven't you?"

"Mr. Ryan, I have heard my husband preach directly from the Bible that faith in Jesus is the only way to Heaven and anyone who doesn't profess faith in Jesus will be going to Hell."

"Including Muslims?"

"Including anyone who refuses to believe in Jesus—including Muslims, but also including other world religions and anyone even without a religion, if they don't believe. That's just what the Bible says."

Preston's next witness was Elder Joshua Bernard:

"Mr. Bernard, are you an elder from the Grace Bible Church?"

"I am."

"That is the church where Preston Curtis has been the pastor, correct?"

"That is correct."

"Were you present in the courtroom when the former Elder Chairman Bob Martin testified that Pastor Curtis was ruining the church and spewing hate?"

"I was."

"Do you agree with those conclusions?"

"Absolutely not. All Pastor Curtis has done is proclaim the truth of God's Word unapologetically. He believes the Bible. I believe the Bible and our congregation believes the Bible. Where the Bible is taught and people are believing, Satan will attack and seek to destroy. I and many others in our church are proud of Pastor Curtis for preaching truth and having a clear and firm conviction about the truth of God's word. Pastor Curtis does not hate. If his preaching causes one person to believe in Jesus and avoid going to Hell, then it will have been worth it for him and the church. What rock do we as believers and church members have to hold onto if we can't believe the Bible and proclaim its truth?"

After presenting evidence from several other church members and two area pastors in support of Pastor Curtis, RT rested his case.

DA Ryan couldn't resist calling Imam Amar again to reiterate the negative impact Pastor Curtis had on him and his Muslim congregation. Amar reiterated how Muslims had been attacked, ridiculed, and abused by words and conduct that was clearly hate speech and prohibited by law.

Finally, Judge Jackson asked Preston to stand for sentencing.

"Mr. Curtis," she asked, "do you have anything you want to say before I impose punishment?"

"No, Your Honor."

"Mr. Curtis, How would you respond to me if I say I will grant you probation and will not send you to prison, on the condition that you agree not to preach hateful speech that Muslims and other religious groups were going to Hell?"

"Your Honor," RT interjected, "before my client responds may we have a minute to confer please?"

"Yes, Mr. Glassman, but I would suggest to you that he answer my question very carefully and wisely."

As soon as they got into the hallway, RT told Preston he had to agree to restrict his preaching to avoid prison. "You can say the only way to Heaven is by trusting Jesus. Just don't talk about people going to Hell!"

"RT, don't you see how I can't agree to that? I can't be put in the position of having to have the DA or this judge preview and censor my sermons. I can't live in fear they are going to revoke my probation over some future sermon! I would be unfaithful to my call as a minister of the gospel and to God's truth if I refused to preach the whole truth. Don't you see the precedent that would be set if all pastors had to also live under this burden? I am not only concerned about myself but about future generations of believers and pastors that will be following me."

Preston's wife Janie hugged him. "Preston, I don't know what we will do if you get sent to prison. Is there no other way?" She cried and Preston just held her.

They spent several minutes discussing how to respond, but Preston's answer always remained the same. The bailiff came out and said the judge wanted them back in the courtroom.

"Mr. Curtis, do you have an answer to the Court's question about whether you would refrain from the hateful speech if I granted you probation rather than sending you to prison?"

"Your Honor," Preston said. "I appreciate the Court's consideration and opportunity you have proposed. I mean no disrespect, but my dilemma is that I am unsure what would be included in the definition of hateful speech. If agreeing to simply preach the Bible is okay, I can do that. But I believe that is all I have done in this case. I also am uncomfortable knowing the DA might be scouring each and every sermon to see if he can find one word that he would say was hateful. I am called as a minister to speak the truth of the Bible—God's word— without compromising the truth. What some might call hate I call love as the way to spend an eternity in Heaven. If what you have suggested would prevent me from preaching the truth of the Bible as to salvation being through trusting Jesus Christ, I cannot compromise or agree. If what you are asking is for me not to use the word 'Muslim' for a period of time, I could do that. However, rather than having to live with the DA trying to censor each and every sermon, I feel compelled to respond as Peter and John did to the Sanhedrin in Acts 4: 19-20:

'Judge for yourselves whether it is right in God's sight to obey you rather than God. For we cannot help speaking about what we have seen and heard.' Therefore, Your Honor, while I absolutely do not want to go to prison, and I do not believe I preach hate when I preach the Bible, I can't agree or tell you I will do something that I can't do. It would compromise my integrity as a minister of the gospel."

As Preston was speaking, RT could once again see the red color beginning to move up the judge's cheeks.

"Mr. Curtis, the law on hate speech is clear and a jury has found that you intentionally and knowingly violated that law. You have told me you would either be unable or unwilling to comply with the requirements of probation if one term was to require that you refrain from such hateful speech. Therefore, I am going to set your punishment at nine months confinement in the Oregon Department of Criminal Justice. Is there any reason I should not impose this sentence at this time?"

"Your Honor," RT said, "before imposing the sentence, we would request that the Court allow Pastor Curtis to remain out on bond until the appeal process has been completed. We believe this case has serious constitutional issues that should be resolved prior to imposing sentence. He does not pose a flight risk and he no longer has a pulpit in this community from which to preach, because the church has now begun the process of calling a new pastor."

DA Ryan vigorously objected: "Judge, this man is a convicted felon and he has already admitted he is going to continue to spew hate, even though he could have avoided prison if he agreed to refrain from such hateful speech. Leaving him at large under these conditions will only assure that he will continue with the same hateful speech."

"Mr. Curtis," the judge began, "you present a real dilemma to the Court. Because you are no longer a pastor in our community, I am going to defer sentencing until the appeals have been completed. But I must caution you that just because I am not actually sentencing today does not mean that if I hear there are other instances of hate speech between now and the time of sentencing that I will not seriously entertain a motion by the DA to increase the sentence up to the maximum of two years in prison. I will also consider revoking your bond if the DA brings additional future instances of hate speech during the appeals process. Have I made myself clear?"

RT responded. "Yes, Your Honor, perfectly clear."

———◆———

As Judge Jackson returned to her chamber after sentencing, she knew she had performed her job, but somehow sending this man to prison felt hollow. She had tried to spare him prison time, but he left her no choice. Pastor Curtis implying that she was going to Hell, had upset her, and the possibility of that potential outcome gave her great pause.

She went into her chamber, and after hanging up her robe she sat in her chair staring out the window. As a little girl, she had grown up in a Christian home, but over the years God seemed absent and nonresponsive to her prayers, so she had lost interest. With all of the bad things she had witnessed in the courtroom, she couldn't reconcile how a good God allowed such evil. She decided to pull out the old dusty Bible sitting on her bookcase and read Acts 4 that had been quoted by Pastor Curtis. That chapter of refusal to stop preaching by the apostles was puzzling. She remembered someone once telling her that God was love and she should read the gospel of John. She turned to the book of John in the New Testament. She read about Jesus and the miracles he performed, and how he demonstrated love to so many people viewed as worthless. The passages gave her flashbacks of what her parents and others had taught her as a child. She began to wonder if she had missed something very important in life. At that moment, her executive assistant buzzed in and said they were ready for her to hear the next case. *Almost persuaded*, she thought.

Most cases just came and went, one after another, without a lot of impact on her. But this Preston Curtis fella and his dedication to his faith caused her to contemplate her own lack of faith. Finally, she just shook her head and mumbled "Next case."

CHAPTER 44

THE REACTION OF THE MEDIA to the conviction was swift and strong. CNN was interviewing Imam Amar as he proclaimed, "Justice has prevailed. Judge Jackson has demonstrated that hate speech in Oregon is wrong and unlawful, even when uttered by a so-called preacher. Hopefully, Muslims here in Oregon and all through the United States will be free to proclaim Allah's love and message without being the subject of ridicule and hatred by bigoted Christians. Religious liberty means religious liberty for all faiths, not just Christians. Let this be a warning to other religious groups. As Muslims, we take our faith and religion seriously, and will pursue protection of our faith, our God and our message. That is the victory for all Americans today."

The imam was asked by the reporter, "So, does this mean that you and your mosque were behind the prosecution of Pastor Curtis? Is that what you mean by pursuing protection of your faith?"

"Absolutely not," said Amar, "but now that we have this precedent, we have ammunition and backing of a court case to say enough is enough! We had a DA and judge that were willing to follow the law, even if it was unpopular. If the ultimate result is a favorable Supreme Court decision, we are hopeful that other DA's and judges will follow suit and be brave to protect followers of the Islamic faith."

Others on the political left were praising the result. "It's about time those Christians had to pay for their hateful speech," one prominent left-wing leader said.

Fox News and other right-wing media outlets interviewed several pastors and commentators railing against the attack on the Christian faith, the Bible, and the constitutional disappearance of freedom of religion and free speech.

The two camps were polarized, but both sides agreed that the case of Pastor Preston Curtis was headed to the US Supreme Court.

Imam Amar met with his closest friends and laughed, gave out high five's and celebrated. "Only in America," he continued to boast. "This is a victory for all religions, but particularly for the followers of the Islam faith because we were the object of this attack and we can use it to our advantage to attract new members to the Muslim faith. Praise Allah!"

They discussed how they could use this decision and the Muslim organization throughout the US to raise money and empower the various organizations to celebrate the victory, increase their numbers, and silence and prevent attacks by infidels. They also decided to lobby other states to adopt hate speech laws similar to Oregon's.

Meanwhile, Elder Chairman Paul Reed gathered several members of Grace Bible Church to support and pray for Pastor Curtis and his wife—even though the church had decided to seek a new pastor.

As for RT, he just wanted to return to his family and law practice in Texas. He was very discouraged and needed to be refreshed, both physically and mentally, as he continued to struggle with the thought that he had let his best friend down to go to prison simply for preaching the Bible. His law practice had suffered, and his family was frustrated by his absence. His wife had lost her patience, as had his law partner. Still, he couldn't let go. There were bigger principals at stake than his law practice. *How had America gotten to the point where a preacher could be sentenced to prison for simply preaching the Bible?* RT pondered. He felt a moral obligation to help Preston with the appeal, no matter the sacrifice. But he would need help—lots of it.

RT put the word out to conservative religious and political groups that he was looking for experienced attorneys for help with the appeal. Within days, the response was overwhelming.

⸺⸺◆⸺⸺

RT knew that Preston was demoralized and without a job and would need financial help, but he also knew Preston would not take a handout from RT. So, after he returned to Texas, he made a phone call to his pastor.

"Pastor, you and I have talked about my good friend and pastor from Oregon who is being prosecuted for the crime of religious hate speech. His church has decided they need to call a new pastor, and he doesn't have a job yet. Pending his sentencing. I want to help him financially, but I know he won't take it directly from me. Is there a way I could give three thousand dollars a month through the church to be paid to him as a ministry of our church without him knowing who is providing the money?"

"RT, what a generous and gracious thing for you to do. I don't know all the legal or IRS implications, but let me get with our business administrator and figure out a way to do this. Our Benevolence Committee provides assistance to people in need, so we may have to work through them."

Preston and his family had been staying at Janie's parents' farm for free, so RT knew with the $3,000 the church would be sending, and Janie's parents' help, the Curtis family would be okay. But he also knew ministering again would be great for Preston's dignity. He called a good friend who was chairman of the local hospital board.

"Freddy," RT said, "I could use a favor. You know about my high school buddy who is the pastor from Oregon convicted of preaching from the Bible?"

"Of course I do. Outrageous! Glad you're taking this on. How can I help?""

"Well, my client needs some help, both financially and spiritually. So, I was wondering if the hospital hires or use preachers for chaplains or counselors?"

"We do," said Freddy. "Let me do some checking on what's available. I think I heard that we had a chaplain move last month, so there may be an opening. Let me call the hospital administrator and I'll get back to you."

Three days later, Preston was hired as a part-time chaplain at the hospital to help patients and their families deal with sickness and grief. He also led a Sunday morning worship service at the hospital one Sunday a month. He began to feel useful again, both in a community and in ministry.

CHAPTER 45

THE ROUTE TO THE SUPREME Court from the Oregon courts was through the United States Court of Appeals. The Ninth Circuit Court of Appeals was known as the country's most liberal. Cases from that court were reversed more often than any other circuit for what ardent conservatives considered to be judicially active decisions. Over about a ten-year span, about 20 percent of the Ninth Circuit cases were affirmed by the Supreme Court; 19 percent were vacated, and 61 percent were reversed. From 2010 to 2015 alone, of the Ninth Circuit cases accepted by the Supreme Court, 79 percent were reversed. In 2019, 78 percent of the Ninth Circuit cases for which writs were granted were reversed, while the lowest reversal rate among the circuits was the Fifth Circuit at 50 percent. These numbers gave RT hope.

Before the first appellate brief was even filed, RT knew what the outcome at the Ninth Circuit Court would be, and that going through those doors was a mere formality to reach the nation's highest court.

Sure enough, four months later, the Ninth Circuit, by an *en banc* decision of ten to one, issued its opinion affirming the guilty verdict and the sentence imposed upon Pastor Preston Curtis. RT knew the true legal war in the appellate courts would now begin in earnest.

*　　　*　　　*

Lawyers tend to pigeonhole the Supreme Court justices into either the *liberal* or *conservative* camp, even though the issues don't always fit those categories. Liberal justices tend to support an expansive view of the Constitution beyond its express wording. Therefore, the liberal justices could say that the equal protection amendment to the Constitution requires states to provide the same protections to gay married couples as to heterosexual married couples, even though those rights are not expressly mentioned in the Constitution. On the other hand, conservative justices tend to say the strict wording of the Constitution controls and since the words "gay" or "homosexual" are not included in the Constitution, and there was no historical reference for such rights by the Founding Fathers, the Supreme Court should not address that issue or expand the protections of the Constitution beyond its actual words. Inclusion of those rights would be a function of the legislative branch rather than the judicial branch of the government.

Liberals are generally viewed as interested in reaching the correct conclusion and expanding the application of constitutional rights to protect people outside the express wording of the Constitution. Conservative justices tend to say the Court is limited to interpreting the wording and original intent of the framers of the Constitution and accept that, unfortunately, the Constitution may not provide a remedy for every wrong. This view emphasizes there may have been a wrong, but there's not always a remedy unless the legislative branch has provided one.

Scholars and legal writers collect data to reflect each of the Supreme Court justices' ideological leanings and how they would likely vote. RT, in representing Preston, would have to do the same.

Preston's case presented an interesting situation for both the liberal and conservative justices. Liberal justices tended to support free speech, even if very offensive. Conservative justices tended to look at the consequences to see if the speech was appropriate. They might ask whether someone was harmed as a result of the speech. Conservatives also tended to be more protective of citizens from government interference regarding religious practices.

———◇———

Because of this impending clash over religious liberties, the US Supreme Court granted the *writ of certiorari* to hear Preston's case. Only a small percentage of cases were granted a writ by the Court, but this case had such significant constitutional issues that no legal scholar was surprised. There would be two points on appeal: first, whether Preston's conviction violated the religious liberty protections granted by the US Constitution, also known as the Free Exercise Clause; and second, whether Preston's conviction violated his constitutional rights to free speech, the so-called Free Speech Clause.

Having the Supreme Court hear your case was usually a dream come true for most attorneys. But not for RT, who had never handled a case before the Supreme Court. He knew he was in over his head. He just hoped he could convince Preston to let him get some help. And RT would surely need it to make his case.

Any chance at success required an analysis of the predispositions and prior opinions of each of the nine justices. RT had already learned this much:

Chief Justice Michael Robinson was appointed as a conservative but appeared to be moving to the left to "conserve the court." In many cases involving religious liberty, he seemed to be more interested in not upsetting precedent—even liberal precedent. Lately, he seemed to worry more about the Court being perceived as too conservative or too political, even while giving lip service as an 'original intent' jurist.

Justice James Berringer was a conservative, confirmed after a bruising Senate confirmation battle. He was the newest justice and had never been involved with a religious liberty case as a Supreme Court justice. During confirmation, he was attacked as trying to undo all civil rights gains from the past century.

Justice Bobbie Sue Abbott believed the Constitution was a breathing document that had to change with the times. She had worked for the American Civil Liberties Union and had never felt bound by the strict wording of the Constitution. She was also the oldest justice, at age eighty-nine, and was believed to have been trying to hang on until a Democrat was elected president, ensuring her seat on the Court would be filled with another liberal.

Justice Byron Weatherly was seen as a moderate, but routinely voted with the other liberal justices on social issues. He was eighty-one and criticized by pundits on the right as being inept.

Justice Stephen Schroeder was viewed as a very conservative, a strict constitutional jurist who rarely spoke, asked questions during oral arguments or wrote opinions.

Justice Consuello Perez, one of two Hispanic women on the Court, had served as an assistant district attorney for many years in Oregon, and when she was appointed she was represented by the media and colleagues as more moderate on constitutional issues. But she quickly became recognized as a solid vote for liberal positions when it came to civil rights.

Justice Jacqueline Fernandez was the second Hispanic woman on the Court. She had clerked for liberal Justice Thurgood Marshall. She had also been dean of Stanford Law School, and approached every case from a very intellectual perspective. She was recognized for her intellect and keen wit. She almost always voted as a liberal, and tended to support the side seeking to expand rights on socially charged issues, such as abortion and gay rights.

Justice Edward Gould was recognized for his academic and intellectual prowess. He had been Florida's attorney general and had later worked in the US Justice Department. He was viewed as a consistent conservative vote who firmly believed issues like abortion, gay and other civil rights should be left to the legislative branch of government to resolve, rather than the judicial branch.

RT's analysis suggested the Court would likely rule 5-4 in his favor. The wild card, however, was Chief Justice Robinson, no longer consider a reliable conservative vote on social issues.

CHAPTER 46

RT MET WITH PRESTON TO discuss his strategy and to help him prepare for the possibility of an unfavorable outcome.

"It's gonna be close," RT warned regarding the high court's decision.

"How do I prepare my family to be without me for nine months?" Preston asked. "How do I prepare myself for being in prison with rapists, murderers and drug dealers for nine months? I have to confess, I am more scared than I think I have ever been, both for myself and my family."

"Janie thinks her world has been turned upside-down. We're still being harassed by the media. People still call us hatemongers. My job is part time and provides limited income."

RT could see his friend was on the edge of being broken. At that moment, words failed him, and as he hugged Preston, they both choked up.

"Preston," he said, "you, Janie and the kids are going to get through this and be stronger on the other side. I am cautious but hopeful about the appeal, but even if we lose, you are strong, and you have an incredible faith. If anyone can get through this, it is you."

By the following week, RT had regrouped and was much stronger mentally and felt better prepared to continue Preston's legal battle.

"RT," Preston said, "I am so tired from all of this. Maybe I should just drop the appeal and start serving my jail time. I don't really want my name associated with the case that might give district attorneys the right to preview any pastor's sermon."

"Preston, we're not done fighting yet. We knew all along that this fight would not be over until the Supreme Court rules. I believe we have four solid votes to overturn the conviction, and we only need to persuade one justice to vote in your favor. So, while I hear where you are coming from, just keep your chin up! This will be over soon. Plus, come over here, I want to show you something." RT pulled out two file cabinet drawers and asked, "Do you know what those documents are?"

"No," Preston said.

"I had my legal assistant print off all of the emails that I have received from attorneys and organizations who support you and your legal position. You know how many there are?"

"No," he replied.

"Over ten thousand, at last count. Preston, you are not alone. A lot of people and conservative groups have watched you stand up for what you believe is an important issue—protection of religious liberty as set out in the Constitution. While you believe the DA and some in the media want to see you hanging from a tree, I can tell you there are a lot of people encouraged by you and the stand you have taken. I have gotten overwhelming legal support from individuals and organizations with legal staffs. I feel like our case will be strong and we'll be prepared."

Preston just smiled as he stared at the two drawers. "Can I read some of these?"

"Absolutely!" RT responded.

Two hours later, Preston walked out of RT's office, relieved that there were a lot of people and legal authorities who thought he was right. Preston no longer felt alone.

RT had known from the outset that he couldn't handle the appeal on his own. He had never appeared before the Supreme Court, or even filed a brief with it.

"Preston, I don't even know where the door to the Supreme Court is located. I am not admitted to practice there, and my IQ is about ten percent of the IQ of the Supreme Court justices. They will eat me alive in oral arguments. Unless we get some help, we don't have a prayer, literally!"

"RT, I understand, but you know I don't have any money for expensive appellate lawyers, and I trust you and want you arguing my case. But, if you can find a way to get someone to help you, I am okay with it."

RT was relieved and had already accumulated a list of qualified attorneys with Supreme Court experience chomping at the bit to argue the case for religious liberty. At the top of his list was Bill Spearman, the most senior attorney at the largest non-profit legal firm in the country.

"Mr. Spearman, my name is RT Glassman—"

Before he could continue, Spearman said, "I have been hoping you would call."

RT exhaled and smiled.

"You represent Pastor Preston Curtis who has been convicted of religious hate speech. We monitor all cases involving religious liberty, and I had been hoping you would respond to my email. I believe it is a travesty of justice to imprison a pastor for preaching from the Bible. I am a committed Christian, and I have practiced law solely in the area of protecting the constitutionally protected right of religious liberty."

"Tell me about some of the kinds of cases you have handled. Do you only handle cases involving Christians?" RT asked.

"Oh no, religious liberty is not just a Christian issue. We have represented a county that was sued to remove a six-foot display of the Ten Commandments. We have represented Christians, Jews, Native Americans in various kinds of religious liberty cases, and in one case, which is interesting because of the facts of your case, we represented some Muslims who were impacted by a travel ban imposed by the president. I will say that a large percentage of our cases involve Christians, because right now that seems to be a hot area in the legal realm."

"Have you argued before the US Supreme Court?"

"Yes, I have personally appeared before the Supreme Court ten times. Including other attorneys in our organization, we have argued over twenty-five cases at the Supreme Court. We also have six briefing attorneys that do extensive legal research for us, and we have five panels of attorneys and former judges that we present mock arguments to before arguing a case at the Supreme Court."

"Impressive," RT said. "But, as you have already acknowledged, my client is a pastor, and he can't afford lawyers with that kind of experience. I have been helping my friend *pro bono*. Are there any fees to assist us?"

"Not a penny. We're a nonprofit organization funded by donations, so we don't charge our clients."

"You're hired!" RT said. "When can you start?"

"Right now. I'll send you an attorney engagement letter for Mr. Curtis to sign, and we'll start developing a strategy for handling the Supreme Court argument."

CHAPTER 47

ATTORNEY SPEARMAN'S FIRST STEP WAS to review the lower court decisions in the Preston Curtis case, to research all issues, including all relevant Supreme Court opinions, and begin to prepare the appellate legal brief. He and his organization began sifting through the applicable cases. They discovered this was not the first time that Oregon had trampled on religious liberty and attacked Christians.

Aaron and Melissa Klein were Oregon residents who owned and operated a family bakery called Sweet Cakes by Melissa. When a woman asked the Kleins to make a custom-designed cake for her same-sex wedding, the Kleins declined for religious reasons. The state of Oregon attacked the Kleins and forced them out of business with a fine of $135,000 and a gag order preventing them from even talking about their beliefs. That case had recently been addressed by the Supreme Court and amounted to a small victory for religious liberty. The opinion sent the case back to the Court of Appeals with instructions on how to address the religious liberty issue. The Court also did not affirm the fine.

During his research, RT also came across a recent Supreme Court ruling involving a baker who refused to make a wedding cake for two gay men because of religious reasons. RT decided to reach out to an attorney named Davidson who handled the case.

"I'll be glad to visit with you," Davidson said to RT. "The facts of the case are that my client was a baker who had been in business for over ten years. He was active in his community as a Christian, and his religious view is that homosexuality goes against the Bible. So, based on those religious views, he told two gay men requesting he bake a wedding cake that he could not help them. He said he would be glad to bake other things for them, but a wedding cake hit squarely in the center of his religious views, so he declined. The two men were incensed and said they were tired of being discriminated against. So they filed a complaint with the Civil Rights Commission espousing their constitutional right to get married and, since the baker made wedding cakes for straight couples but turned them down, he was discriminating against them. The Civil Rights Commission ruled against my client. The Supreme Court overturned the case saying the Civil Rights Commission had violated the baker's first amendment rights to the freedom of expression. But a critical point for you and your case is that the Supreme Court didn't expressly rule that his conduct was protected based upon his religious convictions, but rather said his speech was protected. They sidestepped the bigger issue and refused to adopt an opinion that said the baker's conduct was protected on the basis of religious liberty. Justice Weatherly wrote the seven-to-two opinion and said, essentially, that the issue of whether a business could refuse to serve gay people 'must await further elaboration.' It is obvious— the Court wants to dodge any religious liberty issues. Your case may force them to address the issue directly."

"The result is encouraging, but hearing you say they want to avoid a decision based on religious liberty is discouraging," RT said.

"Any pointers for preparation of Supreme Court arguments?"

Davidson laughed and said, "Get ready! We probably only gave three minutes of our planned argument out of the allotted twenty minutes! The rest was taken up by questions from the justices. If you can offer an alternative basis for ruling for your client without expressly saying the conviction violates his constitutional religious liberty rights, I would use it. From my experience, the free speech issue is more likely to be successful than the religious liberty argument. Three justices will be hostile to you right out of the gate. They are interested in protecting the underdog, and while normally your client, being charged and convicted, would be the underdog, my guess is that the Muslim community will be perceived as the underdog in your case. In our case, it was the two gay men. Those three justices will argue the necessary constitutional and statutory protection of the Muslims under attack. They will never see a legal need to protect your pastor based on religious convictions. The other argument that was successful for us that you might consider using would be the possible ramifications if the decision is upheld. Do we want our pastors regularly indicted for preaching?

"The inconsistency of application is another problem. The DA in Oregon believes a criminal offense occurred, and a DA in Texas where you live may be appalled at the thought that a pastor would be indicted for preaching a sermon based on Biblical principles. There will be different standards throughout the country. Does the Court want to keep deciding which sermons are okay and which ones are not? The implications of judicial economy and time being spent by the courts on this issue are enormous. Three and maybe four of the justices will be very concerned about those practical implications.

"Finally, I would suggest in your practice sessions you have someone ask some really off-the-wall questions to help you be prepared so you won't be surprised by anything. The justices opposing your position will want to throw you off-balance, and it may be a question that has nothing to do with the legal questions like, Did Pastor Curtis pray about the sermon that morning before he preached it? They toss you an easy one and then come with a hardball question like, 'Don't you think the Muslims' religious liberties should be protected by the Constitution?' Finally, no disrespect to you, but do you have an attorney with Supreme Court experience assisting you?"

"Yes," replied RT. "Bill Spearman is taking the lead."

"Very good," said Davidson. "Bill is an excellent Supreme Court advocate. You will be well represented."

———◇———

It had taken four weeks to complete the brief. One of the hardest chores was keeping it under the Court's fifty-page limit. By the time set for oral arguments there had been forty *amicus* briefs ('friend of the court' briefs) filed by interested parties or organizations in support of protecting religious liberties. The amicus briefs were filed by nearly every Christian denomination and a number of other religious groups. In addition, there were twenty amicus briefs filed by many secular organizations opposing overturning the decision. The group included the ACLU, the Islamic Supreme Council of America, and many non-Christian religious organizations.

Because Preston had been accused and convicted of a crime, the appeal was styled as Preston Curtis vs. The State of Oregon. Thus, the case looked like an appeal by every other criminal defendant convicted of a crime. It placed the power, prestige and authority of the state of Oregon against this small-town preacher.

RT had grown up knowing about David vs. Goliath as a Bible story, and it seemed they were reliving it. He was praying for the same powerful help and positive result that David had. But so far in the legal proceedings, it seemed the giant was winning.

CHAPTER 48

AS THE WEEKS PASSED, LIFE for Preston and his family had settled into a new normal. Life was continuing, but there was a black cloud continuously reminding them of the potential jail sentence.

Preston was given great freedom as the chaplain of a Texas hospital, and as such was not timid about Biblical teachings. He was allowed to privately share his Christian faith and convictions with hospital patients and their families and friends.

Meanwhile, the Oregon CPS required Preston and Janie to file a monthly report and respond to questions, including, "Have you preached at any church during the past thirty days? If yes, state the name of the church and the date of the sermon."

It was obvious that CPS and the DA wanted to catch him in a trap that would revoke his bail and remove his children from his custody. Preston had been invited to preach at Texas churches and to share his story but he felt God had given him the hospital ministry for now. Upon RT's advice, he also didn't want to stir things up while his case was pending.

There were moments when life almost seemed normal again. Sarah had a new boyfriend and had been elected as one of her high school's homecoming queens. Caleb was enjoying his football team, and Joshua had been taking guitar lessons and learning to sing the latest country hits. Preston's wife, Janie, had formed a women's Bible study group at a local church that provided spiritual and emotional support.

But there would be the occasional reminder that Preston's life was anything but normal. He still received threatening calls or correspondence. One morning while he was at the hospital, he received a call from someone who called him a "Muslim hater."

"I hope they take care of you in prison. You're going to need protection," the man said. "Sounds like you're going to Hell before the Muslims do."

Another day he got a letter in the mail that said, "You don't know me, but after your last sermon, my husband was bullied at work and my kids were bullied at school because we are Muslims, and people claimed that Muslims are sending you to prison. You may think we are going to Hell, but you have made our life hell on earth."

There was simply no way he could escape the constant reminders of his plight.

———◇———

Despite the threats and drama, support continued to build for Preston—and his lawyer.

RT's practice had begun to flourish. Nothing attracted clients like his regular appearances on Fox News talking about how liberals were taking away religious liberties. He had added two new attorneys to his firm and had clients in several states, requiring him to either get licensed in those states or keep filing motions to be admitted on a case-by-case basis. One state he had vowed never to set foot in again was Oregon. However, one case there presented enough interesting facts and potential money to lure him back.

There was a local rancher who owned a 14,000-acre ranch. He had leased 6,000 acres to a concrete company to mine sand and gravel. The lease contained annual minimum mining and payment obligations. However, the concrete company had failed to make any payments for three years, and RT accepted representation on a contingency basis of a third of the recovered money. He filed a lawsuit and was able to obtain a swift summary judgment terminating the lease. They were later able to obtain a new sand and gravel lease from another concrete company, resulting in an annual minimum payment to RT of five figures. That was enough to cover the $3,000 per month he was providing anonymously for Preston—and then some. He saw it as God's provision for both himself and Preston.

Because RT knew the level of hostility directed to Preston while the appeal was pending, he felt the need to provide a diversion.

"Kathy," he said, "I talked to Preston today and he has gotten a few anonymous calls and letters in the last couple of days and he seemed down. We need to do something to distract them."

"Okay," she said. "I'll call Janie and work out something."

On a Friday night, while eating their Texas grilled steaks, Kathy asked Janie, "How are you guys doing?"

"We are doing okay. Sometimes life almost seems normal, but then Preston gets a hateful phone call or letter, or one of the kids wants to see a friend in Oregon but we can't go back there with the CPS lady out to get us."

"I know," Kathy said. "I think you and I need a spa day. I can get us in tomorrow. Can you do that?"

"I'd love to, but we can't really afford for me to have a spa day with all that has happened."

"No worries, my treat! I got it covered."

"I can't accept that. You guys have done so much for us already, and with RT doing all the legal work for free, I just can't let you do anything else."

"Nonsense," Kathy said. "It will just be us girls!"

Preston had overheard them. "Spa day? That's a great idea! I can keep the kids."

CHAPTER 49

ORAL ARGUMENTS WERE SCHEDULED FOR the first Tuesday of November. RT had never been party to such intense preparation. For two weeks before the case was heard, they had conducted mock oral arguments before different constitutional attorneys and former judges who grilled Spearman and RT about every positive and negative aspect of each relevant case. They had attorneys both supportive and adverse to their position asking them questions. They wrote and rewrote their oral argument. They knew there was a high likelihood they would never make it through what they had prepared, but they wanted to be ready.

Spearman would make the bulk of the argument and handle most questions; RT would close with impassioned factual implications concerning the consequences if pastors across America started being indicted for preaching the Bible. They knew that the Court was not going to be interested in factual arguments per se, and would want to entertain only legal ones, but they thought the magnitude of the impact, not only to the cause of religious liberty but to pastors like Preston, could not be overlooked.

Additionally, the prospect of courts having to rule on numerous cases, sermon by sermon, seemed like a potentially impossible drain of judicial resources. That chilling possibility would resonate with the Court. This was also the first criminal case with potential imprisonment consequences for a pastor preaching from the pulpit. Did the justices really want to put preachers behind bars? All other cases of religious liberties had only involved civil penalties such as fines. There were high moral arguments to be made, but also practical ones.

On the day set for oral arguments, Preston and the two lawyers approached the Supreme Court building and could have confused it for a zoo. People of differing views were lined up shouting at each other with signs such as "Protect my Bible!", "No prison for pastors," "Christians Hate," and "Go to Hell Yourself!"

As they approached the Supreme Court building, a number of people recognized Preston and charged at him. Police cleared a path into the courthouse. All three men's nerves were frayed by the time they finally got to the courtroom. Fortunately, they were the second case scheduled for argument, so they had time to get their minds settled and organized.

As RT approached the courtroom, there was a sense of awe and reverence. He thought about such legal giants as Chief Justice John Marshall, Chief Justice John Jay and Justice Oliver Wendell Holmes, Jr. who had sat in these chambers. This courtroom had been the epicenter of legal opinions since its creation in 1789. RT wondered what had happened to such great constitutionalists.

The printed guide they were provided set out the rules for the Supreme Court and was nearly twenty pages long, with everything from how you report into the lawyer's lounge, to the duties of the clerk, to the attire of counsel and the banning of electronic devices in the courtroom. They were advised where to sit, how to address the justices and that they would be allotted thirty minutes for argument. It all seemed very daunting to RT who felt relieved to have Spearman at his side.

———————◆———————

When their time came, Spearman started.

"Mr. Chief Justice and may it please the Court—"

Liberal Justice Abbott cut him off. "Mr. Spearman, do you acknowledge this Court has recognized limitations both on the freedom of speech and religious liberty? For example, are you familiar with another Oregon case on religious freedom, the Department of Human Resources of Oregon vs. Smith case, that said employees digesting peyote as an essential element of a religious ceremony could be fired from their jobs?"

"Yes, Justice Abbott, I am aware there are some limitations, but not where a pastor is preaching directly from the Bible from his church pulpit."

Justice Abbott: "This Court has long recognized that accommodation to religious beliefs must not significantly impinge on the interests of third parties. Do you not think saying Muslims are going to Hell impinges on the Muslims' interests?"

Spearman: "No, Justice Abbott, it does not. The Muslim pastor in the pulpit should be free to say Christians are going to Hell, too, if that is their religious belief."

Justice Abbott continued to hammer Spearman for the next ten minutes. Then another liberal, Justice Perez, picked up the same theme about the Oregon student accusing his high school principal of being Muslim. Finally, Justice Gould, in an apparent effort to rescue Spearman, asked if he thought the Supreme Court should be deciding what pastors preached from the pulpit, and therefore opening the door to having trial judges and district attorneys deciding which sermons were acceptable and which sermons were hateful. Spearman was able to articulate the danger in restricting religious freedom and religious free speech.

As Spearman's time expired, RT realized Spearman had made it through very few of the prepared comments. It appeared the liberal justices were trying to push the extreme examples to persuade the deciding swing vote, Chief Justice Robinson, of the rightness of their position. Conservative justices, however, had been mostly silent, which RT found unnerving. The hostility of one segment of the Court to religious liberty and free speech seemed apparent to Preston.

As Spearman walked back to the counsel table, RT thought, *I have never felt so intimidated in all my life! I have got to give the argument of my career. Preston is counting on me!*

"Mr. Chief Justice and may it please the Court. I want to take the remainder of our time to talk about the significant impact and implications if this case is affirmed."

Justice Abbott interrupted. "Counsel, this is a court for legal arguments, not about the impact. We are concerned about the law."

"I understand Justice Abbott, but this decision cannot be made in a vacuum without considering several consequences. The first consequence is the harm to the Constitution itself. The pilgrims left England partially to be free from an imposed and mandated religion by the Church of England. From a historical perspective, and, following through on the intent of the framers of our Constitution, religious freedom and the freedom to worship God in the manner each individual deems appropriate was a basic and fundamental right to our Founding Fathers. This case, if allowed to stand, means that each individual and each pastor will no longer have that power and freedom. That power and freedom will have shifted back to the state and will flow through a district attorney or a judge, which is exactly what the Founders were attempting to prevent.

"The second consequence is a profound consequence as well, with huge practical implications. There are over a half million Christian churches in America, both denominational and non-denominational. These churches teach and preach the Bible as the authoritative word of God each Sunday. In addition, there are many more faiths in America that rely upon the principle of religious liberty. Denominations such as the Jews, Catholics, Mormons, Hindus, Buddhists and even the Muslims. The consequences of upholding this conviction will be profound in the hundreds of thousands of places of worship each week. This decision doesn't just impact one church and one pastor. The Biblical principle of having an eternity in heaven through faith in Jesus is taught in every evangelical church weekly. Other denominations have doctrines to which they hold onto just as rigidly. Suddenly, the pastors, priests, imams or other leaders will have to stop and think whether their words will be offensive to some district attorney or judge. Others will take the position of the New Testament apostles and say, 'I must be true to God and not to the whims of a DA.' Each district attorney all across the states will be deciding whether or not a church leader crossed the line of religious hate speech the preceding Sunday. Also, there will be disparate standards across the country. A DA in Oregon will file criminal charges while a DA in Texas will say 'Amen, preach on, brother' over the same words. Discriminatory enforcement will be rampant, and uniformity will be totally lacking. Suddenly, the floodgates of criminal court cases will burst open. The courts across the United States will have to review sermons to see if they are acceptable. This court will be called upon repeatedly to decide if a pastor preaching the Bible on a given week was OK or that person stepped across the line. Can you imagine the amount of time, energy and expense required for such an endeavor? The potential for using massive judicial resources on this one topic is beyond description.

"Finally, all cases interpreting religious liberty prior to this case have involved situations other than a pastor preaching from the pulpit. Can a baker decline to bake a cake for a gay couple? Can the use of illegal drugs be excused as a religious exercise? Those are the kinds of situations represented in prior Supreme Court cases of religious liberty. But no other case has said a pastor preaching his conviction about the Bible from a pulpit in a house of worship could

be a basis to criminally convict that pastor. Upholding this conviction
will utterly decimate any semblance or vestige of religious liberty in
this country. If there is no religious liberty in the pulpits and houses
of worship all across America, there is no religious liberty. None. It.
Is. Done. Thank you."

RT sat exhausted and mentally spent. *I did my best. God, please
let it be enough.*

———◦———

When DA Ryan went to the podium, he was given clear sailing to
make his presentation for the first ten minutes. Finally, conservative
Justice Berringer spoke up.

"Mr. Ryan, the Supreme Court has recognized that a state such as
Oregon has an obligation of religious neutrality. I see no evidence of
such neutrality from you as the prosecutor, the trial judge or even from
the CPS worker that threatened to take Mr. Curtis' children out of the
home. Can you point me to anything in the record that demonstrates
that any government worker provided religious neutrality?"

"Of course, Justice Berringer. There was no violation of a
requirement of religious neutrality. All any of us did was to enforce
a criminal statute that defined hate speech. It just so happened
that the person promoting the hate speech did so from a pulpit.
Such speech caused great harm to the Muslim community, another
religious group. In essence, it was religious group vs. religious group.
That fact alone would constitute religious neutrality to the extreme."

Justice Berringer: "This Court has recognized the principle
that the First Amendment ensures that religious organizations
and persons are given proper protection as they seek to teach the
principles that are so fulfilling and so central to their lives and faith.
Can you think of anything more basic or important as a principle of
faith than how a person gets to Heaven in the afterlife?"

DA Ryan: "Justice Berringer, I do acknowledge that how a person
gets to Heaven is a basic principle of religious organizations. If Mr.
Curtis had simply stated how he believed a person could get to

Heaven, we would not be here. Where he crossed the line was when he called out Muslims and said that religious group was going to Hell. That constituted hate speech under our Oregon statute."

There was bantering back and forth during the remainder of the time with each respective group of justices. Finally, the time for their oral argument expired. As they walked out of the courtroom, a CNN reporter stuck a microphone in Spearman's face.

"All legal scholars appear to believe the liberal justices are supporting the protection of the Muslim religion rather than the free speech of your client, which would be bad for your side. Do you agree?"

"No, I don't agree. Free speech and freedom of religion is neither a liberal nor conservative issue. It's a constitutional issue that should concern people of all faiths and religious beliefs. Today the attack is on a Christian, but what if tomorrow it is against a Jewish rabbi or a Muslim imam? We are confident of success based upon prior precedent of the Court."

Preston and his lawyers waded through the crowd of hecklers and supporters to an awaiting car that took them to their hotel rooms.

———◇———

At the hotel, the three men sat at a quiet table in the lounge to discuss the case.

"I thought such an important court would immediately say that a pastor preaching the Bible from the pulpit cannot be guilty of criminal hate speech," Preston said. "But it looked like just the opposite in there today!"

"I know," said Spearman. "I'm not going to sugarcoat it. It was obvious the liberal justices were siding with the prosecution and aggressively so. Just remember, there were two justices that were silent, and we only have to get the vote of one of those two justices in order to win. My take is that the justices we saw in there were not really focused on this case as a religious liberty issue going forward, nor the practical impossibilities of courts having the right to approve or disapprove pastor's sermons. It seemed to me they were looking at it only from a political or ideological perspective of protecting the poor Muslim group that was offended. I don't believe that is a proper approach to such a critical constitutional issue, nor is it the approach I believe our Founding Fathers intended, but I fear that is what we saw today."

"Preston," RT said. "I tend to agree with Bill, and I am concerned. But I don't want you to live in fear of what might happen. We have to take it one step at a time and trust God for the results. I have constantly asked myself if there was anything else we could have done to try to increase the chances for a good outcome, and I can't think of one thing we could have done in addition to what we did."

"RT and Bill, I agree that you guys have done a phenomenal job. I never thought that you guys should have done anything differently." He added, "You guys have worked hard, and for free, no less!" he added with a chuckle. "What I struggle to wrap my arms around is the system itself and the idea that our nation has gotten to the point that such a precious constitutional right as religious liberty could be dismissed so easily."

They spent two hours trying to calm him down and persuade him all was not lost. But privately, RT had to agree; they got hammered by the liberal justices. Now all they could do was wait.

For five days after the oral arguments, Preston, Spearman and RT were being interviewed by Fox News and other media outlets. Liberal pundits were predicting victory while conservative pundits were decrying the state of the country where pastors could be convicted of hate speech for preaching the Bible. The wait for the opinion would be excruciating and long, but at least Preston was not in prison.

CHAPTER 50

FIVE MONTHS LATER, RT'S EMAIL box pinged, giving him notification from the US Supreme Court that an opinion had been rendered in Preston's case. His heart almost stopped. He realized that he would soon know if this horrendous burden had been lifted, or his best friend was going to prison.

As he opened the opinion, he noticed that liberal Justice Abbott was the author of the opinion. Since she was the one who had hammered him and Spearman during oral arguments, he suspected the worst. Sure enough, he went to the end of the sixty-five-page opinion and saw the words *Conviction Affirmed*. Preston was going to prison. In looking further at the opinion, their conservative Chief Justice Robinson had sided with the four liberal justices. While there were scathing dissents by the four remaining conservatives on the Court, their opinions did not help Preston stay out of prison. RT couldn't bring himself to read all of the pages of the opinion because at that moment it didn't matter; he had failed his buddy; the legal system had failed his buddy; the US Supreme Court had failed his buddy. And he feared that hostility toward Christians had just intensified in a dangerous manner.

———————◇———————

RT dreaded making the phone call to Preston, but he knew the media would be all over this opinion and that the firestorm would soon begin. He wanted Preston to hear it from him first. He called Preston's cell phone.

"Preston, we have an opinion, and it's not good."

RT could hear Janie in the background. "The Supreme Court ruled, and we lost, didn't we?" She started crying and dropped to her knees.

Eventually, Preston was able to ask, "When do I have to start my prison term?"

"Preston, I'm very sorry," RT said. "We will file an application for rehearing, but I expect it will be promptly denied, and once that happens the trial judge will likely immediately sentence you to serve the prison term. My guess is the process will take in ninety to one hundred twenty days. You need to get prepared. I will let you know when sentencing will occur as soon as I get the word . . . I'm sorry, Preston."

"RT," he said, "you have gone above and beyond anything I could have ever expected. I appreciate all you have done and the sacrifices you have made. Nobody could have done more or anything better."

After RT hung up the phone he couldn't concentrate, he couldn't think, he couldn't focus, and he couldn't speak. This case was enough to make a nondrinking Baptist start drinking! All through this case, he kept asking himself how America could get to the place where a pastor preaching the Bible could be convicted for hate speech. He finally had his answer—because five justices get to define the boundaries of religious liberties and free speech.

Forget the wording of the Constitution or the will of the people; it boiled down to one swing vote.

RT had never been involved in partisan politics, presidential elections or in the significance of the impact of presidential elections and the Supreme Court. The next president would likely be able to appoint one to three Supreme Court Justices. RT felt the decision in Preston's case had been wrong, not just because it impacted his best friend, but because ministers of all religious beliefs and creeds could now come under a hostile DA's radar screen for prosecution. RT thought, *the religious liberty upon which this nation was formed is slipping away.* Never had the significance of presidential elections and the ability to appoint Supreme Court justices been as important or significant as in the next election.

CHAPTER 51

AS EXPECTED, THE APPLICATION FOR rehearing was denied by the Supreme Court and the trial judge quickly set the date for the imposition of Preston's sentence. When they appeared in the courtroom, the DA argued that the sentence be increased to the maximum, but the judge quickly dismissed his motion. With little fanfare she said, "Preston Curtis, you are sentenced to nine months in prison. You are remanded to the custody of the sheriff to be transported to the Oregon Department of Criminal Justice to carry out this sentence. Court is adjourned."

"Your Honor," RT said, "before he is taken off can we please have five minutes in the hall with his family?" The judge looked at the deputy sheriff who nodded approval.

When they got in the hall, Janie and the kids were there and were crying and holding tightly to Preston. Janie choked out, "Preston, I'm so sorry. I don't know what to say except I love you and we will be praying for you and will be here when you get out."

Preston said, "I will think about and pray for you guys every second of every day. Don't worry about me. It is in God's hands now and I trust Him. You guys encourage and support each other while I am gone. I'll write to you often. Never forget how much I love you."

All RT could do was watch in pain. Some reporters started running up and asking Preston crazy questions like, "Where is your God now?" and "Are you going to preach anymore?" and "Are you mad at God?"

As the deputy sheriff came over to put on the handcuffs and escort him away, Preston finally spoke into the cameras. "Some have been asking me how I can keep my faith and whether I feel abandoned by God. The answer is, my faith is stronger today than it has ever been. I am disappointed for my family and I ask you to pray for them. On the night before Jesus' death, He left His disciples with the following words: 'I have told you these things so that in me you may have peace. In this world you will have trouble. But take heart! I have overcome the world.' Jesus knows the pain and brokenness of our lives and has given us peace through His pain. So, as I begin my journey to prison, I am claiming two Scriptures. The first is Romans 8:28 which says, 'And we know that God causes all things to work together for good to those who love God, to those who are called according to His purpose.' The second Scripture is 2 Timothy 1:12: 'For this reason I suffer these things, but I am not ashamed; for I know whom I have believed, and I am convinced that He is able to guard what I have entrusted to Him until that day.'"

Then, as Preston turned and was escorted down the hall, the last thing his family and RT heard was Preston singing a verse from the Casting Crowns song, "Only Jesus."

"And I, I don't want to leave a legacy, I don't care if they remember me, only Jesus. And I, I've only got one life to live, I'll let every second point to Him! Only Jesus. Jesus is the only name; Jesus is the only name; Jesus is the only name to remember. . . "

And with that, he was gone.

—◦—

RT was amazed at Preston's last response and faith. He knew he was not supposed to be encouraged as his friend marched into prison, but he had never been more amazed by the response of his friend. It seemed RT had just witnessed the only encouraging thing about this whole series of events. His faith as a Christian had been bolstered by Preston's approach, response and faithfulness, but his faith in the legal system had taken a big hit.

—◦—

RT struggled with an internal conflict, knowing that his government had failed his best friend and seemingly, there was turmoil at all levels of government, yet knowing that as a Christian he was to submit to the government. Preston and he had discussed this conflict and Preston reminded him of Romans 13: 1-5: "Let everyone be subject to the governing authorities, for there is no authority except that which God has established. The authorities that exist have been established by God. Consequently, whoever rebels against the authority is rebelling against what God has instituted, and those who do so will bring judgment on themselves. For rulers hold no terror for those who do right, but for those who do wrong. Do you want to be free from fear of the one in authority? Then do what is right and you will be commended. For the one in authority is God's servant for your good. But if you do wrong, be afraid, for rulers do not bear the sword for no reason. They are God's servants, agents of wrath to bring punishment on the wrongdoer. Therefore, it is necessary to submit to the authorities, not only because of possible punishment but also as a matter of conscience."

That was Preston's lesson to RT, but Preston's stand and his confidence to act and be defiant to authority came from Acts 5:29 which says that, as Christians "we must obey God rather than man." Trust in God is a hard concept to live out daily, and it is even harder to trust that our real victory is not a political or legal victory, but a spiritual one. *But,* RT thought, *it sure would be nice to see some political victories in this present life once in a while.*

Because of the way the justices sided in Preston's case, all of the political and legal media pundits had characterized the decision in Preston's case as one where the "liberals" had voted against the pastor's ability to have the freedom to preach his convictions from the pulpit. Because of that characterization, conservatives were fired up about electing a president to appoint justices who would overturn the decision in Preston's case. The liberal base believed since the fight had been one religion, Christian, against another religion, Muslim, the decision would have no long-term effect on religious liberty, but the underdog Muslims needed to be protected, and one religious group should not be able to cause harm to another religious group through speech.

----◆----

Not since the ruling on abortion in Roe vs. Wade had the political fires burned as bright. Conservative Christians had a million-person march in Washington DC, carrying their Bibles with signs and chanting, "Preach on, Protect our pastors, and Imprison criminals, not pastors."

At every political rally, the Republican presidential nominee excoriated liberals as hatemongers, and claimed that the framers of the Constitution would roll over in their graves knowing that a preacher was jailed for teaching the Bible. "Our pastors should not have to get permission from a district attorney to preach from the Bible, or be faced with a prison sentence," the Republican candidate demanded.

The Democratic presidential candidate tried to deflect the Supreme Court decision as not being a political matter, but a legal matter based upon different interpretations of the constitution. However, all across the country, many people of faith found their voices and expressed strong convictions that religious freedom was a significant right that needed to be protected, and they didn't want their pastors threatened with imprisonment for preaching the Bible. As the political fires raged, there was a growing realization that the decision in Pastor Curtis' case was no longer simply about one man being sent to prison. It ignited a movement.

———◆———

District Attorney Mark Ryan was the first to fall. Conservatives from all across the country contributed five million dollars to the campaign of his opponent. Local pastors in the Portland area, including those in the Portland Ministerial Alliance that had refused to take a stand in support of Preston, suddenly saw the light and got on the bandwagon opposing DA Ryan. Ryan had been in office for fifteen years and was totally stunned by the opposition he had drawn over one case. Ryan lost the election by twenty points. Leading much of the political opposition to DA Ryan were members of Pastor Curtis' former church—Grace Bible Church.

Another event fueled the flames of the presidential election. Two weeks after Pastor Curtis' sentencing, Justice Abbott, author of the opinion affirming Preston's conviction, died in her sleep. Everyone knew that the direction of the Supreme Court, and even the future of religious liberty and free speech, would be decided by her replacement, further stoking the already polarizing and white-hot discourse of the presidential campaigns.

Central to that contentious debate was the fight for religious liberty. Pastor Preston Curtis serving his sentence in prison became a poster child for those on the right who were seeking to regain religious liberty for their country. Preston prayed that people would not get caught up solely in the political fight which he above all others knew was important. He prayed that instead, the love of Christ in the Bible would be seen, and that the love demonstrated by Christians committed to the Bible would result in many people becoming believers in Christ for their eternal destiny.

AUTHOR'S NOTES

I WANT TO THANK YOU, the reader, for taking a chance on this first-time author! I will never take you for granted!

The foundation for this book began years ago when, as an attorney, I was called upon to defend my pastor in a deposition and subsequently a court hearing because of a sermon he preached. The topic of religious liberty has grown in importance to me as I now have a son and daughter in ministry, and have seen some politicians use the Covid-19 pandemic as an excuse to demonstrate hostility to religious worship—of all faiths— throughout our country. The actions described in this book set out a logical next form of attack on our religious liberties.

I also want to acknowledge and thank some of the people who played such a vital role in helping this book become a reality.

To my lawyer buddy (you know who you are!), who took the time to study the manuscript and make significant suggestions to convert it from a legal "position paper" to a readable fiction book.

To many friends who also provided valuable support, encouragement and input including Scott and Carrilyn Baker, Bobby Albert, Shelli and Brian Littleton and Melinda Caruso.

To Amanda Rooker, who helped with plot development, editing and direction for the next steps.

To photographer Marlo Collins, who helped me look much better in a picture than in real life!

To John Koehler and all of the folks at Koehler Books for all of the editing, handholding and support, including Joe Coccaro, Marshall McClure, and Danielle Koehler with Dalitopia Media.

I need to give a special shout-out and thanks to my biggest fans— my family—including Mindy, Amy, Curt, and especially my wife, Donna. She had to read and revise many drafts and patiently encourage me through the process. I love you!

Finally, to those in America and across the world whose religious liberties are under attack: be encouraged, and stay strong in the Lord!

For more Author's Ramblings, please go to my website: judgeroysparkman.com